G000067775

LEFT FOR DEAD

PAUL J. TEAGUE

ALSO BY PAUL J. TEAGUE

Morecambe Bay Trilogy 1

Book 1 - Left For Dead

Book 2 - Circle of Lies

Book 3 - Truth Be Told

Morecambe Bay Trilogy 2

Book 4 - Trust Me Once

Book 5 - Fall From Grace

Book 6 - Bound By Blood

Morecambe Bay Trilogy 3

Book 7 - First To Die

Book 8 - Nothing To Lose

Book 9 - Last To Tell

Note: The Morecambe Bay trilogies are best read in the order shown above.

Don't Tell Meg Trilogy

Features DCI Kate Summers and Steven Terry.

Book 1 - Don't Tell Meg

Book 2 - The Murder Place

Book 3 - The Forgotten Children

Standalone Thrillers

Dead of Night

One Last Chance

PROLOGUE

1984 - Sandy Beaches Holiday Camp

The blustery wind carried away Charlotte's cries as she ran through the outskirts of the holiday camp, frantically looking behind her, wondering how long it would be before Bruce caught up.

She should have escaped from the relationship earlier. She was a feminist, for Christ's sake. How had she got trapped? It was the first commandment of not being stupid: *Thou shalt not jump into bed with a psycho, just because he's good-looking and it's only a summer fling.*

He was closing on her now. She was such a stupid cow sometimes - it had been obvious he was getting more controlling. Ever since Will had arrived to work at the camp, her sense that things might turn sour had proved to be true. Bruce was convinced she was sleeping with Will. He was an *'if I can't have you, no-one can'* kind of guy. So when she and Will had argued in the bar, she should have just headed directly for Sally's chalet - or even Will's or

Abi's come to that. In spite of everything, even Abi would have been a better option than Bruce.

Instead, like an idiot, she'd run towards the beach, taking the fork at the half-constructed paddling pool in the middle of the camp rather than the safety-in-numbers option of the chalets.

This was the culmination of everything that had come before it: every put-down, every suspicion, every loaded remark, every threat. Her heart burned with the effort of running as she struggled to keep going. Then she shuddered to a halt as his strong hands clawed at her shoulders and he wheeled her round to face him. She gasped in fear as she looked into his face and saw the brutality there.

He sunk his clenched fist into her stomach, forcing the air out of her lungs. Choking with the sheer shock of it, in that instant she knew he was capable of killing her.

She cried out, her voice competing with the waves crashing on to the shore just beyond the stone wall which marked the boundary between the holiday camp and the beach. In the moment he took to pull back his arm, she saw her opportunity and darted away from him. All she could do was try to out-run him, to make it as far as the beach and hope a courting couple would be there to save her. But on a night like this, nobody would be on the beach; they'd be crazy to go anywhere near those waves.

Charlotte pushed open the wooden door at the edge of the camp and ran down the small grassy bank towards the beach, her feet crunching and sliding on the pebbles. The game was up; it was impossible to run on the shingle in those shoes. He was almost upon her.

Exhausted, she knew she would have to submit to whatever punishment he had in store for her.

Bruce caught Charlotte's arm, spun her around, struck

her face with his hand and pushed her to the ground. The wind and waves drowned out her screams. In any case, there was no one there to help.

He unbuckled his belt and unzipped his flies, pushing her back down to the ground once again.

'I'll show you, you bitch!' he screamed at her, his face full of fury.

Bruce pushed Charlotte down to the floor, hitching up her dress and tearing off her underwear with a single movement.

'No!' she yelled.

He lowered himself onto her body, pushing her legs open, pinning her down, probing.

Panic rose up in her throat as she struggled against his brute force. Her hand reached out, desperate, searching for a way out, any escape from this torment.

She heard the crack of stone on skull and for a moment everything was silent, frozen in time. She held the stone in her hand, waiting and wondering. Bruce seemed to be suspended above her, neither moving nor shouting.

Charlotte struck him once again. This time he slumped immediately, a massive lifeless weight falling on top of her. She dropped the stone and turned her head to see a wave rolling in, covering it and rinsing away the blood.

She tried to roll Bruce off, pushing and twisting until she managed to squeeze out from underneath him. Charlotte didn't check to see if he was alive or dead. All she cared about was that he had stopped, that he could no longer hurt her. She retrieved her torn underwear, now in a soggy mess, and she stumbled back towards the gate, leaving Bruce where he lay. As she looked back, she thought she saw him move. Maybe she imagined it, but she wasn't hanging around to find out.

The holiday camp was still now, the bars and pubs closed for the night and everyone locked up in their chalets, ready for the next day of family tensions and gloomy, grey skies. Charlotte opened the door to her chalet and double-locked the door. She was relieved that Jenna wasn't there. She had a good idea where she'd be, waiting - waiting for Bruce.

Charlotte was relieved. Slowly, still terrified, she took off her clothes, washed herself in the sink and examined the bruise on her ribs. It was only when she lay on her bed and drifted off into a fearful sleep, exhausted by the events of that evening, that she realised her necklace was missing. The necklace that her mother had given her, just before cancer had beaten her. The one with her mother's name engraved upon it.

CHAPTER ONE

Present Day - Morecambe

'And smile once more please...'

Charlotte's mouth was aching already. The photographer had set them up in several ridiculous poses and she'd had enough now. Her one consolation was that they did not have to hold a large cardboard cheque, the size of which no sane person would ever use in real life. Such was the imaginative prowess of the local press. At least the kids had been spared the ordeal, Olli in particular being unwilling to get involved in the feature in the local press.

'That's all we need when we're starting a new school, Mum. If it wasn't bad enough you moving in the middle of my 'A' level year, the humiliation of appearing in the local paper will murder any chance of social acceptance whatsoever.'

That was Olli, always one for the over-dramatic.

'Remind me again why you had to uproot us from the home we loved to take over a bloody...'

'Olli!' Will chided.

'...to take over a crappy old guest house in a seaside resort which had seen better days in the seventies, let alone in the 21st Century.'

'That's enough!' Will intervened, sensing that his attitude might be all Charlotte needed to tip her over the edge on a day that was stressful enough already.

'You know why we moved. It's a curse of middle-age, you'll find out for yourself one day. If the robots haven't taken over the earth by then...'

Olli had laughed. Will could always make the kids laugh. Charlotte wished she had the same skill. Instead, she just chided, nagged and made life generally dull for them. Her one saving grace was that she kept the clean clothes flowing. Her role of mother had become reduced to that. In the end, both Olli and Lucia had gone off to their first day at their new school, reluctant and begrudging.

Redundancy. That was the official reason for the move. A nervous breakdown was the unofficial reason. Only Charlotte, Will and Doctor Sutton would ever know that. Charlotte wasn't so ill that she couldn't see how the stigma of a breakdown might tar her with the mental health brush for the rest of her life. The life insurance premiums would go up and it could provide a problem if she ever - God forbid - returned to teaching. No, it was best dealt with quietly, in the hope that she made a full recovery. That way it couldn't screw things up later, if the guest house didn't work out and she had to go back to work. She shuddered at the thought, recalling the moment in Room 10a when she'd finally flipped.

She still couldn't believe that she'd done it. Slapping Kenny Mason around the face like that and just storming out. But it had given her a sudden and massive sense of relief, even though she'd probably be suspended, charged with the assault of a minor and eventually lose her job. Kenny Mason was no minor. He was built like a brick shithouse and had the devious mind of a Bond villain.

Whatever the outcome, the look of pure astonishment on his face when she struck him was worth it. It had simultaneously shocked and silenced him. The rest of the class had given her a round of applause, but she only heard it from along the corridor as she stormed out. She'd made directly for the head teacher's office, telling Mr Vernon exactly what she'd done. Then she left Bishopbriggs Science Academy and resolved never to teach again.

Fortunately for her, Kenny Mason's parents also thought that he was a little shit, so didn't press charges.

'Stoopid idiot deserves everything he got!' Phil Mason announced to Mr Vernon, striking his son much harder than Charlotte had. With that, the matter was closed, but there was no way Charlotte could return to education again. She'd had enough. Her mind was frayed, her confidence blown to pieces and her ability to work gone up in smoke.

'Could you just give your wife a kiss... move along a little bit further so you're directly under the sign. That's perfect. Hold it there please...'

Charlotte's mind returned to the here and now. She wondered what life was like for Nigel Davies, as a reporter working on a local newspaper in a rundown seaside resort. Back in the eighties, when they'd been students, it would have been a big deal. Things didn't seem to have moved on that much in the fading resort since they'd been away. She wondered if it was still a cause of excitement.

'So when will the article be in the newspaper?' Will

asked, always set on the practical. There was no disappearing into flights of conjecture, panic or fantasy for him; he always knew what to do. It had been his idea to buy the guest house. He'd run the numbers and looked like he'd hit the jackpot.

'This place has a sixty-one thousand pounds turnover every year, twenty-five thousand pounds of which is profit. It has a housekeeper who runs the place, a family flat at the top and it's cheap as chips compared to Bristol. All you have to do is run to the cash and carry twice a week and watch the bookings come in. Simple!'

Not for the first time, Charlotte had agreed to something that she was less than certain about. She knew that she had to bring in some money - fast - and that the thought of going back into education was unbearable. Just thinking about it made her sweat all over, her hands shaking at the prospect of going back into that classroom. Will had been as patient as anything for the first seven months, but the first time they'd missed making a full mortgage payment, he was furious.

'We can't carry on like this. We have to make a plan, or we're going down!' he'd announced.

So, there they were, smiling for the camera and hoping like hell that owning a guest house in Morecambe would simultaneously allow them to balance the books without Charlotte having to return to the workplace. Any workplace. Much as he could see they were in financial trouble, Will knew his wife well enough to understand that she was still very fragile.

'The news story is online already,' Nigel replied to Will's question. 'We can't hold on to anything these days - the internet is like some insatiable beast which has to be fed.

I'll add the photo as soon as I'm back in the office and the full feature will get published in Friday's newspaper. How does that sound?'

'Sounds great to me - what do you think Charlotte?' Will asked, desperately searching her face for some sign of enthusiasm, even the smallest glimmer of hope.

'Yes, sounds great,' Charlotte replied, her mind elsewhere. It was always elsewhere these days.

'So, just to check, you're booking guests into the first-floor rooms and still decorating the middle floor?'

'Yes,' Will replied. 'It had been empty for so long when we bought it, it needed a refresh. We've made the ground and first floor look great, but we'll use the income to redecorate the middle floor. That's the plan, anyway!'

'It's good to see someone taking a chance on the resort, rather than abandoning it,' Nigel replied. 'We need a bit of hope around this town. This row of guest houses used to be Morecambe's finest. It's so sad to see what's happening to the place.'

'How long have you lived here?' Charlotte asked, genuinely interested. She liked Nigel Davies; he had an enthusiasm that was infectious. She needed a bit of that.

'Same as you,' Nigel smiled. 'I went to the university in Lancaster, met my wife and we settled here.'

'It wasn't quite the same for us,' Will told him. 'I was at the university; Charlotte was at the teaching college. We actually met in the eighties at Sandy Beaches Holiday Camp, if you can remember that? We were two hard-up students, paying off our overdrafts. We lived in Bristol for years after we left the area, but we thought it would be nice to come back to our roots.'

Not much had changed as far as Charlotte was

concerned. They were still hard-up; they just weren't students any more. And although the resort did hold many happy memories, it was also the place where a terrible thing had happened. An event that had lain buried for over thirty years. One which she'd never quite believed that she'd got away with.

CHAPTER TWO

Present Day - Morecambe

'So, come on. We've got one more day before I start the new job. How about we take a drive around, see how the old place has changed?'

Charlotte didn't feel like a drive around. Her anxiety levels were already rocketing in anticipation of the first dribble of guests arriving later that week and it seemed a distraction too far. As usual, Will succeeded in cajoling her.

'It'll be good for you,' he'd reminded her, 'It'll get your head out of what happened. You remember what the Cognitive Behavioural Therapy guy said: you need to be more present.'

Charlotte had heard what the CBT guy had said, but it was easier to read in a pamphlet than it was to carry out in real life. Her phone made the distinctive *ding* sound, announcing that a Facebook update had arrived.

I hate this place already. It's a tip!

She had every sympathy for Olli and Lucia having to

tear themselves away from their life in Bristol and start again. But if she and Will didn't salvage their relationship... well, school would be the least of their problems. It had seemed like a good idea at the time, returning to the place they'd met, a town with happy associations for them. Where they'd got their degrees and married in the local register office. Where they'd both taken their first teaching jobs. When Will had put it like that, she couldn't refuse him. After all, he didn't know what had happened there.

'I still can't get used to the gears in this car,' Will cursed as he reversed out into the narrow alleyway at the rear of the guest house.

'Well, selling the decent cars paid for the redecoration work, so beggars can't be choosers.'

'Yeah, I know, but...'

Charlotte cursed in her head. Maybe the CBT guy was right. She seemed to frame everything as a negative since walking out of the school. It was a cycle she couldn't break out of. The glass was always half empty rather than half full. She couldn't help it; her words just came out that way. Will was doing his best.

Charlotte's phone dinged again. Lucia.

They all hate me. They're already in their cliques. I'll never fit in here.

She wanted to scream. She hated herself for forcing this upon the kids. But what choice did they have? Olli and Lucia were probably too self-absorbed to have sensed the tensions between her and Will. They'd made sure the counselling sessions were in the daytime, so the kids would never know about those. Maybe if they made it to their Golden Wedding, they might laugh about it then, when life had been safely tucked in behind them.

Will was doing his best; he had done everything the

counsellor advised. Now he was encouraging her to share old memories of their early years together as a way of cementing what they'd built together. Maybe it was time she got with the programme. But she felt so worn down all the time, she just wanted a break... from Will, the kids, from life. She needed some time, a little space - but life was a carousel which insisted on turning.

'Doesn't it feel good to be back?' Will said as they drew out of the junction, back onto the sea front.

It was a beautiful, clear day - a rarity - and they could see the Cumbrian hills in the distance, beyond the shimmering sea. Even though it was a weekday, pensioners and parents with toddlers were walking up and down the front. It would have been good, if it wasn't for what had happened.

'Remember the pier?' Will asked. 'That disco we went to as students. You could see the sea through the floorboards, talk about scary!'

Charlotte laughed. Will had been dressed up in his Duran Duran gear that night. He'd even ventured a touch of makeup. It seemed so funny now, looking back at it.

'I remember spending half an hour on my hair and when we stepped off the bus, the wind was wild - by the time we'd walked along the deck and got in, I looked like some wild beast from a horror movie!'

They both laughed, Will taking his hand away from the gear stick and placing it on her leg.

'It's good to hear you laugh,' he said, looking over at her. 'Hey, this is where I failed my driving test for the first time, do you remember that?'

They passed a slip lane in the road and Charlotte nodded.

'Undue hesitation wasn't it?' she asked.

'Yes, I was so relieved to have a moment's pause, I just stopped in that lane and didn't move. The driving instructor asked me if everything was alright. I'd gone into a daze; I was so relieved to be out of the traffic flow!'

Charlotte laughed out loud at that.

'It's good to be back, isn't it?' Will said earnestly.

She knew how much he wanted the marriage to work. She did too. Everything just seemed so difficult. 'We certainly have a lot of good memories here.'

'Oh no, look, Adventure Kingdom is all boarded up!'

Charlotte looked away from the sea, towards what was left of the amusement park that they'd frequented every summer as students. Her phone dinged again. She ignored it. *Live in the present moment,* the CBT guy had said.

'Oh no. We had so much fun in there,' she answered, thinking back. 'Do you remember your brother in that Crazy Mouse ride? I honestly thought he was going to jump out of it, he was so scared.'

Will smiled, that big, broad beam that she fell for every time. Charlotte was a quick learner after Bruce, soon realising that guys like Will - skinny as a rake, with zero athleticism and completely useless with anything related to tools, cars or motorbikes - guys like that were usually a lot nicer. They had to be; they couldn't trade on their bodies. She was still a sucker for that smile.

'We'll be okay, won't we?' Will asked out of the blue. 'We won't end up like all our college friends, divorced and bitter? I know it's been difficult, but we'll be okay here, I'm sure.'

Charlotte gave a nod but couldn't muster a verbal response.

'I wonder if they'll knock it all down and build an Aldi?' Will commented.

'It's sad though,' Charlotte said thoughtfully. 'All these places we used to frequent as kids - the funfair, the pier, the arcades. They even used to come here with the Radio One Roadshow, don't you remember? We got one of the worst DJs every year, never a breakfast presenter. I wonder what makes a place like this struggle?'

'It's far from dead yet,' Will replied, keen to defend their decision to relocate there. 'You saw the accounts on the guest house. I can't believe you can still generate a decent income like that. Somebody must still be visiting this place!'

Charlotte was looking from side to side now. They had reached the end of the promenade and were now entering the West End.

'This bit still looks run down,' she said, wondering if the three-storey buildings had once been hotels and accommodation for holiday-makers. Now they had been demoted to houses of multiple occupancy, and the West End had become the location of choice for the terminally unemployed.

'Hey, we've got time. Why don't we drive out to Heysham and take a look at the old holiday camp?'

Charlotte tensed immediately, feeling her face reddening. Her phone dinged. She resisted looking once again. If it was Lucia giving her a running commentary of how much she hated her new school, she might scream.

'Do we have to?' she replied. 'It was always a dump back then. Besides, they shut it down, didn't they?'

'Yes, I think so. Remember how the holiday-makers used to arrive on the Fun Bus on a Saturday afternoon, and the look of disappointment on their faces when they saw where they were staying for the next week? Some of the poor buggers were stuck there for a fortnight!'

Charlotte remembered. She recalled everything about that place. Her one small consolation was that it was where she and Will had met.

'Let's go and take a look,' Will insisted. 'For old times' sake. We haven't been back there since we finished that summer season in '84. We don't have guests in tomorrow, so we can spare the time.'

Reluctantly, Charlotte agreed. She'd known this would come up. But she'd resolved to take it in her stride, so what harm could it do? It was almost forty years ago. Where had the time gone? Besides, Bruce was long gone. Maybe not from her nightmares, perhaps not from her deepest fears. But wherever he was now, he was out of their lives. He couldn't get to her now.

Sandy Beaches Holiday Camp was approached via a winding country lane, bordered on each side by fields. There was no indication of being anywhere near a beach until static caravans began to appear at irregular intervals and a nuclear power station loomed up in the distance.

'I forgot about the power station,' Will said. 'Can you imagine spending all that money on your summer holidays, only to share the beach with a power station? People must have been so disappointed.'

They turned a corner, passed a static caravan site and directly in front of them was the Sandy Beaches Holiday Camp. Will drew up in front of it, now surrounded by protective fencing with *Danger. Keep Out!* signs liberally attached around the perimeter. In a small clearing to the side, three bulldozers lay in wait. The sign was still there, on a big wall which at one time had heralded the arrival of thousands of holiday-makers to the area. *Sandy B-aches Holiday C-mp.*

'I'm tempted to steal one of the letters myself,' Will said, looking at the sad gaps between the once-proud lettering. 'Or maybe we could re-arrange them to make a rude word, like they used to do at the beginning of Fawlty Towers on the TV?'

Charlotte's phone dinged again. She was surprised she could even get a signal so far out from the resort. They hadn't had mobile phones back in the eighties, so it wasn't even an issue back then.

'Let's take a look around, shall we?' Will asked, getting out of the car already.

Charlotte could resist no longer; she took her phone out of standby and checked the notifications. It was Facebook. A friend request - that was unusual. And she didn't recognise the name.

'Are you coming?' Will asked. 'I want to lock up the car.'

Charlotte made a move, like she was on her way, but stopped to examine the friend request. It was from an Andrew Stranger, but there was no image. A Stranger - was this a joke or some weirdo guy chancing his luck?

There was a message attached. She moved her thumb and opened it.

I saw you online in the local paper. I have your necklace. I've had it for years. Want it back?

CHAPTER THREE

1984 - Sandy Beaches Holiday Camp

There were two new arrivals that day, both of them students. Among the staff at the Sandy Beaches Holiday Camp, there was very much an 'us-and-them' divide between the students and the other seasonal recruits. The students were usually there to pay off overdrafts, levelling up their cash to enable them to spend the next academic year in the bar, much as they had done the year before. Some of the students were dismissive of the other staff, thinking that their impending degrees made them somehow superior.

The divide between the students and the regular workers was further exacerbated by the fact that the Easter starters all knew each other - and the system - extremely well by the time the students started to show their faces. However, for the young men and women who worked all summer, then having thrown the benefits staff off their scent, returned to their bedsits over winter, students were a romantic prize that was much sought after.

The prospect of some 'posh totty' was worth the fight through the smouldering resentment of being uneducated. After all, the students got grants which enabled them to get better-paid jobs, comfortable accommodation, refectory meals and a roller coaster life of booze and parties. On benefits, there was no work and the accommodation tended to be worse. Either way, it was the government bank-rolling it all, but the students seemed to get the better deal.

Mickey Lucas was showing round two new student recruits. Mickey had a higher status than the other non-student workers. Having returned to the camp over a period of several years - starting as a kitchen porter, then moving up to waiting on tables - he was now what passed as lower management at Sandy Beaches Holiday Camp. He presided over a team of waiters, waitresses and nippies - the title given to the female-only staff who cleared tables in the cafeteria.

Mickey quite clearly had the hots for the new girl, whose name was as yet unknown. Charlotte was standing at her station, her tables already set, awaiting the arrival of her first diners. As a waitress she was allocated three tables of eight people. Sometimes they were couples, at other times families, occasionally solo holiday-makers. Each day, they were given a choice of three starters, three main courses and three sweets. There was nothing ambitious on offer; it was a couple of notches up from a school dinner.

While Mickey quite clearly had his eyes on the young woman, Charlotte had clocked the guy already. He was rating extremely high as far as she was concerned. They were in the lull between getting the tables set up and their workstations ready and awaiting the first guests to dribble in. The guests had a window of up to two hours to grab their lunch, so it was always anybody's guess when they would show their faces.

'Hot stuff at three o'clock!' Jenna whispered.

'I see him,' Charlotte smiled, 'Hands off, he's mine.'

'You're with Bruce already,' Jenna reminded her. 'Whereas me? I'm still floating.'

'Maybe I won't be with Bruce much longer...' Charlotte began.

'Oh yes? Is all not going well with the new love birds?'

'I'll tell you about it later,' Charlotte replied. 'They're heading over here. Tits out, best behaviour, you know the drill!'

'Hi Jenna, Charlotte...' Mickey began, surveying their tables before making the introductions. 'Jenna, you might just want to straighten some of your cutlery. It looks a bit slapdash from over here.'

Charlotte watched as Jenna's face reddened. Mickey had made an early power play, showing the new girl who was boss. It was important for Mickey to let new recruits know who ruled the roost.

'This is Will and Sally,' Mickey began. 'They're starting today. I'm handing them over to shadow you today and tomorrow, then I'll assign them their tables once they've got the hang of everything.'

Charlotte couldn't have been happier. Will was just her sort: skinny, completely unmacho and with a ready, friendly smile. His arms were too long for the white jacket that he'd been allocated and his bow tie was slightly askew. Sally was blonde, with a soft complexion and gentle features.

Charlotte had never encountered women as coarse and crude as the Easter intake at Sandy Beaches Holiday Camp. They talked openly about their sex lives and wore love bites on their necks as trophies of conquest. They called it chalet rash in the kitchens, but the currencies among the non-student staff were the love bites on your neck and the number of different people who'd given them to you.

The students tended to avoid that game, though a few got caught up in it. But none could compete with Abi Smithson, a woman with startling grey eyes, reputed to be sexually voracious, whose sole aim was to work through every single male member of staff during the course of the summer. That was according to holiday camp folklore. She had a trail of love bites leading from her neck, down to her cleavage. Beyond that it was a matter for conjecture as to how far down they went. For Charlotte it felt more like cannibalism than a sign of affection and she'd told Bruce in no uncertain terms that he was not to bite her. That was the first time she'd seen what he could be like.

Will and Sally exchanged pleasantries.

'Charlie and Jenna are thick as thieves - they both attend the teacher training college in Lancaster,' Mickey told them.

'We're from the university,' Will said, 'Paying off overdrafts!'

'Are you a couple?' Charlotte asked, perhaps a little obvious.

'No, I'm here with my boyfriend,' Sally chimed in. 'He's in the entertainment team, a Purple Coat. I didn't know Will before today. It's a big campus at the uni.'

'A Purple Coat, eh?' Jenna teased. Purple Coats trumped Mickey in the hierarchy, as prestigious as it came, even getting better accommodation than the regular staff. Confident and cocksure, they were the entertainment heart of Sandy Beaches Holiday Camp. Their role gave them access to everybody and they would regularly dine alongside the customers, not having to rough it in the staff canteen like the others.

'Yes, he's a singer and a comedian,' Sally told them. 'I'm here to spend the summer with him, rather than go home to my parents.'

Mickey interrupted them. 'Let me take you to the kitchens, then these two can show you the ropes. The diners will start to arrive soon.'

He whisked them away, leaving Jenna and Charlotte with a few minutes to exchange notes.

'I wish he'd stop calling me Charlie!' Charlotte cursed, the moment they were out of earshot. 'What gives people the right to think they can mangle your name without permission? It's really rude!'

'They seem nice enough,' Jenna said, attempting to divert her. She'd heard the name rant many times before.

'Yes,' Charlotte agreed, checking out Will's butt as he disappeared through the swing door. She still wasn't quite sure why she'd got together with Bruce. He wasn't really her type; Will was much more like it. She resolved to have another try at ditching Bruce later that evening. It wasn't that she didn't fancy Bruce. A bit of muscle and supreme confidence between the sheets had been quite a novelty, but she'd realised quickly that she needed much more than brawn and a limited repertoire of bedroom moves. Somehow she didn't think he would quite hit the mark in the long term.

'Sally's lucky being with a Purple Coat,' Charlotte continued. 'That means she won't be confined to the bad chalets like we are.'

'Lucky cow...' Jenna agreed, then looked over towards the entrance to the dining room. 'Oh look, prunes lady is here!'

'Ha, I wonder if she's had a bowel movement yet,' Charlotte laughed.

It was a constant source of amusement for the waiting staff. Many of the pensioners would order prunes as their first course at breakfast or as their sweet at lunchtime or dinner. Jenna had an old lady assigned to her tables who constantly ate prunes. As far as Charlotte and Jenna were concerned, prunes were such an abomination as a food type that only somebody in dire need of relief from constipation would eat them. Even funnier to them was the strained look on the woman's face.

'She'll come in one morning looking calm and relaxed and we'll know she's finally defeated the logjam!' Jenna had laughed.

Jenna switched on her smile and welcomed the old lady and her husband, seating them at the end of one of her tables. Charlotte was still awaiting her first guests, so looked over to the kitchen door to check on the progress of the new recruits. The swing doors to the kitchen had safety glass in them at eye level, to protect the waiting staff from being clouted by an opening door while they had their hands full of plates stacked with hot food.

Bruce was watching her from his station in the kitchen, through the glass portal, awaiting dirty dishes to stack into the plastic trays which sent them through the industrial size dishwashing machine. Whenever she looked over he seemed to be watching, like a sentinel, ever alert. She'd need to have that conversation with him - and soon.

CHAPTER FOUR

Present Day - Morecambe

For a moment, parked outside the derelict remains of the holiday camp, Charlotte thought she'd given the game away. She could feel the colour draining from her face. Surely Will would notice. And here, of all places. What a time for that Facebook message to arrive.

'Charlotte, come on!' Will cajoled. 'Is that a message from Lucia? She's been bitching about school all day; my messenger app is full of her moans.'

'Well you can't really blame her, can you? We take her out of the school she's been in since the age of eleven and relocate her to a place she knows nothing about. Morecambe might have some happy memories for us, Will, but remember, it's new to the kids.'

'Would anybody have given a damn about what we thought when we were kids? My mum and dad used to move us around all the time. They could never settle in one place. We give the kids too much say in things these days.

When I was young, I had to like it or lump it. I can remember my dad smoking at the table at mealtimes and we'd all be coughing away. But his attitude would just be a *Screw You!* We're too soft as parents. We're all too soft these days...'

Charlotte was thankful that Will was off on one of his favourite rants. The softening of attitudes over the generations - that one never grew old.

It bought her a few more seconds to look at the message. It was completely anonymous: no image, no contact details, no other Facebook friends. It was obviously a spoof profile.

This was something different from the cruel messages the kids at school would send. It was focused, meant just for her. And whoever had sent it knew about the necklace. How, though? She'd never spoken a word about that night. When she'd returned to check on Bruce the moment daylight had broken, he was gone. She'd panicked, fearing at the time that she'd killed him and he'd been washed away by the sea.

But nobody reported Bruce missing, even though he didn't turn up for work the next day. And all Mickey Lucas could tell her was that Bruce had slipped a note under the door of the admin offices, informing them that he had quit.

'That's really screwed up my rotas.' Mickey had cursed. 'He won't get his wages either, not if he didn't work out his notice.'

Who knew about the necklace? She'd never worn jewellery since. Charlotte had managed to lose the one thing that was most precious to her. She'd unclasped it from her mother's neck - aged eleven - because her mum was too weak to do it herself.

'It's yours Charlotte,' she'd whispered, so drained by the treatment in the hospice that she could barely say the words. 'You've always loved it and now it's yours. I'll always be with you my precious girl, always.'

Those had been her last words to Charlotte. She'd worn the necklace every day since her mum had died. And she'd never forgiven herself for losing it that night on the beach.

Will was getting impatient now.

'Charlotte, will you please put that phone away and come on. I want to lock the doors.'

He had the car remote poised to secure the vehicle. Charlotte slammed the door and the car cheeped as Will activated the locks. She slipped her phone into her jeans back pocket and walked up to Will.

'I don't know why you're locking the doors,' she remarked, 'The place is all cordoned off, we can only get a view from a distance anyway.'

'Screw that!' Will said. 'The great thing about being middle-aged is that you can get away with almost anything. It's so remote out here that nobody will see us anyway. But if they do, we'll just tell them that this is where we met, and we were having a last look around for old times' sake.'

He was already unlatching one of the wire safety panels from its clip. Before long, he'd removed the lower clip, tilted one of the panels to the side and was down on his knees, squeezing through the gap.

'Aren't we a bit old to be sneaking into building sites?'

'You're never too old to break into a building site, Charlotte!' he smiled. 'Besides, we're not here to steal anything, we're just here for a look around.'

Charlotte remembered, of course she did. She remembered every inch of that place. She'd scoured the whole holiday camp after Bruce had disappeared, barely able to believe that she'd got away with it, looking for clues, searching for her necklace. She didn't really know what clues she was looking for, but she did it anyway.

As the days passed, there was no investigation, no police visit and no awkward questions. Everybody knew she and Bruce had split up by then, so he was none of her business. The only response she could get about Bruce's disappearance was that he was a prick for leaving them in the lurch like that. He should have worked his notice, but because he hadn't, he wouldn't get his wages. Mickey liked to repeat that one, as a warning to the rest of them not to do the same thing.

Reluctantly, Charlotte got down on her knees and pulled herself through the fence and into the grounds of Sandy Beaches Holiday Camp. She stood up and looked around. It was exactly as she remembered it, only run down, the paint flaking on the doors and windows, weeds growing along the paths and road, the once-manicured flower bed now completely overgrown.

To the left was the old porter's lodge, the place where she'd first got off the holiday bus and made her presence known, nervous about what working at a holiday camp might entail. To the right was the admin block, the place they used to go every Tuesday to collect their wages. The money would be handed over in small, translucent envelopes, the corners of the notes sticking out of the top so that they could be counted without breaking the seal. It all seemed so long ago; Charlotte could barely believe that she was old enough to remember receiving wages that way.

Directly ahead of the porter's lodge was the family pub - and the wishing well that gave it its olde worlde charm.

'Look at those chalets!' Will scoffed. 'That was the biggest surprise of my life when I arrived. Those units look like inner-city housing. There's no way you could describe that accommodation as a chalet.'

'They were the pits, weren't they?' Charlotte replied, thinking back to the one room that they had shared towards the end of their summer stint. They'd even got a double bed, much to the envy of other couples on the site.

'Do you remember that bed?' she continued. 'It was so funny; you'd see people moving them about on the landings as couples got together and broke up.'

'I was once offered forty pounds for ours.' Will smiled.

'You never told me that. That was a week's wages in those days. Who offered you that amount of money? I'm surprised you didn't take it.'

'No way!' said Will. 'There were only four or five double beds available to the catering staff, and they had to be shared out between over fifty of us. Most couples had to make do with pushing two single beds together. Once I got hold of one, there was no way I was letting it go. Besides, we were young and in love. I couldn't believe my luck when you and I got together.'

For one moment Charlotte was able to recapture a moment in time and feel that excitement as if she were actually there, back in 1984. It passed in an instant, but for a few seconds she felt the rush of new love and the relief that Bruce was out of her life - somehow - and that sense of having her whole life ahead of her.

Her thoughts were interrupted by the sound of an Alsatian barking ahead of them. They'd been spotted by a security patrol. They were barely through the fence and they'd been caught already.

CHAPTER FIVE

Present Day - Morecambe

'George? That can't be George.' said Will.

'It might be, he'd be an old man now. He's coming up to us anyway, so we'll soon find out.'

The Alsatian appeared to have much more enthusiasm for the job than the security guard did. The man was old and slow. Clearly whoever now owned the site didn't have high expectations of it being invaded by criminal masterminds or the like.

'You realise you're not supposed to be on these premises, don't you?' he said, as if assessing the level of threat. He relaxed immediately, evidently concluding that Will and Charlotte were of minimal danger.

'George Newlove, that is you isn't it?' Will asked.

Yes, I'm George Newlove,' the guard replied, scrutinising Will's face as if desperately trying to figure out how he knew his name.

'I'm Will - Will Grayson. I was here in 1984...'

'A lot of people passed through these gates over the years.'

'Yes, but you remember. Me and Charlotte. We used to come into the porter's lodge and drink tea with you. You would sometimes thrash me at pool in the family pub.'

George looked at Charlotte with a slow realisation.

'I remember you! You're Charlotte-not-Charlie! And Will. My God, what are you doing here? It's great to see you. And look at you, you're still together after all these years. That's so nice to see these days.'

Will took George's hand and shook it, clasping it firmly. He was genuinely choked up to see George again, a friendly ghost from the past, someone he'd barely thought about since leaving, but who'd become so much more important to him in the rear-view mirror that middle-age provided.

'I remember you two, you were one of the nicer couples that passed through these gates. Most of them used to pass me by. Very few staff or visitors took the trouble to get to know me. It's wonderful to see you. I guess I don't have to ask you why you're sneaking through the security fence? It's pretty obvious really.'

'Hello George,' Charlotte smiled, giving him a hug.

'I'm seventy in June,' he said. 'Can you believe I'm still here?'

'Wow, that's amazing!' Will replied. 'Have you worked here all this time?'

The Alsatian seemed to take its lead from George as Charlotte stroked him. It had made its own threat level assessment and had concluded that it was happy to be fussed by her.

'No, not continuously,' George responded. 'I retired at sixty, in the year this place closed. It's been boarded up for years, but they finally managed to sell the land. My Una died four years ago, and I thought I'd be on the scrap heap then. But when I saw this job advertised, I thought I'd take it. Nobody ever comes this way, so it's safe enough for a doddery old fool like me. Until the expensive building supplies arrive that is. I suspect they'll ask me to move on when something worth stealing arrives.'

'I'm so sorry to hear about your wife,' Charlotte said, fussing the Alsatian which had now metamorphosed into the softest creature in the canine kingdom.

'Yes, we met here, did you know that? She came on holiday here with her mum and dad in 1969. I was twenty years old and new to the porter's job, she was just eighteen...'

'That's the same age as we were, pretty well,' Will commented. 'This place must be responsible for hundreds of marriages!'

'Well, it's funny you should say that,' George continued. 'The strange thing about a place like this is that it either drew people together or it split them apart. For me and Una, it was true love. It looks like it was the same for you too?'

Will and Charlotte looked at each other. Charlotte returned to patting the dog a little sooner than she should, unsure how much she wanted to dwell on their own relationship at that moment in time.

'Anyway, it's good to see you. You want a tour?' George asked.

'Can we?' Will asked. 'I'm sorry about sneaking through the fence, but we couldn't resist it.'

'It's no trouble,' George smiled, 'But I'd appreciate it if you could set that security panel back right - I'll kill myself if I have to bend down that far!'

Charlotte burst out laughing. 'I know the feeling, I

almost did myself a mischief when I crawled through that gap.'

'She likes you,' George said, as the dog's tail wagged furiously, ecstatic at the attention it was receiving.

'She's called Una,' George admitted sheepishly. 'I spend most of my day talking to my Una, so it seemed the best thing to do. At least it doesn't confuse the dog.'

'No harm in that,' Will reassured him, 'You must miss her terribly after all those years ... I know I would.'

'There's not a day goes by that I don't think of her,' George said, his eyes reddening. 'And it helps to be wandering around here all day, in a place that's full of happy memories for me. It was one of the saddest days of my life when they closed it down. Everybody's hopping on EasyJet and holidaying abroad now. I guess it was bound to happen.'

George led the way towards the narrow road that ran through the centre of the old camp. He was slow in walking, but Will didn't hurry him.

'What sort of hours do they keep you here, George?' he asked.

'Oh, it's only part-time; I'm not even sure I could manage it full-time now. I'm not here every day. Basically, I turn up for twenty hours a week, at random times, and it just gives the appearance that we have security on site. Nothing ever happens here...'

George stopped and thought a moment.

'What?' Charlotte asked.

'I was going to say that nothing ever happens here, but that's not entirely true.'

'Go on,' Will urged, sensing a story.

'Well, I've been here for three months now, ever since the land was sold and the fencing went up. They start building next month. The planning permission just got passed last week.'

'What are they building here?' Charlotte asked.

'Where are they digging?' Will said at exactly the same time.

'It's going to be a retirement village. How ironic is that for me? I worked here all my life and there's no chance I'll be able to afford one of these places once they're built.'

'Where are they digging?' Will asked again.

'Well, those diggers that you see, they'll be creating a car park area for the contractors first of all, over there, well away from the main buildings and the dust.'

'By the tower?' Will asked.

The tower was the most distinctive feature of the holiday camp, apart from the main entertainment complex which had been built in the shape and form of an ocean liner. It was another irony about that place - creating a bricks and mortar image of the type of seaborne holiday that would eventually lure the holiday camp's clientele away from the charms of a UK-based vacation.

Circular in shape and built entirely of stone, a single storey in height, with distinctive battlements, the tower was a complete anomaly, bearing in mind the entertainments complex that had been built around it. Equally unusual was the fact that nobody seemed to know its history. Everybody asked, but nobody knew. It was difficult to date the structure. It had seemed older to Will as a teenager, but looking at it through adult eyes, he thought it was probably late-Victorian, perhaps even early twentieth century.

'Yes, just around the tower,' George confirmed. 'They're not taking it down though; they're going to renovate it and make a feature of it. I reckon it puts at least twenty thousand pounds on the price of each of those retirement homes.

They're going to rename this place Sandside Tower - how expensive-sounding is that?'

Will laughed, thinking George was probably right about that. 'Can we take a closer look at the tower?'

'Do we have to?' Charlotte asked. Una looked up at her, expecting further fussing.

'Why not?' said Will. 'Everything else is boarded up now, so we can't get a proper look inside. It's our last chance to take a tour. This place will be all locked up when they start spending money on it.'

He took Charlotte's hand, encouraging her towards the structure on the grassy bank which, along with a wall, separated the camp from the beach. But she trembled and pulled her hand away, as a look of panic passed across her face.

'I'm sorry, I've got to go. I need to head back to the car. I'm sorry George...'

Charlotte ran off back along the road, leaving the two men looking at each other, wondering what had just happened.

CHAPTER SIX

1984 - Sandy Beaches Holiday Camp

Jenna and Charlotte were in the thick of a lunch shift by the time Will and Sally had completed their tour of the dining room. Mickey deposited the new recruits at their work-station.

'I'd like you to shadow Jenna and Charlotte until teatime tomorrow, then I'll allocate you your own tables when the new guests arrive on Saturday. How does that sound?'

Will and Sally nodded, and Mickey was away, fussing around elsewhere in the dining room.

'One moment,' Charlotte said to Will, 'I'll just deliver these lamb cutlets and I'll be with you.'

Will watched as she walked briskly to the serving area, loaded two plates up with the aforementioned food, and dropped it off at her table.

'They're all on main courses now. That gives us five minutes for a chat. Have you ever served on tables before?'

'No,' Will replied, 'Just a bit of bar work in the town. I've dropped off a couple of ploughman's lunches in my time, but that's about the length of it.'

'Well, don't worry, you don't need any experience to survive in this place. It's pretty basic stuff; not a lot can go wrong. Just make sure you get the orders right and don't spill it all in their lap. Apart from that, you're good to go!'

Jenna and Sally were already serving together. It seemed to Will that Sally had done it before.

'So, you're at the university?' Charlotte asked.

'Yes, studying English Literature. God knows why, my real interest is in photography. How about you?'

'I'm at the teacher training college. I couldn't quite make it to university. Besides, I've always wanted to teach. I'm doing English as my second subject.'

They hit it off straight away, so much so that they were interrupted by one of the guests in mid-flow.

'Excuse me!' she announced. 'As if it weren't disappointing enough that we're stuck in this godforsaken place all week, it would be nice if we could get fed while we're here. I can't think of a worse place to starve in!'

Charlotte's face reddened; this wasn't a good start to her mentoring duties.

'I'm so sorry,' she apologised, 'I'll come and take your order now.'

'No worries, I'll do it,' said Will, smiling at the lady. She relaxed immediately, flattered to have such a nice young man attending to her. Will escorted her back to her table and took the family's order. Within two minutes he had them eating out of his hand and laughing their heads off.

'See, a little bit of patter and they're like putty in my hand. Now, I've got their order, but where the heck do I get the food?'

Will was quick to learn, not that there was much to pick up. The food was all stored in industrial-sized warmers which lined the far end of the dining room. On the cafeteria side, the guests had to help themselves. On the table-service side, they got to order from the same school lunch menu, but the waiters and waitresses dished it up and delivered it to them.

The entire system was based on a conveyor belt process. You picked up a tray, grabbed some warm dishes, got the servers to place the order on the plate, then off you went to get it delivered to your tables before it started to go cold.

'Breakfast is the time you need to get strategic,' Charlotte explained. 'Fried eggs are at a real premium, 'cause they're slow to get cooked and hard to keep warm. Get to know the serving staff who are delivering the fried eggs and you won't go far wrong.'

Will manoeuvred a couple of lamb cutlets onto a plate.

'Hey man, wait to be served!' a thickset man in a grubby apron shouted over to him.

'They can be quite territorial over the serving duties. If you serve yourself, make sure nobody's looking. And if you piss them off, they'll give you the broken or rubbery eggs in the morning. I'm telling you, this place is like one massive negotiating table - it's all about who you know.'

Will apologised to the serving assistant - a Scot called Stevie. The way he'd spoken to Will made it sound like he was about to tear his head off.

'You'll get used to the Scots,' Charlotte reassured him. 'They sound terrifying, but they're really nice. No wonder the Romans decided to call off their invasion and just build a big wall to keep them in.'

Jenna and Sally joined the queue for food, lining up their trays on the counters next to Will and Charlotte's.

'Do you fancy coming out tonight?' Jenna asked. 'Apparently, Sally gets left on her own most evenings because her man is entertaining the crowds all evening. How about a crawl around the bars?'

Charlotte hesitated for a moment. One of the few benefits of working at Sandy Beaches Holiday Camp was the bars that were spread out over the site. There was the family pub and the Old Codger's bar, in which a keyboard and singing duo played old-time hits all evening, plus an entertainment and show area which became packed at night. Every night on stage, before nine o'clock, there'd be some form of family entertainment. The kids were sent off to bed and the cover bands then appeared on stage, along with the occasional comedian. And, if they ever fancied getting away from the site, there was the pub in the next village, which also made a pleasant change.

'Yes, how about it?' she replied. 'I'm up for a night out. Krazeee are on stage tonight. They always play some decent cover versions - let's do it!'

The time passed a lot faster than normal, thanks to the novelty of Will and Sally being there. It wasn't long until they reached the post-meal hot drinks and the end of the shift was in sight.

'I need to teach you how to sort the teas and coffees,' Charlotte began to explain to Will. 'They're a bit of a pain - sometimes the urn in the dining room runs dry and you have to use the back-up urn in the kitchens.'

She walked him over to the urn and lifted off the lid, peering inside.

'See, it's as good as empty. I wish they'd just put another one out here. If you're not careful they'll get a cup full of limescale and then the customers will start bitching. Look, I'll just about manage to squeeze a teapot for two out of this water. If you go into the kitchens and turn immediately right, you'll see the second urn. Just take care when you come through the door, in case someone sends you flying.'

Will watched how Charlotte presented the tea, then grabbed a tray, set out the cups and saucers, took an empty metal teapot and headed for the kitchens.

He'd barely taken it all in when Mickey had taken him and Sally on their tour, and he'd already forgotten the names of the staff in there.

'Hey, big man!' shouted the guy who was unloading the dishwasher, sticking up his thumb in an enthusiastic welcome.

'Hi!' Will responded, 'Is it over here to use the urn? Alright to just help myself?'

'Get in there, big man!' came the reply.

Will moved over towards the steaming container, placing his tray on the sturdy table on which it was supported. He lifted the lid and peered inside, as Charlotte had done with the urn in the dining area. Will was aware of somebody approaching from behind, and turned to see who it was.

'So, you're one of the new guys?'

Will turned around to see who was speaking. He recognised the man as the dish washer, his massive arms covered in tattoos.

'Yes, hi, I'm Will Grayson,' he began.

'So what do you think of Charlotte?' the man asked.

Will was taken aback; he'd expected an outstretched hand and a friendly greeting.

'Charlotte? Oh, well, she's nice. She's been very helpful... is she a friend of yours?'

'Listen pal, I'm no fan of you students, prancing around like you own the place.'

Will was immediately on his guard. He recognised behaviour like this from his school days.

'And I certainly don't like it when your type swan in here and smile sweetly at all the girls, you get me?'

Will just stared at him in amazement, still not sure where this had come from.

'Is there a problem here?' he asked. 'Have I offended you in some way?'

'Have I offended you in some way?' the man echoed back in an effeminate voice. He took hold of Will's hand and placed it on the tray, directly underneath the spout of the tea urn. He placed his other hand on the tap which switched the flow of water on and off.

Will jolted his hand to try to free it. He'd been caught completely off his guard, in no way expecting an encounter like this, not five minutes after walking into the kitchen.

'Yes, Will, you've offended me in some way,' the man seethed directly into his face. 'Charlotte is my girl and I don't like it when student types like you walk in here like you own the place, thinking you can just give them a charming smile and sweet-talk them into bed with all that learning nonsense.'

'I really wasn't hitting on Charlotte. Besides, isn't it up to her who she speaks to?'

Bruce held Will's hand firmly to the tray and flicked the tap so that a trickle of scalding water ran onto his hand. Will's impulse was to snatch it away, but the man held him firmly. Faced with that power and strength, Will was no match for him physically.

'Leave Charlotte alone... or else!' the man said, moving in so close that Will could taste his breath.

He released Will's hand and returned to his workstation, not bothering to glance back, with the self-confidence of a man who was used to physical intimidation.

Will rubbed his hand, scanning the kitchen to see if anybody had noticed what just happened. There were no witnesses; everybody was busy trying to get cleaned up and finish the shift.

He carried on preparing the teas and delivered them to the table, returning to Charlotte's station to see what was needed next.

'Did you meet Bruce in the kitchens?' Charlotte asked. 'He's my, well I guess he was my... Bruce is my friend.'

Will looked at her directly, wondering whether he should say anything. He moved his scalded hand behind his back so that she wouldn't notice. He'd need to run it under a cold tap as soon as possible to ease the scalding.

'I think I just met him. He's the dish washer, right?'

'Yes, that's him. Did he introduce himself?'

'Yes, you might say that,' Will replied.

CHAPTER SEVEN

Present Day - Morecambe

'I still can't believe you ran off like that! George let me out of the side gate, so I could catch up with you.'

Charlotte couldn't figure out if Will was annoyed or embarrassed.

He shook his head in despair. 'George is a good guy - what must he think of us?'

'I'm sure he's seen it all before. Don't worry, I'll go back and apologise some time. I'll make it up to him.'

'But whatever came over you?' Will asked. 'I thought we'd got through all of this?'

She was as desperate as he was to see an end to the panic attacks. But it didn't work like that. Sure, they were much less frequent now. She'd been a wreck after the incident in the classroom - any little thing would set her off. It was the sight of the tower and the dilapidated holiday camp. And the Facebook message. She'd just felt overwhelmed all of a sudden.

'What did you say to George?'

'I apologised of course! He was really concerned about you. He's such a nice guy, he always was. I just felt really embarrassed.'

'I'm sorry if I embarrass you, Will.'

'I didn't mean it like that! Come on Charlotte, I've been patient...'

'I told you before, Will, this isn't something that just gets fixed. I can't take a tablet and it's gone. Anxiety doesn't work like that.'

He moved his hand from the gear-stick over to hers. The car wasn't running yet.

'Come back any time,' George had said. 'But make sure Charlotte is okay. Take care of her first.'

'How did you get out?' Will asked, squeezing her hand.

'I came out the same way we went in ...' Charlotte answered. 'Don't worry, I put the fence back as it was.'

'Are you okay to head back home?' Will asked.

Charlotte nodded. They drove back to the guest house in silence. Whenever Will's attention was taken fully by the road, she'd open up the Facebook messages once again, trying to figure out who it could be.

She thought she'd killed Bruce Craven that night. She really believed he was dead. She was too scared to leave her room afterwards, in case he found her. She was terrified by what had happened on that beach. Yet her conscience urged her to confess and tell all.

When Bruce had gone in the morning, when it appeared he was alive and well, she didn't know what to think. Nobody seemed concerned. The police never came around asking questions. After what happened, she never wanted to see him again. He simply disappeared off the face of the earth.

Charlotte thanked her lucky stars many times over that social media was not a thing when she was young. Bruce knew nothing more about her than she was a student at the college in a town ten miles away. They didn't even have phones in those days. When Charlotte needed to call home, she'd have to save up her change and queue on the corner of her street to use an open-air public phone. There was no privacy - everybody could hear your conversation, loud and clear.

There were no selfies; very few photographs were taken, and most communications were sent via letter and Royal Mail. She wondered how Lucia might cope in a similar situation. Nowadays, the kids seemed to exchange personal details within minutes of meeting. They had access to each other's phone numbers, their social profiles, their dating information. They often shared intimate photographs within days of knowing each other. She shuddered to think there might be a day when her daughter got into a similar scrape with a man.

It had been terrifying and unsettling for her, but ultimately she'd been able to walk away. Bruce Craven had disappeared. He hadn't tried to trace her, and after she'd left the college and married, there was no way he'd ever find her anyway.

'Are you okay?' Will asked again, looking over to Charlotte. 'I was really concerned about you back there. I don't want to be a nag, but you've been so much better recently. It was a bit of a shock to see you racing off like that.'

'I'm fine, honestly,' Charlotte said. 'Have you heard from Olli today? Has he said anything about school?'

'Just a message at morning break,' Will replied. 'It was something like *Same drill, same old nonsense*. You know

Olli, he's never been one for enthusiasm where academia is concerned.'

'I know the feeling.' Charlotte smiled back, wanting to offer him something. She needed to figure out this message on her own. She'd never told Will. How could she? She was going to - the morning after she struck Bruce on the head with that rock. But she didn't have to. He'd gone, he'd handed in his notice, she was rid of him. She and Will were free to get on with their relationship, without the threatening shadow of Bruce Craven lingering in the background. Besides, they had some making up of their own to do after the way the evening had ended.

Will had never made anything of it at the time.

'Thank God he's pissed off!' was all he'd said. 'Good riddance to him. I'm pleased he's out of our lives. If he's gone back to Newcastle we'll never see him again. He won't be missed; he was violent and aggressive.'

That was it. Will wasn't normally one to bad-mouth people, but when it came to Bruce Craven, his invective ran freely. He'd made their lives hell over that couple of weeks at the holiday camp. They never spoke about him again, but both felt the gush of relief that comes when any toxic relationship is finally over.

'Lucia is being a right pain,' Charlotte continued. 'She's done nothing but bitch all day. Have you heard from her?'

'Yes - they need to be a bit stricter about their mobile phone policy at that school. She can't have done much learning today with all the messages that she's sent. Do you want to stop at the pub for a sandwich? For old time's sake?'

They'd reached the village at the end of the winding road that led to Sandy Beaches Holiday Camp. In the few weeks they'd been a couple at the site, they'd often taken a walk up to the village in the light, summer evenings to get away from their friends at the camp. Neither had a car as students, so it was buses or walking - and there was no convenient bus at that time of day.

'It's right at this corner isn't it?' he asked.

'Yes, it was just there, wasn't it?'

'It's gone!' Will said, disappointed. 'It's just a house now. I suppose everybody buys their booze from the off-licence these days, so there's not much call for village pubs this far out. It feels like they're putting up the shutters on our memories, and everything we did as youngsters is being sold off in a fire sale.'

Charlotte's phoned cheeped. They were back in the land of the living and her signal had returned.

'Voice mail,' she said, examining the screen. 'I'd better check it out, it might be Lucia deciding to run away on her first day of school.'

'I wouldn't put it past her.' Will laughed to himself, turning the car around in the ample drive of what had once been a very nice village pub.

Charlotte keyed in her numbers and listened to her message.

Hi Charlotte, it's Nigel here, Nigel Davies from The Bay View Weekly. We've had quite a reaction to the online article already. It seems a few people are glad to see you back in the area. There was one lady who was quite persistent - she wanted your phone number. I told her I can't pass it on, but I said I'd get in touch and let her know. She's called Jenna Manson - you knew her as Jenna Phillips ...'

'It's Jenna!' Charlotte announced. 'She still lives locally; can you believe that?'

'It's not that surprising,' Will answered. 'Not everybody was in such a rush to leave after they graduated. I'll bet loads of our old chums ended up getting jobs here.'

'She wants to meet up for coffee,' Charlotte continued. 'Nigel Davies has passed on her number. It'll be great to catch up with her. I lost track of her after we moved to Bristol. If you missed one house move or a change of address in the old days, you lost contact forever. I guess things cooled a bit after that summer. No wonder I couldn't find her on Facebook - she must have married. It'll still be good to catch up though.'

'We're not still eighteen years old, you know,' Will reminded her. 'At our age she could be a grandparent by now. She might have four marriages behind her. None of us are spring chickens.'

'I always wondered what happened to Jenna. She was such a great laugh at college. It's sad how we go our separate ways, isn't it? You must lose contact with so many people during your lifetime.'

'Well, some of them I'm pleased to see the back of,' Will replied. 'I can think of some people we knew here that I'm very happy never to see again.'

For a moment, Charlotte really thought he was going to say his name. After all those years. It would have been fitting, having just visited the holiday camp. Charlotte figured that Will must have thought about him again, but decided against mentioning it. Bruce Craven was like a marital problem that neither partner wanted to bring up in conversation, because it stirred such heated emotions.

Even if Will wasn't going to say the words, she couldn't bury her head in the sand any longer. She opened up Facebook on her phone and responded to the anonymous message.

'Who are you?' she typed. 'What do you want?'

CHAPTER EIGHT

Present Day - Morecambe

'I'm going to meet Jenna this afternoon, at the Costa shop on the sea front. Hope you don't mind?'

'That was fast,' Will replied. 'You don't waste any time, do you?'

'Well, we have the first guests in tomorrow, so there's no time like the present. Besides, now we've left all our old friends behind in Bristol, it'll be good to rekindle some old friendships up here. Especially with Jenna. She always made me laugh.'

'It'll do you the world of good,' Will agreed. 'Do you want me to go to the cash and carry this afternoon?'

'Would you?' Charlotte asked. 'I know it looks like I'm skiving before we've even got started, but I'd love to see Jenna again. How many years is it now? It must be thirty-five or thereabouts.'

'Heck, we're getting old!' Will laughed. 'Look, you go ahead - there's nothing that can't wait back home. I'll do the cash and carry, so long as you can be back to see Isla when she pops in. Is that okay?'

The plans were made. After three hours of making up beds, adding soaps, towels and toiletries to rooms and writing a list of the final purchases that needed to be made at the cash and carry, Will and Charlotte headed off in their separate directions.

It was bracing walking along the sea front. The sea was out, and her walk took her past the Sailing Club building, the town hall and the bingo. She and Will used to love a game of bingo in the arcades further up the promenade. She still had a toy rabbit tucked away in a cardboard box somewhere, won in the arcades on one of their visits to the resort on a day off.

Will was probably right; they'd forged so many happy memories in the area, it would be good for their marriage. God knows, they certainly needed it. Things had been tense enough, what with the anxiety, the kids and the money stress. No wonder they were feeling under pressure. Things would even out soon, she was sure of it. And meeting Jenna would be part of that process. It would feel like a fresh start, even though Jenna was part of their past.

As she passed the RNLI building and saw the clock tower in the distance, Charlotte began to feel the slightest hint of a flutter in her stomach. She was actually nervous about seeing Jenna again. They'd shared a room at the holiday camp for a short time, then drifted apart when Will arrived on the scene.

'You haven't changed a bit, you old cow!' Jenna said, rushing over to give Charlotte a hug. 'Look at you! Great tits still, no grey hairs and still a complexion to die for. I hate you already!'

They laughed and hugged. It felt good to see her again,

as if her very presence rolled back the onward march of time, taking her back to a period in her life when everything had seemed much simpler. Had it really been simpler, or did it just seem that way in hindsight? She wasn't entirely sure.

'How about me?' Jenna asked. 'How am I wearing? Choose your words carefully!'

Charlotte took a look at her old college friend. She looked worn out, her roots were showing and she had bags under her eyes. She looked terrible.

'You look just like the Jenna I remember,' Charlotte replied diplomatically. People often said she and Will looked younger than they were. They'd been lucky like that.

'You lying cow,' Jenna teased. 'What are you having? Espresso, Americano, Latte, Cappuccino, Cortado or Flat White? Jesus, do you remember the old days? It was so much simpler then. Tea, coffee or water. Like it or lump it!'

'Me and Will used to go to one of the bigger arcades near the old amusement park,' Charlotte began.

'I can't believe you and Will are still together!' Jenna interrupted. 'After all these years. You always were two lovebirds - you fancied him from the minute he walked into the dining room with... what's his name?'

'Mickey,' Charlotte replied.

'You've got a good memory,' Jenna replied. 'Anyhow, what were you going to tell me about Will?'

'We used to go to an arcade towards the far end of the sea front on our days off. They used to have a sign outside. *A nice cup of tea or a good cup of coffee - only 10p.* Can you believe that? It costs a fortune to drink in these places. And it was a nice cup of tea, too. We used to watch the guy making it. He would squeeze the tea bag to death; God knows how many cups he managed to get out of one bag.'

'It's great to see you, Charlotte. Where the hell did you go? We just lost contact...'

'I thought I had your address. And you changed your name - you got married.'

'Twice!' Jenna said. 'I've been married twice. I had none of your luck in that department.'

'Are you still teaching?' Charlotte asked. She was genuinely interested.

'No, I gave it up years ago. The paperwork just ground me down. That and an eviscerating relationship with a man called Alan...'

'One of your husbands?'

'No, the married head teacher of the school I was working in. It all went bad, and I had to leave. It just seemed to be a good place to stop. I'd never really enjoyed the job, so I decided to walk away from it.'

'What are you doing now?' Charlotte asked.

'A bit of this and a bit of that,' Jenna replied. 'What do they call it, a portfolio career? That's what I've got these days. But what about you? You're property owners now, you must be loaded! I read the article online, I couldn't believe it was you and Will.'

'Well, it looks more impressive than it is...' Charlotte began.

'You always were modest!' Jenna teased.

'No, seriously. We had a little money left in our place in Bristol, enough to buy an old guest house on the sea front. They're honestly not that expensive when you compare them with the property prices further south. And we're living there too, it's our home as well.'

'If you ask me, you and Will did alright,' Jenna replied. 'To think we all started in the same place... and look at you now!'

Charlotte decided not to protest the issue too much. Instead, they ordered their drinks and took a table, eager to catch up with each other's news. They were chatting for over two hours, laughing about college life, their time at the holiday camp and some of the antics they used to get up to as young adults. It was only when Charlotte was walking back along the sea front, having connected with Jenna on Facebook and entered phone numbers into their mobiles, that she realised she still didn't know that much about Jenna's present life. She hadn't a clue where she was living, what work she was doing or even if she was in a relationship at that moment in time. She hadn't even found out if she had any children.

When she reflected back on everything they'd said, Jenna had said lots but told her nothing. The entire conversation had been one way. Why she'd left teaching, how Will was making his living, what the kids were like and where they went to school. Jenna had barely told her anything that she didn't know already. And there was that issue with her debit cards when it had come to settling the bill – she'd ended up paying for both of them.

She reached the front door of the guest house and paused a moment before walking in. There in the porch were Will's shoes, the ones he'd been wearing when they went their separate ways earlier that afternoon. Only now, they were caked with mud. They were so filthy, there was no way the cash and carry could have been his only destination that afternoon.

CHAPTER NINE

1984 - Sandy Beaches Holiday Camp

Will was surprised by the knock at the door. He'd been fortunate so far; he had a room to himself with two single beds. With the holiday season getting busier now, it wouldn't be long before he'd be forced to share his room with some unknown staff member, much like inmates thrown together in a prison. He was making the most of it while it lasted.

He walked towards the door through a mist of Blue Stratos deodorant. He wasn't expecting anyone to knock. After finishing the evening shift, they'd arranged a place to meet up at eight o'clock.

Will was put out to discover that they didn't get private facilities in the chalets. In fact, the last thing he'd call his accommodation was a chalet. Having lived a privileged, middle-class life up the point where it was necessary to start paying his own bills, Will was inclined to describe the facilities as being more akin to social housing. As for sharing a bath and toilet, he hadn't banked on that.

The chalets were configured so that the doors to the rooms were opposite each other. Two rooms shared one toilet and one bath, and the doors to those facilities separated each neighbour. The chalet blocks were built over two storeys and Will's room was based on the upper level.

He opened the door. A stunning woman with long blonde hair, immaculate make-up and a flesh-revealing top was standing across his doorway, one arm stretched above her head, displaying the curves of her cleavage with no attempt whatsoever at concealment.

'Hi, you must be Will?' she grinned.

'Er... yes,' he replied, taken aback by this sudden force of nature. He dropped his hand to conceal the red mark from the burn. Cold water had taken away the worst of it, but it still hurt, and he didn't want anybody asking what had happened. If they did, he'd lie. He still wasn't sure quite what had happened with Bruce in the kitchen. It had come from nowhere.

The woman made a melodramatic smelling motion and reached out to touch his arm.

'That's Blue Stratos isn't it? It's one of my favourites. Very nice - very sophisticated.'

She steered him gently to one side and walked into his room. Will had barely had any time to unpack. He was picking clothes and toiletries out of his suitcase, one at a time, on an 'as-needed' basis.

'Excuse the mess in here,' he apologised.

'I'm Abi,' the woman said, holding out her hand. 'Abi Smithson. Pleased to meet you!'

Will took her hand to shake it. She gave it a gentle squeeze, then placed her left hand over his. He was locked in and she held it that way for slightly longer than was comfortable.

'Will Grayson,' he replied, gently trying to remove his hand from her clasp. 'But I think you know that already?'

'Oh yes,' Abi replied, releasing him now and taking a good look around his room.

'No roommate, I see. Rooms like this are at a premium in this place. You just can't get any privacy in these chalets.'

'No, I got lucky. Sounds like it won't be long until I have to double up though.'

'The best strategy is to come as a couple,' Abi continued. 'Get one of the double beds and hitch up for the summer with somebody you're happy to share a room with.'

Will had been trying to figure out what the marks were on Abi's neck. At first he thought she might have some sort of rash, though quite what it was, he couldn't work out. Then the penny dropped. They were love bites.

'So, I take it you're my neighbour?' Will asked, trying not to count the love bites. Four. Four and a half if you counted the half-bite peeking out the rim of her vest top.

That must hurt.

'Yes, I'm just across from you,' Abi replied, sitting on one of the beds. 'We get to share a bath every day. You can't say that about most jobs!'

Will felt his cheeks colouring. He would not have classed himself as adept with women; in fact he could be positively awkward. But even he could tell what Abi's game was. He felt like a wildebeest being manoeuvred across the plains by a hungry lion.

'I don't think I saw you in the dining hall, did I?' Will asked, anxious to steer the conversation to safe ground.

'No, but I saw you!' she smiled. 'I'm what's called a nippy. We work at the other side of the dining hall, for the self-service customers. We're a bit of rough compared to you waiters. That's if you like a bit of rough, of course?'

'Yes, Mickey explained about the nippies,' Will picked up, feeling like he was trying to steer the boat one way while the tide had other things in mind.

'I'm hoping to join you sometime soon,' Abi said. 'This is the third year I've worked here. I think they like you students working as waiters because you all sound so posh and educated. For people like me, we have to do the shit jobs because they don't think we're up to serving on tables.'

'Is that what you'd rather be doing?' Will asked.

'I'd rather be singing as a Purple Coat,' Abi replied. 'But the chances of that are almost zero. I'm not the right kind of person to do that sort of thing.'

'You sing?'

'Yes, when I can,' Abi answered, standing up now. 'But I'll settle for being a waitress in the meantime. It adds another ten pounds to my wage packet every week. God knows, I need it.'

For a moment, Will glimpsed sadness in Abi's eyes.

'Where are you from Abi? Is this your main job?'

Abi laughed at him.

'You students! For you this is just a way of paying off an overdraft so that you can clean the slate to spend the next academic year pissed out of your brains. Yes, this is my main job. If you don't work hard at school, this is how you end up, Will. No choices. I work all summer while my mum looks after my daughter, and that way I can keep my benefits for the rest of the year. For some of us this is living, not just a nice way to save up some money over summer.'

'I'm sorry,' Will said, chastened. 'I'd never thought of it like that. You're right, we are a bunch of tossers, us students.

Compared to everybody else, I mean. How old is your daughter?'

'She's two,' Abi replied. 'I miss her every day, but it has to be done. I go and see her on my days off. If I'm out the door after the evening shift, I can be home by midnight, then back in time for my shift when I need to be.'

'Well Abi, I'm pleased to meet you. I can see that things can be a bit hostile here between the regular workers and the students. I know we might seem like privileged snobs sometimes, but please give me the benefit of the doubt. I'm not all bad!'

'I'm sorry Will,' Abi said, now looking sheepish. 'I got a bit heavy there. I like you students, really I do. One day I'd like to go to university myself. Once I've got my 'O' level in maths out the way, that might be a start!'

She laughed at herself, as if the idea of somebody like her bettering herself was preposterous.

'Don't rule it out Abi,' Will tried to reassure her. 'There's no reason why you can't do a degree. Peoples' lives are different, and sometimes you need to take a different path. I'll be happy to help if you want?'

'Would you?' Abi asked. She seemed taken aback that something might be offered out of kindness rather than the desire for a romantic interaction. This was clearly not the relationship currency she was used to dealing with.

'I'd love that,' she replied softly. 'I've tried three times to pass that exam. I go to evening classes in the autumn, when this place closes down for the season. But it's just so intimidating. Everybody seems so clever compared to me.'

'Next time you visit your daughter, bring your textbooks back with you. I'd be happy to help with some tutoring, if I can help. It'll be no problem.'

'I'm off out!' came a voice from just outside Will's door.

A red-headed woman with a thick scouse accent appeared. She was wearing black high heels, a skirt so short that it was just possible to see her crotch, and a tight T-shirt on which was emblazoned the wording *Frankie Says Relax*.

Will watched as Abi transformed in front of his own eyes. She'd softened - just for a moment - but now she was back to full force, a whirlwind of personality and suggestiveness.

'Alright darlin', where are you headed?'

'Over to the family bar - they've got a disco on after the kids piss off to bed. You comin'?'

'Maybe later,' Abi replied, looking towards Will.

'Oh, you're welcome to tag along with us tonight,' Will suggested. 'I'm going out with Charlotte, Jenna and Sally.'

'You're a fast mover, sunshine!' Abi's mate laughed. 'Still, you've got plenty of beds in here to go around. Give us a knock if yer lookin' for anyone to make up the numbers.' Her shrieks of laughter could be heard, even as she made her way along the landing and headed off into the night.

'Your roommate, I take it?' Will asked.

'Yes, that's Reese. She's a great laugh. But she makes a racket when she's shagging blokes in our room.'

For a moment, Will considered that she didn't appear to be guilt-free in that department, but he admonished himself. Abi was not quite what he was used to, but he liked her, and he felt sorry for her.

'She's from Liverpool. The girl's a scream on a night out. A real man-eater too!'

'So, do you fancy tagging along this evening? I don't know if you already know the other girls. You won't know Sally, I suspect - she started the job with me, earlier today.'

'Yeah, I'd love to,' Abi replied, touching his arm gently.

'Just give me five minutes to tart myself up a bit more and I'll be back over, ready to go.'

Will smiled at her, walked with her to the door and shut it gently behind her. It was turning out to be quite a day. He hadn't even spent a first night at Sandy Beaches Holiday Camp and here he was making friends already.

CHAPTER TEN

Present Day - Morecambe

'Where did that mud come from?' Charlotte asked, before she'd even had time to exchange pleasantries about the day.

'Isla's here,' Will replied from the downstairs kitchen, a hint of a warning in his voice.

Charlotte could tell he was letting her know that Isla Thomas was in the building and that anything of a domestic nature might be best getting parked for half an hour. She softened her tone, picking up on his cue.

'Oh, hi Isla, sorry I'm a bit late - I've been catching up with a friend.'

Isla Thomas was the blessing that had made the purchase of the guest house possible. Charlotte and Will hadn't a clue how to run an establishment like that. Sure, they'd worked in catering while they were students, but the day-to-day running of the place was a mystery to them. Thanks to the kindness of the previous owners and the reluctance of Isla to retire, they managed to secure not only a key member of staff, but also a complete blueprint as to how to run the place on a day-to-day basis. What with some free business support from the local Chamber of Commerce, they felt good to go - the rest they'd have to learn on the job.

Charlotte joined them in the kitchen, where Isla was sitting on a wooden stool and Will was perched against the metal counter of the food preparation area. He'd unloaded the cash and carry purchases from the car and broken into a catering pack of five thousand tea bags to make them both a brew.

Charlotte gave Isla a hug, already being on familiar terms.

'So, D-Day tomorrow!' Charlotte announced.

'Yes, you'll be alright my darling.' Isla smiled at her. They hadn't been able to figure out Isla's age - and they'd been too polite to ask - but they reckoned at least sixty-nine, possibly early seventies.

They'd argued about whether they should base their new business on Isla's expertise.

'I don't mean to insult her, but what if she dies on us?' Will had said.

'Isla Thomas will out-survive us!' Charlotte argued. 'She's sturdy as anything, that woman and she's worked in the guest house for years. You heard what she said. *I'd rather die on my feet than be a prisoner in an old folks' home.* She wants to do this; we're doing her a favour by employing her here.'

'But what if she falls ill and leaves you on your own?' Will hesitated. 'Do you think you could cope?'

'I'm not sure we have any other choice, do we? We have

to find a way for me to bring in some money and keep a roof over our heads, and we agreed that this is the best way - for now. And if something does happen, there must be a hundred like her out there, working in guest houses all over Morecambe.'

'So long as you're sure?' Will checked.

'I'm not certain about anything these days, Will. But we have to try it; we were dying slowly in Bristol. We couldn't carry on as we were - we couldn't afford that house.'

When Isla hugged Charlotte, she felt the warmth she'd missed since her mother had died. It wasn't a feeling a man could give her; it was simply a gesture offered in kindness and concern. It made her feel cherished in a way that the judgement of a father or the expectations of a husband could never offer. Isla Thomas soothed Charlotte; she'd noticed it the moment they met.

'Everything is ready,' Isla began. 'I'll let myself in for the breakfasts, so you don't need to get up for me. It's nice to have some help with the sheets now - I find the double beds difficult. The laundry pick up is at ten o'clock. I'll be back for evening meals by four o'clock and we're all done by seven. It's simple when you get the hang of it. When this place was closed for the year it was on sale, I didn't know what to do with myself. Do you know, the only time I was ever ill was when I stopped working here. This place is keeping me alive!'

Isla laughed, and Charlotte gave Will a glance, claiming victory for her previous stance.

'We'll run on low numbers for at least a month with just the lower bedrooms, then we'll start to build up the bookings as the rooms on the top level are decorated. That'll give everybody a chance to get up to speed. Are you sure I've got you everything you need from the cash and carry?' Will asked.

Isla nodded. 'Yes, relax both of you, we're all ready to go. All you need to do is check in the guests as they arrive. Charlotte, if you help me with the sheets in the morning, the rest will run like clockwork. How many do we have tomorrow?'

'Three rooms full tomorrow,' Charlotte replied. She'd committed the first week's guests to memory. 'We have two couples and a single lady with a child. The couple have been here before, apparently. Mr and Mrs Roach. Ring any bells, Isla?'

'Oh my goodness, they've been coming here for years!' she smiled. 'They're a lovely couple - you'll have no problems with them. What a lovely way to re-open the guest house. It'll be like launching a new ship.'

Charlotte loved the positivity that Isla brought with her. God knows she needed it. She had the easy simplicity of an older person, something that seemed only to be forged in a post-war Britain and a quality sadly lacking in Charlotte's generation.

'I'll be in first thing tomorrow. You'll hear me creeping around, but don't let it bother you. Then I'll come in a little earlier than I normally would to get ready for the evening meal. You've done right to limit the menu at first. Most people visiting Morecambe are happy to eat traditional food. They don't like anything too fancy.'

Isla touched Charlotte's arm and moved towards the kitchen door.

'Have a lovely evening my dears, see you tomorrow!'

They waited as Isla made her way through the entrance hall and out through the back door. Charlotte inspected the purchases from the cash and carry.

'How was Jenna?' Will asked. 'Did you enjoy your afternoon?'

'I thought she was looking a bit tired,' Charlotte replied, removing some bags of sugar from one of the boxes and placing them on the worktop. 'Do we need this much sugar? Most people don't take it these days. Type 2 diabetes has ruined all our fun.'

'I thought I'd better. It's not like it goes off. And Isla likes to bake.'

'Fair enough. Yes, Jenna has had a tough time of it I think. Man trouble. And work problems too. Remember when we first started work, we thought we'd get a job and that would be it until we died? What happened, I wonder? You're lucky if you stay anywhere for more than three years at a time these days. You're either made redundant, worn out by the work or you move on because the management is so terrible. I wonder whatever happened to good old-fashioned career progression.'

Will laughed. 'Speaking of which, I've got my teaching timetable at last. It's not bad either. I'll be able to help around here on Tuesday mornings and Friday afternoons. It looks like they give up on Fridays at the college, so I can be around for weekend check-ins. I do have to be in late on Wednesdays though. All in all, it's not a bad timetable.'

'Why were your shoes so muddy?'

Will looked at her, obviously wrong-footed by the change of subject.

'I take it the cash and carry hasn't been relocated to a farmyard?'

'No, no, nothing like that.'

Charlotte could tell he was stalling her.

'Well, you can't go leaving them around like that when we have guests. We share our house now, remember, we have to clean up after ourselves. How do you think that's going to play out in the reviews? *Nice sea view but mud all over the entrance hall. Two stars because of the mess.*'

'Yeah, you're right, I'm sorry, it's just that I was late for Isla.'

'You had loads of time to go to the cash and carry. Whatever kept you?'

Charlotte kept pushing, intent on knowing where the mud had come from.

'Nothing, really. You know how it is. It's easy to get distracted in the warehouse, there's so much stuff in there.'

The front door slammed. Moments later it opened again, and Olli's voice could be heard calling after Lucia.

'We're in the kitchen!' Will shouted.

Olli appeared, his rucksack swung over one shoulder.

'So how was it?' Charlotte asked. She felt compelled to ask, but she didn't really want to hear the answer. If the kids couldn't settle at the school, she didn't know what she'd do.

'Usual nonsense,' Olli replied. 'They're way behind us in English Lit, but I hadn't got a clue what they were talking about in Physics. I'm sure I'll catch up. Oh, and there are drugs in the school.'

'Jesus!' Will exclaimed. 'Why can't they just educate the damn kids? Secondary school life is becoming more and more like prison every day.'

'What about Lucia?' Charlotte asked. 'I take it the slammed door tells us everything we need to know?'

'She's had a bad day,' Olli replied after some time. 'I don't think she made any friends and she couldn't pee all day because there's a gang of girls who lurk in the toilets taking pictures over the door with their smartphones. And then to top it all, she got hassled outside the school gates by some guy...'

'What kind of guy? Someone from school?'

'She wouldn't tell me. She described him as *some old guy*. He had faded tattoos, she said. Reckoned he knew her. She told him to get lost. That's what's shaken her most, I think.'

CHAPTER ELEVEN

Present Day - Morecambe

'So who was he, this man?' Charlotte asked, handing Lucia the cornflakes.

They'd decided to give her a wide berth the night before, sensing that she was in dire need of decompression time. But Charlotte couldn't let it lie. There was an uneasy feeling in her stomach that she hadn't experienced for some years. And it was growing stronger.

Will had walked round to the corner shop. Charlotte insisted he didn't use one of the large catering bags of milk that they stored in the big kitchen downstairs, so he'd popped out to the newsagent to pick up something a little smaller. Really, Charlotte just wanted him out of the way, to give her a chance to talk in private with her daughter.

'Just some creep,' Lucia replied. 'You always get them at the school gates. I mean, we did at our old school. There were usually some weirdos hanging around at home time.'

'Why have you never told me this before? Where are the teachers when all this happens?'

'The teachers are usually too busy sorting out the lower years. If they're not scrapping, they're screaming as they go down the street. I guess they just assume the older kids can take care of themselves. We call them the short skirts brigade. Well, that's what we called them at our old school.'

'And what do they do?'

'Often they're older guys with construction jobs and stuff like that. Sometimes they're dating some of the older girls. But you think how attractive all those young girls are to the old perverts. Some of them can't resist making leery comments.'

'What sort of comments?'

'Just stuff like how gorgeous we look, or what they'd like to do to us if they were younger...'

'You're kidding? Please tell me you're kidding.'

'No. I just assumed it went with the territory of being a woman. The minute they can't get thrown into prison as a paedophile, they think you're fair game.'

'You were only fifteen when you were at your previous school,' Charlotte reminded her. 'And what have I told you about sexism? It's never acceptable.'

She wondered if all those Spare Rib Magazine issues had been a waste of time. And had the Spice Girls' career been completely in vain?

'Was this chap leery with you?' Charlotte asked after a few moments. 'Because if he was, I'm going to complain to the school.'

'Mum, no! I've only just got there. If you start causing trouble already, I'll never find any friends. He didn't do anything pervy, okay?'

'But you were clearly upset when you came home last night.'

'Look, he was just the final straw at the end of a very bad first day, alright? It was just that...'

She stopped short, clearly thinking better of it.

'What?' Charlotte asked.

'He knew my name, that's all,' Lucia replied. 'How did he know my name?'

The door slammed at the bottom of the building. Will was back. She had the time it would take him to run from the bottom stair to their private accommodation at the top of the guest house to communicate with her daughter.

'Are you certain you've never seen him before? And he had tattoos along both of his arms?'

'Most guys do these days, Mum.'

'Yes, but they were old, you said. How old was he?'

'Well, you know. Old. Old like you and dad...'

'Hey, we're in the paper!'

Will was out of breath; he'd run up the stairs.

'I bought two copies; this is definitely one for the scrapbook. Look!'

He laid the two papers flat on the small kitchen table. Lucia moved her cornflakes to make more room. They were on the front page.

Morecambe's Brand New Dawn? the headline read.

'Listen to this,' Will began. 'The reopening of the Lakes View Guest House on Morecambe's historic promenade is being hailed as the latest in a series of positive signals heralding the rise of the popular resort.'

'Ugh, they've used a picture of all of us. And you can see my spots!'

'Well, I did advise you to be in the new picture when

Nigel Davies came around, but you refused. He used that old one from last year to show the whole family.'

Lucia grabbed the spare copy and began to scrutinise it more closely.

'Mum! Dad! I'm going to be a laughing stock in school! Look what it says... *Siblings Oliver and Lucia will be an asset for Morecambe's secondary school. Oliver was head boy at his previous school in Bristol whilst Lucia was their top-performing student at GCSE.* I am never going to live this down. I'm going to be a social pariah after this.'

'I think you're overreacting just a bit, don't you?' Will suggested. 'Besides, all your school chums are way too cool to read the local newspaper. Only their parents will see this, and they're bound to be impressed by you and Olli.'

'Did I hear my name?' Olli asked, walking into the kitchen, his hair still wet from the shower.

'Hi Olli, how did you sleep?' Charlotte asked, eager to take some of the wind out of Lucia's sails.

'Bloody seagulls!' he exclaimed. 'Can't anyone else hear them?' They're so noisy!'

'We don't hear them at our side of the house,' Will remarked. 'Did I hear somebody downstairs?'

'It'll just be Isla,' Charlotte replied.

Olli pulled up a chair and for the next five minutes, they huddled around the two newspapers, occasionally laughing at the turn of phrase used by the local reporter.

'Ooh, look, they talk about how you and dad met!' Lucia teased. Charlotte figured at least she'd changed the focus from herself.

Charlotte and Will met as students at Sandy Beaches Holiday Camp in 1984 and they've been happy campers ever since.

'Are you really that old?' Lucia asked. 'They didn't even have mobile phones then, did they?'

'I don't recall seeing my first mobile phone until the nineties,' Will remarked. 'And in those days, we only had a black and white TV, that's if we even had one at all. We didn't have a TV at the holiday camp. They were only available in some of the bars and social areas.'

'I can't believe things were so primitive back then,' Lucia teased. 'You two really are dinosaurs. How can you even stay with the same person that long? Aren't you completely bored with each other?'

Charlotte was relieved when Will used that as his cue to leave the table and clean his teeth.

'Better get a move on,' he said. 'I'm not sure of the bus times. They seem regular enough, but I'd better leave a bit earlier for the first week. Just in case.'

Olli's cornflakes barely touched the sides. He was away in minutes, leaving Lucia still nursing a cup of tea. Charlotte picked up the paper and studied some wording just below the banner on the front page.

'You know that chap last night? He probably just recognised you from the paper. This says *Early Edition* on the top. I bet he just recognised you from the front page. Anybody can see it; they don't even have to buy the paper. I'm sure that's all it was.'

'Yeah, probably,' Lucia replied, not sounding entirely convinced.

Charlotte was barely convincing herself. She heard more movement downstairs.

'You finish getting ready for school, Lucia. I'm just going to go downstairs and say hello to Mrs Thomas. It's going to take some getting used to, having other people letting themselves in and out of our house.'

Charlotte gave Lucia a kiss on the head, which she greeted with the obligatory look of disgust and a thorough wipe with her hands. She made her way down the stairs, along the carpeted corridor, and into the kitchen.

'Isla? Isla? Are you here?' she asked.

She looked around the kitchen, as if Mrs Thomas were a mouse and might have been hiding in the corner, then she darted into the dining room. It was immaculately set up and ready to receive the first guests later that day. The red-checked tablecloths and the perfectly arranged cutlery looked fresh and welcoming. Charlotte was pleased with it.

Next, she made her way back along the corridor to the lounge area. There was still no sign of Isla.

'Will - have you seen Isla this morning?'

'No, but I thought I heard somebody moving around downstairs, that must have been her.' he said to her, running down the staircase two steps at a time.

'Gotta go, I don't want to be late on my first day!'

He hesitated a moment, then gave Charlotte a kiss and was out of the door a moment later.

Olli and Lucia followed him, bags thrown over shoulders and phones in hand.

'I'm sure it will be better today, darling,' Charlotte tried to reassure her daughter.

'I doubt it,' said Lucia, darting to the side to avoid any body contact which might have been heading her way.

Olli accepted a kiss. She knew they hated it, but it didn't feel right not trying.

Charlotte paused a moment, unsettled by what Lucia had told her at the kitchen table. She was tempted to call the head teacher there and then, to complain about not taking better care of their wards at the school gate. No, she understood what Lucia had said: it was too early in the day to be causing trouble at a new school. She had something else in mind. She'd drive up to the school later and wait in the car at a safe distance, and watch her kids leaving at home time. They wouldn't know she was there, but she just wanted to be sure. She had to be certain. It was that feeling in her stomach again; she couldn't shake it.

Isla Thomas walked through the doorway. She was wearing a headscarf but had given up on her umbrella.

'Good morning Charlotte, and how are you today?' She smiled as she stepped inside.

'Did you just nip outside, Isla? We thought you were here earlier.'

'No my dear, I decided I'd come in a little later this morning and give you all some time to get yourselves organised in your routine. This is the first time I've stepped through this door since I saw you last night.'

CHAPTER TWELVE

1984 - Sandy Beaches Holiday Camp

Will was regretting inviting Abi along to meet up with the others for drinks. He sensed the tension the moment they arrived.

Charlotte, Sally and Jenna had already taken a table at the Old Codger's Bar. That's what the staff called it. Its real name was The Golden Nights Bar, but it amounted to the same thing. This was where the more mature members of staff pulled pints and spent time talking to the customers. In the corner was a keyboard, a drum machine and a bass guitar, all plugged into a single amplifier and running through two speakers. The hum of the mains could be heard when the buzz of conversation took a lull and the musical instruments sat there, promising an evening of middle-of-the-road entertainment. Nothing too raucous.

Charlotte and Jenna had told him earlier that they'd taken to starting their evenings in this bar. When you were sober, you could hear yourself speak, they'd said. It was always quiet until after ten o'clock. At that point, like vampires rising from their graves to inhabit the night, the oldies would spontaneously rise and begin to dance in the way only old people can. They knew the steps off by heart, coordinating their movements like two hearts beating together in perfect time.

'I think you know Abi already?' Will said, smiling at the girls around the table. Charlotte seemed particularly keen to see him, but a frosty chill swept the small group as Abi grabbed a seat and placed herself directly between Jenna and Charlotte.

'I don't know you, do I?' Abi spoke to Sally, holding out her hand. Abi had a small tattoo on the inside of her fore-arm, one of those that could be found inside the wrappers of chewy sweets. Sally obviously clocked it but was gracious anyway. She seemed more preoccupied with the love bites and how far below her top they traversed.

'Abi is in the room opposite me,' Will continued. 'I hesi-tate to call it a chalet - I don't want to perpetuate the myth.'

Charlotte's smile disappeared, and her eyes bored into Abi, fixating on the marks on her skin. Will followed her gaze, sensing now that Abi was a negative force in this envi-ronment.

'Sally's bloke is a Purple Coat!' Jenna announced.

She was drinking a double vodka. If that was her warm-up drink, Will wondered what she would choose once it got later into the night.

He topped up Jenna's drink and bought a round for Abi and himself. Sally and Charlotte were pacing themselves a little better.

'So, how was your first day?' Jenna asked.

'I'm getting the hang of it,' Will replied. 'There's a lot to remember though. I'm sure it'll become routine pretty fast.'

He reached out to pick up his pint and Sally winced loudly.

'My God, Will. What have you done to your hand? It's red raw!'

Will forgot to conceal the burn that he'd sustained earlier at Bruce's hands. He'd run it under a cold tap in the toilets afterwards and the discomfort had subsided. However, it had left a red patch on the skin that would take some time to disappear.

'Oh, idiot here splashed hot water all over himself in the kitchens. I haven't quite got the hang of those catering kettles yet. I guess I won't be doing that again.'

'It's easily done, Jenna replied. 'I'm doing it all the time. Usually because I'm chatting away and the teapot overfills.'

Will noticed Charlotte was studying him. Like she knew.

'Where's your bloke tonight?' Abi asked. 'You're still with Bruce, aren't you? How's that going?'

Charlotte seemed distracted, then realised that Abi was speaking to her.

'Oh, he works the bars in the evenings. He often double shifts it. A lot of them do it in the kitchens - they can double their wages.'

'You want to watch that Bruce,' Abi said. 'I've been working here for three years. He's a right one, believe me. Just be careful.'

Will, Jenna, Sally and Charlotte looked at Abi, a look of astonishment on their faces. Abi looked like she'd just let off a stink bomb in church. Charlotte's arms retracted a little in her sleeves and she touched her right shoulder, only for a moment. Will saw all of it.

The musicians walked up to their equipment and got ready to perform.

'Hey look, it's Chaz and Dave!' Sally laughed.

She was right too. The duet - who called themselves *The Pure Notes* - looked like they'd modelled their entire stage image on the seventies performers. Both had beards which would have attracted the speculative attention of any nearby nesting bird. Their ample grey hair protruded from their flat caps and both wore Union Jack waistcoats.

There was the smallest ripple of applause as they walked over to their instruments and readied themselves to play. The bass player - Guy according to his name badge - threw the strap over his shoulder, adjusted the instrument so that it was comfortable in his hands, then moved his fingers over some of the strings to ensure that it was correctly connected to the amplifiers.

Both had microphones, warming up with the customary *One-Two-One-Two* vocal test, throwing in a *three* every now and then for good measure. The keyboard player tested a few notes, then, like a married couple who knew every routine of their relationship, they looked at each other, nodded, and in perfect unison began to play an old crooner's hit from the fifties.

There was a ripple of recognition throughout the bar, which was far from packed at that time of night, as the assembled audience picked up on the song and were instantly transported back to their youth.

'Well, you lot know how to party!' Will laughed. 'It doesn't come much wilder than this.'

'The thing is, you can hear yourself speak in here, that's why we always start in this bar.' Jenna explained. 'The club area gets noisy, so it's best to go there when you're pissed and too far gone to find any words.'

'Are you alright Charlotte?' Will leaned over to speak directly to her. He'd noticed how distracted she'd become when Abi mentioned Bruce. He was eager to talk to her on his own, if the opportunity arose.

'Yes, yes. I'm fine, honestly.'

'Is Bruce okay with you being out with me tonight?'

He was anxious to check, to avoid any trouble. Bruce had already demonstrated he could be fiercely protective of her.

'Well, I'm not out with only you, am I? I'm out with Jenna and Sally... and Abi now. Besides, he's working in the club bar, and it's always heaving in there. There's barely time to breathe when that place gets busy.'

The small group stayed an hour in the Old Codger's Bar, until the Chaz and Dave lookalikes started to invite members of the audience up to join them in a song.

'Oh, that's our cue to go!' Jenna warned them. 'A lot of these old dears are good, but some of the blokes aren't.'

'I'd like to give it a try,' Abi announced. For the second time that night, they all looked at her.

'Abi sings,' Will explained. 'She'd love to be a Purple Coat one day. Have you ever sung here before, Abi?'

'No,' she replied. 'I've been working here for three summers, but I've never even been in this bar at this time of night. I wish I'd known they did sing-along.'

'Come on ladies and gentlemen, don't be shy! Who's going to get the ball rolling tonight?'

Abi was up on her feet. There was a collective gasp from the group. Until that point, they'd seen her as uneducated and a bit blunt, not really their sort. And now they were bracing for embarrassment, as if Abi couldn't possibly be hiding any talent under those love bites.

Will watched as Abi chatted to the two musicians and they found a tune that they all knew.

'Ladies and gentlemen, introducing Abi Smithson, a

first-timer in The Golden Nights Bar. She's going to sing *Goldfinger* for us this evening. One, two, three...'

The familiar introduction began to play and Abi stood awkwardly by the microphone which *The Pure Notes* had placed at her disposal. Will could have reached out and touched the atmosphere of trepidation among his drinking buddies, who seemed aghast at the prospect of Abi - just a nippy - singing.

The first sound from her was stunning. Her voice was strong and confident, even though she herself seemed terrified. There was an enthusiastic round of applause from the growing audience as they all came to the realisation that they were in capable hands.

Abi was stunning. This rough, coarse girl, who appeared to be covered from head to toe in love bites, was an incredible singer. It seemed like a freak of nature that such a sound could come from such a body. The Chaz and Dave lookalikes smiled at each other as they played. They'd been in the business long enough to know when they'd struck pure entertainment gold.

The bar was getting busier now, as if the frisson of excitement caused by Abi's performance had sent a spark around the holiday camp and word had got out that something very special was happening.

'She's absolutely amazing!' Sally said. 'I've got to tell the Purple Coats team manager; she needs to be on the big stage in the theatre.'

The applause was enthusiastic and effusive. Abi seemed blown away by the response, as if she couldn't quite believe that they weren't booing her off the stage. Will thought she looked completely overcome by it, as he stepped forward to offer her an arm.

'You were absolutely incredible!' Will told her. 'You're a

superstar in the making, Abi. You have got to do something about your singing career. Look, they all love you here.'

Abi was half-laughing, half-crying, completely over-come by it all.

There was a crash of glasses up ahead. Will was drawn to it straight away, sensing trouble immediately. As he walked with Abi back to the table, he saw Bruce Craven marching Charlotte out of the bar, his hand firmly gripping the top of her arm.

CHAPTER THIRTEEN

Present Day - Morecambe

Charlotte knew exactly where she was going the moment she left the house.

'So you're sure you're okay getting on with things on your own?' she asked Isla.

'Yes, my dear, I'm fine. I'll get everything ready for evening meals and do a final once over on the bedrooms. You'll be all set to go when the first guests arrive.'

She paused a moment.

'Are you alright my dear? I mean, is everything really okay? I had depression once myself, you know. I thought I'd never get over it. But here I am. I know what it's like.'

Charlotte looked at Isla. She'd never discussed her breakdown with her, but somehow, she could tell.

'Is it that obvious?' she asked.

'When you get to my age, you've seen it all,' Isla reassured her, touching her arm. 'It's nothing to be ashamed of, my darling. If you need to talk to somebody, I'm always here. You can get through it, whatever it is.'

'I appreciate it Isla, I really do,' Charlotte replied. 'I didn't realise it was quite so obvious. But I'm alright, really I am. This is a fresh start; I'm putting the past behind me.'

'Well, you know where I am if you need me,' Isla repeated. 'Sometimes it's easier to talk to somebody who's not involved.'

Charlotte studied Isla. She wondered if at her age there was any crisis or problem that she hadn't encountered at least once in her life. She craved Isla's confidence, the surety that anything could be got through, however bad the scenario.

'Just for a couple of days, while we're all getting used to each other, can you give us a shout up the stairs in the morning when you let yourself in?' Charlotte asked.

'Of course my darling. It must be a bit strange, letting someone have the front door key to your house for the first time. Is anything the matter?'

'No, no. It's just that we thought you were downstairs earlier on. It sounded like somebody was in the rooms on the ground floor. I guess we'll just have to get used to the sounds of a new home. Olli's been cursing the seagulls.'

'Oh, you'll soon get used to them,' Isla laughed. 'Just like you'll get used to the roar of the sea on a windy night. It's part and parcel of life by the seaside.'

Charlotte smiled and left Isla in the kitchen. She walked over to the small check-in desk that was tucked away to the side of the hallway. Locked in the bottom drawer of the desk was a laptop. She fired it up and checked the bookings. There were seven new bookings to approve. Charlotte scanned the names; they were mostly couples.

The previous owners had warned them off using the

Seaside Stays website to manage bookings, but so far it was giving them a steady flow of bookings. Sure, they had to pay commission for the referrals, but they'd reckoned they could rely on the website for the first year or so, then try to go it alone and secure more bookings without having to pay their hefty fees. She checked that day's calendar. The first check-in was after half-past four. The trains to Morecambe tended to arrive just after the half-hour.

That was another thing the previous owners had told them - most of the guests arrived on the train. They were not, on the whole, car owners. Charlotte had thought they'd probably be taking their breaks abroad if they were.

'Okay Isla, that's me out now. I'll be back for the first arrivals. See you later.'

Charlotte was taking the car. With Will on the bus and Lucia and Olli doing the same, or walking if the weather was good, that gave her freedom during the day. She understood the dynamics of the day would change as the guest house became busier. But for now, that sense of space and free time was just what she needed.

She could barely believe she was making the trip back there already. But she'd seen in the paper that the diggers were moving in at the end of the week. She wanted to go there one last time - without Will - to say her own, private farewell to the place.

Charlotte took her time driving over to Middleton. Will was right: there were so many memories for them there. She drove past the bedsits and multiple occupancy rentals that dominated the West End and on to the houses on the road to Heysham, where the great and the good of the resort lived. She'd tutored a child there once, when they were students. The family's house had seemed so grand back then, compared with their shared small, double room in a student house, where the walls were losing their battle against the creeping mould and the single glazed windows struggled to keep out the cold. Life had changed so much since then.

Charlotte chose to check out the pub in Middleton, which they hadn't really explored the other day. As a young couple they'd spent many a happy night in the Old Roof Tree Inn. At first, they were furtive evenings - before she was fully confident she'd got rid of Bruce. They were safe from his ever-watching eyes in there - they only went when Charlotte was certain he was working late in the camp's bars. It was a three-mile walk along a narrow country lane, but it was worth it, to be alone with Will. And after Bruce was gone - really gone - that was when she finally started to relax, when she and Will really became a proper couple. And the bruises on her arms had long since faded.

She paused the car outside the former pub and, this time, took a few minutes to have a proper look. In spite of it having been painted, she could still see the markings from the old pub signage. She turned the car around and drove the final miles to the holiday camp. She needed to do this alone. And she wanted to apologise to George.

She could see that there had already been some signs of activity at the former Sandy Beaches Holiday Camp. Huge plastic bags filled with sand and pallets packed with breeze blocks had been neatly stacked to the side of the temporary car park. Charlotte pulled the car in tight so as not to obstruct any lorries which might arrive while she was visiting.

Her first instinct was to sneak through the fence, as she and Will had done the day before, but it had rained since then and there was a puddle of mud where they'd been able to crawl through previously. The rain had come while she and Jenna had been meeting for coffee. That's when Will had come home with mud plastered all over his shoes. She dismissed the thought; she was letting her mind get out of control again. The CBT had been a waste of time, but she did recognise the need to rein in her thoughts. She could be her own worst enemy at times.

Charlotte walked over to the old porter's lodge and looked through the fencing.

'George!' she called.

Una came running up to her, barking, not as a guard dog this time around but as the animal that she'd petted the day before. George followed more slowly, smiling at her.

'Hello Charlotte-not-Charlie,' he said. 'How nice to see you.'

'Hello George. I just wanted to apologise to you for yesterday. I'm really sorry I rushed off like that. It's just been quite - well, quite emotional really.'

'You don't need to apologise to me,' George replied. 'I'm just delighted to see that you're okay. I take it you're back for a tour? Before they bring in the diggers?'

'Is it okay if I take a look around? I've forgotten so much about this place. There are a lot of memories here, not all of them good, I'm afraid. They just rushed at me too fast yesterday. I was overcome by it all.'

'You're thinking about that boyfriend of yours, the one before you met Will?'

'Do you remember him? I hope my memory is as good as yours by the time I retire. Or should I say semi-retire?'

George laughed.

'He was a bad one, that boy,' he said. 'I'd watch you walking with him sometimes when I was patrolling the camp. It was clear from your body language. I was so pleased when you and Will got together. You can tell when a couple are made for each other.'

Charlotte thought back to how they'd been. She'd always been tense around Bruce. Not at first, but after... she just wanted to get away from him then. But it took some time; she couldn't just walk. Not from a man like that, anyway.

'Do you mind if I take a walk around?' Charlotte asked. 'You don't need to come with me. I promise I won't get up to any mischief.'

George chuckled.

'I think we're all getting a bit too old for any mischief, don't you?' he smiled.

Una was ecstatic to have Charlotte back, ruffling her fur.

'Why don't you take Una with you?' George suggested. 'She's a patient thing, but I'm sure she gets fed up with me plodding around this place. I'm much slower than I was.'

'I'd love to. Come on Una!'

Charlotte took the lead from George's hand and began to walk down the long drive.

'I thought you'd be back,' George called after her. 'I was surprised you didn't come back with Will yesterday.'

Charlotte stopped and turned. Una looked up at her, eager to continue their journey.

'Will was here? Yesterday?'

'Yes, he got caught in that rain. He seemed very intent on looking around before the demolition work starts. I just left him to it.'

CHAPTER FOURTEEN

Present Day - Morecambe

The uneasy feeling in Charlotte's stomach had returned. The first time she'd ever experienced it was at the camp. And now she was back, so was that sense of constant apprehension.

She still couldn't put her finger on it. Did she imagine it? Awfulising is how the CBT guy had described it. Making mountains out of molehills in non-psychobabble speak. Or in pub talk, *you're probably a bit doolally.*

There were so many things going on now. Lucia at the school gate. The unaccounted-for movement in the guest house kitchen. The anonymous Facebook request. Even Will returning to look around the camp without her. It just didn't feel right.

She thought about what the CBT guy had said.

'If ever you feel anxious, touch something solid and ask yourself, is everything okay now? Will everything be okay tomorrow?'

She tried it out. Everything was fine at that moment. But how could she know about tomorrow? Or the next day?

Charlotte walked past what remained of the family pub. They used to call it the Tudor Bar back in the eighties. The small pond in the beer garden was overgrown now, evidently drained some time ago. The whitewashed pub was boarded up, vandals' messages now sprayed against the walls. Even the tiles on the roof were beginning to break loose. It was remarkable how quickly the dilapidation began.

She recalled great times in that pub. After Bruce. She even remembered a couple of nice evenings in there with him. Before the possessiveness began.

The entire site was boarded up: the chalets, the big ship in which the entertainments complex was based, the family theatre - everything was inaccessible, biding its time until the diggers arrived.

Charlotte wanted to put her bad memories behind her. She needed to walk to the old stone tower and look out at the beach beyond it, through the gate. She'd reached the end of the camp's grounds now, with the tower to her right and the gate to her left. She couldn't recall if the tower had been locked up then. They probably hadn't taken much notice of it, with that general disinterest that kids have in anything historical.

Una was panting and Charlotte stopped to pet her. She had never owned a dog before. She liked the feeling of having undemanding company, a pal who knew when to shut up and stay quiet. She played with Una some more, deciding she might quite like to have a dog. Sometime in the future. Will didn't like dogs as a rule.

The two of them made their way up to the tower. It was chained, but the door opened slightly. If she was younger and slimmer, she might have been able to push through. As it was, it was too narrow a gap.

She walked along the bank, Una looking back at her regularly as they made their way through the long grass.

'Good dog,' Charlotte encouraged her. 'Who's a lovely dog?'

As she'd expected, the gate into the beach was chained. However, she still gave it a shake when she got there. The chain slipped through the handle and dropped to the ground. It had been recently cut. Although the chain itself was heavily rusted, the cut was shiny and new.

Charlotte had to pull the door open a little to get through. The grass had grown high on either side of it, so it took some force to pull it open. A piece of rotten wood broke off. She threw it aside. It wouldn't matter - the builders would level the place soon.

There was the beach. She tried to recall the events of that night. Why had she run in this direction? Why didn't she find sanctuary elsewhere? She could have gone to see George and his mates in the porter's lodge, or doubled back to the chalets. Anything would have been better than running this way.

She tried to cut herself some slack. She wasn't even twenty years old at the time, and it was difficult to recall quite how naïve she'd been at that age. Bruce was the second man she'd been with. Will was only the third. All those years with the same man. Dating sites and Tinder had completely bypassed her generation, even though they used computers and were happy with technology. She didn't want to be divorced. She didn't want to be Jenna, alone and apparently single, with no roots set down in a long-term relationship.

Charlotte closed her eyes, picturing that night. She

tensed, recalling how angry Bruce had been. They'd split up by then, and she thought he was done with her. But that night, she and Will had had a lover's tiff. Just a stupid thing, something about Abi getting too close to him. But she'd stormed off like the silly cow she could be sometimes. And that's when he'd chosen his moment. There was still no doubt in Charlotte's mind that Bruce intended to rape her that night.

She pictured the struggle on the beach, her striking him with the stone, his body collapsing onto hers. She still remembered his weight; he was so heavy to move. She'd panicked and run. And lost the necklace. The necklace that somebody now claimed to have.

She took out her phone and opened up the message once again. There was no signal at this side of the camp, but she wrote a reply anyway.

Describe it to me. Who are you?

It would get sent when a signal returned.

She thought about herself, running back along the beach, terrified that she'd killed him. She daren't go back, yet she hardly dared step forward.

A strange disorientation came over her, as if she might faint. She found a large piece of tree trunk that had been washed up at the edges of the beach where it met the grass, and took a seat there.

Would she have done anything differently? Even now, at her age?

For starters, she'd have known better than to start dating Bruce. Even if he had been perfectly charming at first, she liked to think she'd see through him. If she'd been in the same situation now, she'd still have no choice but to strike him with whatever weapon came to hand. Even if it had been present day, there was no signal on her phone. She couldn't have even sent a Facebook message to Will or Jenna, though there'd probably have been wireless connections had the camp still been open.

She was spiralling again; CBT guy had warned her. It started with a simple question and before she knew it, she was out of control. No wonder she felt so dizzy; she'd put herself in a spin.

Charlotte felt ready to stand up once again. Una was poised and waiting, eager to walk by her side. She did her best to re-fasten the wooden door with the chain. Even though it was a pointless exercise, she thought it best to leave it as she found it.

She walked down the bank, heading back towards the main camp, but taking the same route she did that night, veering to the left towards the staff chalets. There was one thing she'd never quite recalled about that panicked run back to her room that night. Maybe being back on the site would help her remember. She'd passed the crazy golf on her right and the arcades on her left. The bright, coloured paint which had once adorned the concrete obstacles on the crazy golf course was now faded and flaked. The fake, green grass was torn and weathered. There was a discarded fruit machine outside the boarded-up arcade. They'd had so many laughs playing Pac-Man and Donkey Kong back in 1984. She closed her eyes again, trying to transport herself back to that night. She was sure there was a storage area at the end of the arcade.

'Come on girl,' she said to Una, who'd found something to sniff.

She was right. There wasn't much left of it, just enough to confirm she wasn't imagining things. As she'd rushed past the gas canister storage area, fleeing from the beach, she'd had a terrible feeling that somebody was hiding there. She'd been much too scared to go back and investigate, but in her memories of that night, she thought she'd made out a figure lurking there, trying not to be seen.

She walked over to it, standing up inside and lining up her head with the brick wall. The roof had long since rotted away, but she'd remembered it correctly - there was room for an adult to stand up in there.

Charlotte stopped and took a deep sigh. She'd drive herself crazy if she continued this wild goose chase. Bruce was gone. He must have been scared that she'd report him and had made himself scarce. He was gone, he was out of her life, so why was she obsessing with it still?

Charlotte heard a ding in her pocket. Her phone had found a signal now she'd moved back into the heart of the holiday camp. She moved Una's lead to her left hand and took a look at her phone. It was a Facebook message. Probably Lucia was moaning about school again. Or perhaps Will, updating her on his first day at the college.

It was neither. The message was from the unidentified person who'd connected with her previously. And whoever it was had gone one better than describing the necklace that she'd lost on that beach over thirty-five years previously. They'd sent a picture of it. There it was, right in front of her: the necklace that her mother had given her just before she'd died.

CHAPTER FIFTEEN

1984 - Sandy Beaches Holiday Camp

The first days at Sandy Beaches Holiday Camp passed in a blur for Will. He wasn't used to the constant cycle of shifts, having never worked a full day at a job in his life. By the time his first six days were completed, not only had he graduated to his own workstation, but he was also due a day off.

'You need to get up and leave the site early,' Abi had warned him. 'If someone is off sick, they'll come and knock you up for a breakfast shift to cover for them. You need to be off the premises at the crack of dawn and don't even think about coming back until the evening shift is done.'

Will was sitting in the staff canteen between shifts, coaching Abi with her maths.

'You know, you're doing alright here Abi. I'm not sure why you keep failing the exam. You've just completed half of a past paper and that's a pass score if ever I saw one!'

'Really?' Abi asked. 'Was that a past paper?'

'Yes, I tricked you,' Will smiled. 'I've a feeling you suffer from what doctors call *white coat syndrome*. I think you get into such a state before an exam, you can't see the wood for the trees. When I gave you exam questions and you didn't realise it, you did fine.'

'I can't believe you're helping me with this,' Abi said. 'I've felt like I was on my own for so long. I've only known you a week and look at me! They've given me a regular Sunday night at the Old Codger's Bar and I'm doing better with my maths than I've ever done. Thank you Will, thank you.'

She leaned over and kissed him on the cheek. Will got a close up of her cleavage as she leaned in, and noticed that the love bites were beginning to fade. They hadn't been replaced with a fresh batch either.

His cheeks coloured and he smiled awkwardly at Abi.

'It's no problem Abi, seriously. I'm happy to help.'

'You like Charlotte, don't you?' Abi scowled. 'I felt it just then, the way you tensed when I kissed you. I don't bite you know!'

The irony of that comment appeared to have been lost on her, Will thought.

'I really like you Abi - a lot - and I'm very happy to help you out. I can think of nothing more satisfying than to set you up for an 'O' level pass in maths as a by-product of working here over summer. But it comes without strings, you know. And yes, I am interested in Charlotte, but she doesn't seem to be so interested in me.'

'She'll have a problem getting away from that Bruce,' Abi replied, 'He's a nasty piece of work. Whatever made an attractive girl like her get together with an idiot like that?'

'Is he a regular here?' Will asked.

'I've been back three summers in a row now; he was a fixture when I arrived. He's a bit of a ladies' man too. He had another girlfriend before all the students started arriving. A nice girl called Lynn. She'd been here more summers than I have. One day, she just left. No explanation, no fanfare, she just packed her bags and left. Charlotte and Jenna arrived soon after, once the universities and colleges started finishing for summer. And Bruce was straight in there. I've made my fair share of bad choices with men, but I know enough to leave that one well alone.'

'Yes, I've seen him in action twice now. You know that night in the bar when everybody was making a big deal about my sore hand? That was Bruce's work.'

'Did you tell anyone?' Abi asked, looking at his hand to see how it had healed.

'No, nobody saw him either. I'm a veteran of school bullying - I know how this stuff works. Casual intimidation, no witnesses, nothing that can't be explained away as a fall, a bump or a clumsy accident. I'm just giving him a wide berth for now, but what can you do? I'm really worried about Charlotte. I've tried to get her to talk about it, but she changes the subject. She's caught I think - scared. But what can she do if she's trapped like that?'

'Just be careful with Bruce,' Abi warned. 'Be careful you don't wade in over your head. I know you want to help Charlotte. But make sure it's not you handing in your notice and packing your bags like Lynn did.'

That conversation bothered Will all night. He barely slept, churning it over and over in his mind. At least he still had the room to himself; he'd heard some real horror stories about mismatched room shares. Abi had to put up with noisy love-making every night from her red-blooded roommate Reese, who seemed to return to the chalet with a different man every night.

The few double beds that were available were moved

from room-to-room, landing-to-landing, as relationships started and ended and deals were struck to secure the much-coveted furniture. Rumour had it that £40 or more was often paid to secure a bed swap, almost a week's wages. He'd never had a life experience like it before.

His restlessness ensured he was up at the crack of dawn on the morning of his first day off. He'd checked the bus times and figured out his strategy. He would take breakfast in one of the on-site fast-food bars which opened at half-past seven in the morning. That way he was out of his room early and didn't have to use the staff canteen, where he might be apprehended to work a shift if anybody had reported in sick. The first bus into Morecambe was at half-past eight, so he'd nurse a cup of tea and read the newspaper until it was time to move on. He reckoned he was safe that way.

Will was running a little late for the bus, which was laid on for the benefit of the holiday-makers who wanted to spend a full day in the nearby resort. It was one of the few staff perks, so they all made use of it to get off the site. It was a double-decker on which were painted the words *Sandy Beaches Holiday Camp - Your Seaside Adventure Begins Here!*

'Damn right it does,' Will thought to himself, running towards the vehicle as fast as he could manage on a full stomach. He'd just seen the black smoke from the diesel engine belch out of the exhaust. It looked like the driver was loaded with passengers and ready to go.

Will jumped on board just as the doors were about to close. The driver gave his staff card a cursory inspection and waved him on.

Surveying the lower deck, he could see the majority of the seats were taken, so he opted for the upper deck. The driver was taking no prisoners; the vehicle lurched forward as Will thrust out his hand to grasp a nearby railing. Walking up the small staircase felt like a battle with centrifugal forces as the driver turned the bus around and headed out towards Morecambe. Eventually, he made it to the top deck, which was much less crowded, so he took a vacant seat.

Following Abi's advice, he was clear of the camp for the day. He wouldn't take the last camp bus back because it always arrived in time for tea. Abi recommended taking the municipal bus service, which sent the last bus out at half-past ten.

As Will settled into his seat, he looked out at the view from the top window. The nuclear power station dominated the coastline, which was dotted with static caravan parks. Predominantly though, it was very rural, with the winding lane to Heysham lined with open, green fields.

'Hi Will, is it your day off too?'

He turned around to see that Charlotte had spotted him from one of the rear seats and had moved to sit behind him.

'Hi Charlotte, fancy seeing you here.'

He scanned for Bruce. There was no sign of him.

'Are you on your own?'

'Yes,' Charlotte replied, 'I managed to get a day off at short notice. I did a swap with somebody.'

He noticed the hesitation in her voice. She was holding back.

'What's your plan for the day?' he asked, figuring she'd tell him if she wanted to.

'A day in Morecambe. No particular plan. I just needed to get away for a day.'

'Any reason?' Will chanced. 'Is everything okay?'

Charlotte paused a moment, as if considering whether to trust him.

'Yes, I'm fine thanks. I just wanted to get away from the place. It can all feel a bit claustrophobic after a while. The same faces, the same shifts every day. You haven't been there long enough to be sick of it yet. How are things going with Abi, by the way?'

'Oh, we're not an item or anything like that.'

'I wasn't suggesting...'

'No, I'm just helping her with her maths. Wasn't she amazing in the bar the other night? Did you know the guys in the band are paying her to sing on Sunday nights? She can't believe her luck. She's over the moon.'

'What do you make of her?' Charlotte asked.

'I like her. I know a lot of people find her a bit much to take. But I think she's got a heart of gold. I also think that somebody needs to show a bit of faith in her. She has zero self-confidence. Why do you ask?'

'Well, I only found this out after we'd started seeing each other. Apparently...'

'Go on,' Will encouraged. 'What happened?'

Charlotte swallowed hard and looked at him.

'Apparently, according to Sally's Purple Coat boyfriend, Abi and Bruce used to be an item.'

CHAPTER SIXTEEN

Present Day - Morecambe

Charlotte felt light-headed. Who could possibly have her mother's necklace after all these years?

She sat down cautiously on what was left of a bench, half expecting it to collapse, and studied the photograph carefully. She knew every millimetre of that piece of jewellery. She'd played with it and coveted it as a child. And when her mum had passed away, she'd guarded it like a treasure. Until that night.

She had always assumed it had been taken by the sea. It seemed the obvious answer. After all, when she'd left Bruce, the waves had been splashing around their feet. At first, she'd been terrified that his body had been swept away by the sea. She'd actually felt a sense of relief that he was still alive. It had come as an even greater relief to hear that he'd packed his bags and left too. For years she had hated herself for losing that necklace, the one last thing that made her feel close to her mother.

Was it Bruce contacting her on Facebook? Surely not, after all this time. Had he harboured a resentment for all these years? Was he seeking revenge?

Charlotte didn't have any answers. But she knew that she had to engage with whoever was sending the messages. She couldn't bury her head in the sand.

What do you want? she typed, immediately erasing it, thinking it made her feel like a victim.

We need to meet, she typed, looking at the words. *Somewhere public. Or are you too afraid to show your face?*

She considered the last sentence for some time. Was it too confrontational? Perhaps. She erased it and sent the remainder of the message. She watched for a few moments to see if it would get a tick mark to show it had been read. It did not.

Charlotte felt an overwhelming sense of panic wash through her and for a moment she thought that she would lose it again. Ever since the incidents at the school, she'd felt only one step away from everything collapsing. She couldn't tell Will; he must be sick of her already. She was holding on by a thread.

It was Una who distracted her from her anxiety. She began to tug gently at the lead, encouraging Charlotte to move on.

'It's okay Una, I'm coming,' she said, running her hands gently along Una's back, making the dog's tail wag.

There was one more stop she wanted to make before they started bulldozing the place: their old room.

It had been Will's room, but he'd managed to survive the summer without getting a roommate. All the other staff members would tease him, asking if he had some kind of disease or if he was a werewolf, too dangerous to assign anyone to. He'd just got lucky; they seemed to have over-looked him. Which meant that when Charlotte and he had begun their relationship, they'd had a bolt hole, providing some privacy. They'd spent many hours in that room, chatting, laughing and getting to know each other. Officially, she'd kept her shared room with Jenna, but as the summer progressed, she spent more and more time over at Will's. It was where they'd taken their first steps as a couple. Besides, Jenna had also moved on by that time.

She could still remember the route to the chalet. Past the nursery, turn left, towards the laundry and into the second chalet block. The accommodation looked wrecked now. The textured cladding, which concealed the low-quality building materials underneath, was beginning to flake off, and the metal windows on the upper levels were severely rusted. Those on the ground floor were boarded up and covered with spray-painted messages.

Charlotte walked over to the bottom of the concrete staircase which used to lead to their room. It was blocked by a single section of builder's fencing, chained to each side of the stair railings.

She tied Una's lead to the lowest railing and pushed the fencing panel over to one side, attempting to create a gap to squeeze through.

Una looked at her, her long, pink tongue hanging out as she panted.

'Don't tell anybody how undignified this looks,' Charlotte said, ruffling her fur. 'Stay there, good girl. It's just for a moment.'

She crouched down and began to pull herself through the small gap that she'd created. The railings pushed against her back and for a moment she thought she might actually get stuck. However, she persisted and although she sustained a couple of small scrapes in the process, she made it through.

Charlotte walked up the staircase. The vandals hadn't made it this far. Lightweights.

She stopped at the top of the stairs and took a breath. The feelings of panic had subsided now and she was feeling on a more even keel.

The doors and windows on the upper levels were free of the chipboard which protected the ground floor. Charlotte wondered why they'd bothered; the vandals might have demolished the place themselves if they'd left it long enough. She walked along the concrete landing, past the room that Abi and Reese had shared.

Of course, there had been life at the camp after she and Will had moved on. It had stayed open another nine years before it closed to holiday-makers. She wondered how many other couples had met or broken up in those rooms. She passed Abi's window and turned left, into the recess which led to the doors. Left and right were the entrances to the rooms, and opposite were the toilet and bathroom. There was Chalet 12.

Charlotte placed her hand onto the metal handle, pushing it down and pressing gently in the hope that the door would open. Below her, Una barked.

'It's okay Una, I'll be back in a moment,' she called.

The door was shut, but the weather had worked its way in and she could see that it was beginning to rot. They were going to demolish the place anyway, so she forced it with her arm. There was the crunch of rotten wood and with two more pushes, she was in. There it was, Will's room. The place where they'd first made love. The room where she'd decided that he was possibly *the one*.

She didn't really know what she was expecting but being there fed her soul. It transported her back to 1984, that feeling of excitement and a newly discovered love, the thrill of a relationship creating a spark of energy for young passion to ignite. She could see them sitting on the bed, writing letters to friends and family, laughing, comfortable in each others' company. She felt like a spirit from the future, almost able to reach out and touch the memory.

It created a wave of nostalgia in her and a sense of what life had torn from them over the years. Kids, jobs, money - it had left them tired and worn. She'd even had suicidal thoughts at times. She was certain she wouldn't do anything - as sure as she could be - but she'd thought about it and the possibility continued to rear itself as a way out should things ever become so bad that she couldn't cope. If only they could press the reset button.

She still loved Will; being there in that room made her see it clearly. It was life that had stripped them of their joy. He was still the same old Will, the boy she'd fallen in love with at Sandy Beaches Holiday Camp, the man who'd taught her what a good relationship can be like.

He'd never raised a hand to her - he'd never been anywhere near it. Neither had he struck the kids. Will was a good man, and she still loved him. Somehow, she had to find her way back to him.

The room had been completely stripped. The cold, drab wallpaper had been removed, with a more modern look achieved through the simple addition of a dado rail. There was patterned paper below the rail and plain above, and it had started to peel off the walls.

All the furniture had been removed. The only things left were the sink in the corner of the room and the mirror above it. She laughed as she recalled how they'd peed down the sink at night, rather than having to throw on some clothes to use the shared toilet on the landing. Looking at the height of the sink, she reckoned she'd put her back out if she tried it nowadays.

She closed her eyes and absorbed the echoes of their youth one last time. It felt good. Will was right - coming back to this place had been a good thing.

Una barked again. Charlotte pulled the door as firmly as she could, then looked over the barrier on the landing to let her know where she was.

'Over here Una!'

The dog looked up and started to wag her tail, content that all was well.

Then Charlotte remembered something they'd completely forgotten in the intervening years. It came back to her with complete clarity.

She went back into the room, made for the windowsill and crouched down so that she could see underneath it. It was still there. The message they'd left all those years ago. She and Will had got drunk on cheap Liebfraumilch and she'd dared him to carve their initials into the woodwork. It had seemed so daring at the time, vandalising holiday camp property like that. Here it was, surviving after so long, remaining hidden for all that time. WG loves CT 1984. Tyson, her maiden name. It was so long since she'd thought about it.

Charlotte heard her phone ping. She removed it from her pocket and studied the screen. There had been nothing from Lucia that day. Hopefully that was a good sign. Olli too had maintained radio silence. It would help if the kids settled quickly.

She'd got her reply from the anonymous contact. As she

opened up the message, that sense of calm was wrenched from her.

Charlotte fainted before she read the rest.

Don't worry, I'll find you.

CHAPTER SEVENTEEN

Present Day - Morecambe

Charlotte woke to the sight of George's face.

'You gave me quite a fright there,' he said. 'If it wasn't for Una, you might have been here for ages. She raised the alarm with her barking.'

Charlotte ran through the events in her head. The message. The overwhelming sense of order crashing around her. The hard fall to the ground, hitting the cold concrete of the balcony.

'My head hurts. Did I fall badly?' she asked.

'I think you hit the railings on your way down,' George said. 'There's a bruise and a bit of blood. You might want to get that checked out at the hospital or by your doctor. You have to be careful with blows to the head, you know.'

For just one second, Charlotte thought George was trying to convey something to her. No, she was being paranoid, she was imagining it.

'What time is it?' she asked, suddenly thinking about

their guests. She wanted to get to the school too, to make sure that Lucia was safe.

'It's half-past two,' George replied. 'I'd take a moment if I were you.'

'I can't' she replied, touching her forehead. She could feel a raised area where the bruise was forming. 'I have to go to the school. I have to get back!'

'Take it easy.' George tried to steady her. 'You've had quite a shock.'

Charlotte was up on her feet.

'Look, I'm so sorry I keep screwing everything up, George. You must think I'm out of my mind...'

'I thought no such thing,' he reassured her.

'Thank you for letting me take a last look around. It means so much to me. Thank you. But I've got to go.'

She placed her arm on George's shoulder and rushed off, along the balcony and down the stairs. George had removed the chains which were securing the barrier, so the exit was now left unobstructed. Charlotte said farewell to Una and rushed off.

So determined was she to get to the school gates in time, that she used the route she and Will had taken on their first visit, squeezing through another narrow gap and caking herself in mud in the process. She didn't care. After the message on her phone, she had to check on Lucia. She needed to make sure that her precious daughter was in no danger.

She ran to the car and activated the locks. Noticing an absence in her back pockets, she cursed as she realised she'd left her phone on the balcony. There was no time to retrieve it. It was safe with George; she'd have to fetch it from him another time.

Charlotte started the car and roared along the country

lane, heading back towards Heysham and Morecambe sea front. It was only when she passed a speed monitoring van that she took her foot off the accelerator and adjusted her speed to match the limit. She wanted to be at the school gates before the kids came out. It was imperative that Olli and Lucia did not see her there; they'd be horrified if they ever thought she was checking up on them.

Even though she was ten minutes early at the main school gate, there were still parents and taxis hovering like vultures. Many of them would have come to the school gates immediately after work, on the non-stop parenting rollercoaster. The contract taxis were there for the special needs kids and travellers, but being located centrally in town, there were no school buses. All the secondary school youngsters used the municipal services.

Charlotte found a parking space opposite the entrance, but not directly in front of it. Their car, an ordinary Ford, blended in nicely. She took out her sunglasses from the front glove compartment and put them on. It wasn't particularly sunny, but it wasn't so dull that she looked ridiculous. It would have to do; she couldn't risk being spotted.

If it turned out she was being paranoid, she'd be home before the kids got back and they'd never even know she was there.

The school bell sounded in the distance, marking the end of the day. She felt a twitch in her stomach. For years her working days had been punctuated by bells like that. She wondered if the apprehension they caused would ever leave her.

The children left the school premises like a stampede being filmed for a David Attenborough nature show. First came the outliers, then the mob left the playground in their noisy and boisterous groups, tearing through the peace and quiet like a violent thunderstorm. She was so pleased this was no longer her life.

A teacher appeared at the gate, a cup of something in her hand. Every now and then she'd chide the youngsters or exchange a bit of banter with them.

Three boys had managed to balance themselves on a single bicycle and were careering dangerously through the crowd.

'Boys, walk with the bike!' she shouted.

They just grinned at her and rode on.

Next, a fight broke out among a group of girls, probably only fourteen or fifteen years old. They were kicking a girl with such ferocity it made her wince, but she'd seen it all before; she knew how wild some of them could be.

The supervising teacher split it up, making the children shake hands in a cursory attempt to smooth it all over. She sat with the bullied student for a few moments before sending her on her way. As if the two-minute head start would keep her safe - the little bitches would be waiting around the corner, ready to finish off what they'd started. Charlotte had done it herself, sometimes so anxious for the school day to end that she'd paper over the cracks and send the kids packing, knowing she wouldn't have resolved the issue. Anything for a bit of peace and quiet and an uninterrupted mug of tea.

Charlotte had been distracted; she'd almost missed her. There she was - she'd darted out of the school gate and was now dawdling near a tree, checking her phone. She had no friends yet. It made Charlotte want to cry.

Then, from across the path, a man with a shaved head moved towards her. He was thickset, tattoos on both arms, wearing jeans and a t-shirt. Why was he going up to her daughter? Was this Bruce, back all these years later to screw up their lives?

Charlotte opened the car door, causing another vehicle to slam on its brakes to avoid crashing into it. She held up her hand by way of apology, shouting 'Sorry! Sorry!'

The man who was driving the van opened up his window and shouted 'Watch what yer doing luv! Bloody wimmin' drivers.'

She ignored him, rushing across the road towards Lucia.

'Hey, piss off you! Just piss off and leave my daughter alone!

Charlotte grabbed the man by the arm and spun him around, shouting into his face.

'You bloody nutter, you screwed up my life before, now piss off and get out of here!'

The man looked bemused. Even as Charlotte shouted the words, she knew that it could not possibly have been Bruce Craven. Everything about him was wrong, even thirty-five years on.

'Hang on a minute darlin', I was only asking her the time,' the man protested. 'She was lookin' at her mobile phone - I just wanted to know what time it was.'

The teacher at the school gate had observed the near-miss in the car and was now approaching at some speed to attempt to sort out the altercation.

Lucia was horrified, screaming at her mum to get a life and leave her alone.

'You're such an embarrassment. Why did you have to do this in front of everybody at school? I hate you, Mum!'

Lucia stormed off. Charlotte moved to pursue her, but the teacher took her arm gently.

'Excuse me,' she said, using her best authoritative tone.

'You can't just come to the school gates causing trouble like this. We have a duty of care to our children.'

'She's a bloody nutter, that's what she is!' the accosted man protested, cutting his losses and beginning to move away.

'Is everything alright here Miss Weir?' came a man's voice from behind them. 'One of the sixth formers told me something was happening at the gates.'

Charlotte watched as Lucia ran off, well ahead of her now. The man had made good his exit, sensing that there was no more benefit to be had from causing a fuss.

'It's alright Miss Weir, I'll handle this,' came the commanding voice.

The teacher released her loose grip on Charlotte's arm and she took a step back.

Charlotte turned to face the man and her eyes fell on his name badge.

Mr E. Hyland, Head Teacher

She'd made a fool of herself, and now she'd have to explain herself to this man, her children's new head teacher. The embarrassment of it. She wanted to shrink into her shoes.

'Let's go to the office shall we? I'm afraid I'll need to determine if the police should be involved in this matter.'

And as he led her through the school gates, towards the main entrance, she was greeted by the final indignity. Olli burst through the doors, laughing alongside one of the sixth form girls. He did a double-take as he passed Charlotte being escorted into the building by Mr Hyland.

'Mum? What are you doing here?'

CHAPTER EIGHTEEN

1984 - Sandy Beaches Holiday Camp

When Charlotte and Will looked back on that summer, they both agreed that the day out in Morecambe counted as their first real date. What started with a spark of recognition and friendship on the bus, ended in a day that would have repercussions for years to come.

Will seemed cagey after the conversation about Abi. Charlotte could sense there was something troubling him, but he seemed conflicted about whether to share it. She tried to probe, but he was having none of it. So she decided to shut up and enjoy the bus trip into the resort.

It wasn't the best of starts. Sitting on the top deck of the bus, moving along the winding country lanes, it was inevitable that somebody was going to get travel sickness. In this case it was Charlotte who struggled to hold onto her stomach as a passenger.

'Can we move to the front of the bus?' she asked, 'I'm feeling a bit queasy.'

Thankfully the front seat was vacant. After a few moments, Charlotte started to relax.

'That's better, my stomach is settling now, and we get a better view from up here anyway.'

As they rounded the turn from the West End, they could see the sea and the Cumbrian hills far off across the bay. It was a beautiful day and the light blue cloudless sky suggested it might even stay that way.

'What great weather for a day off!' Will said, as if invigorated by the thought of some time away from the holiday camp. 'No Bruce with you today?'

Charlotte hesitated in her answer.

'No, we... er... couldn't get our shifts off together,' she stuttered. 'You know how it is in that place, it's a nightmare even getting your own day off, let alone coordinating with someone else.'

'You can say that again,' Will replied. 'I had to run a covert operation this morning to make myself scarce before I could be pulled back in for a shift. How did you manage it?'

'If you're first in the staff canteen for breakfast, you can be in and out before anybody gets a chance to catch you. I got my free breakfast there, then waited in the lobby of the Welcome Hall until the bus arrived.'

'Welcome Hall? Is that what they call it?'

'Yes, welcome to Hell, more like.' Charlotte laughed.

They were so high up on the bus that they had an excellent view of the illuminations which were being erected along the length of the sea front, ready for the switch on towards the end of summer.

'Where are you getting off?' Will asked tentatively.

'At the pier,' Charlotte replied. Testing the waters with similar caution, she asked where his stop was.

'The pier sounds fine to me,' Will said. 'It's central enough ... what have you got planned?'

'Nothing, really. I just wanted to escape for the day. You?'

'Same here. I just wanted to get away from the camp, so I don't have to serve any of those wretched lamb cutlets. Have they even been anywhere near a lamb, do you reckon?'

Charlotte laughed. She felt at ease with Will, a feeling that had been absent from her time with Bruce for some weeks now. When did the problem start? She couldn't put her finger on it. It had come slowly, creeping up on her. And now, here she was. Trapped in what was supposed to be a holiday romance and scared to end it.

Dare she suggest it? 'How do you fancy teaming up for the day and exploring Morecambe together?'

Will had given his answer before she'd even finished her sentence.

'I'd love to.' Then he hesitated. 'Will Bruce be alright with that?'

Charlotte saw his hand move to the sore spot where he'd claimed to have had an accident with the tea urn in the kitchen. He touched it, as if reminding himself it was not yet fully healed.

'He's working shifts all day,' she began, 'Besides, what he doesn't know won't hurt him.'

She felt brave and rebellious saying it, but at the back of her mind was fear and trepidation.

'Are you certain?' Will checked. 'I mean, I'd love to spend the day with you, but I don't want to cause any trouble between you and Bruce. He seems to be the possessive type.'

'The chances of anyone seeing us together are pretty

low. Besides, Bruce needs to get over himself. We're only friends, right?'

Will paused before answering.

'Yes, friends. It's just a harmless day out.'

They'd managed to convince themselves, even though Charlotte felt sicker than she had during the early part of their bus journey, as she thought about her defiance against Bruce.

'This pier has seen better days,' Will commented. 'Do you ever come here during term time?'

'Rarely,' Charlotte replied, happy that Will was taking her mind off Bruce. 'None of my friends has cars, so we tend to stay in Lancaster. Anywhere else is a foreign land as far as I'm concerned.'

'I've been a couple of times. I'm really looking forward to having a proper look around. Where to first, then?'

In spite of the beautiful weather, the promenade was windy, and the pier even more so, exposed to the chill of the sea.

'Do you reckon places like this will survive?' Will asked. 'It's beginning to look a bit run down. This pier for starters - it's seen better days.'

'I hope it'll survive,' Charlotte replied, deep in thought. 'I love these old seaside resorts; it would be a shame if they didn't pull through.'

The morning passed at great speed after their visit to the pier, with a walk up the far end of the promenade to Happy Mount Park, passing the town hall, the bingo club and the rows of guest houses that lined the front.

'Have you ever stayed in one of those places?' Will asked, surveying a row of small, family-run hotels that looked out over the bay.

'Not sure I fancy it,' Charlotte replied. 'It'd be like

sharing your house with a load of strangers. It's bad enough at college. They're probably worse than they look from the outside. You've heard what the holiday-makers say at the camp. Most of them can't believe they fell for the pictures in the brochures.'

Will laughed. 'To be honest with you, I fell for the pictures in the brochures too. I had this image of what it would be like to work there over summer. It's much rougher than I expected it to be. Not just the staff either - the guests can be a bit of a shock too.'

'Oh yes, what's happened now you've got your own workstation? Do tell.'

'I've got a couple of younger girls on holiday together. Can you believe that they asked me back to their room for a threesome? While I was serving them both with a banana sundae, too!'

Charlotte felt her face reddening. She wanted to know if he'd taken them up on their offer.

'And no, I didn't accept their kind offer,' he laughed. 'I think they might have eaten me alive.'

Charlotte felt a sense of relief and wasn't entirely certain why.

They called in at a small café on the front for lunch: *Julian's Pantry*. It looked like it would be cheap and basic. As they were waiting for their toasties and tea to arrive, Charlotte leaned over the table to return the menu to its wooden holder. As she did so her sleeve pulled up to reveal a red mark just above her wrist.

Charlotte yanked her sleeve back down, aware Will had got a clear view.

'I'm as clumsy as you are,' she said, trying to summon up a reason for the markings. 'I ran the bath too hot last night.

That'll teach me to take more care when I'm testing the temperature of the water...'

'He's hurting you, isn't he?'

There was silence. The waitress put two cups of tea on the table.

Will looked into her eyes. 'Tell me to be quiet if I'm wrong. But I think you're scared of him.'

Charlotte tried to hold back her tears. She couldn't admit it to Will. She was like a dam holding back a massive force of water, but the barriers were beginning to crack and she could anticipate the power of the flood if they gave way.

'You can tell me,' Will reassured her. 'Look, see my burn? Bruce did that. He was threatening me to stay away from you.'

The dam burst. The waitress must have wondered what was going on as she deposited two toasties on the table. One cheese and ham, the other cheese and tomato.

Will placed his hand on Charlotte's arm to reassure her. He only kept it there for a moment, uncertain as to whether it would be welcome.

It was such a relief for Charlotte to talk about it at last.

'It's my own silly fault!' she blurted through her tears. 'It was just a stupid summer fling. I've never really got seriously involved with guys before. I just thought it would be a bit of fun and I'd learn more about - well, I'd find out what men liked. It wasn't supposed to turn into something like this. I feel like I'm trapped.'

'It's not your fault,' he reassured her. 'It's never your fault.'

Will let her cry.

'We need to get you out of this relationship, Charlotte. We can't allow him to behave like this.'

He placed his hand on her arm again. This time, Charlotte made sure he knew to keep it there.

CHAPTER NINETEEN

Present Day - Morecambe

Mr Hyland was a pompous ass of a head teacher. Charlotte took an instant disliking to him, immediately regretting having sent the children to the school.

'So Mrs Grayson, what exactly happened out there?' he said in his most imperious voice.

'I thought that my daughter - Lucia Grayson - I thought that she was at risk...'

'At risk?' Mr Hyland queried, before allowing her to finish the sentence. 'How would you suggest that your daughter is at risk outside the gates of our school, with full teacher supervision provided for the pupils?'

Charlotte hesitated. Should she mention Bruce Craven? He'd think she was mad. Will would think she was mad. Even she was beginning to wonder if she was going crazy.

'Lucia had said she was approached by a man at the school gates. She said that it's a common thing for school girls of her age, weird men at the school gates, not just here but in Bristol too...'

Charlotte could feel the hole getting deeper and deeper. What had she hoped to achieve by going to the school? What evidence did she even have to suggest that Bruce was back? Just some anonymous troll on Facebook claiming to have her necklace. But that *was* her mum's old necklace. How had they got it? It had to be Bruce, surely?

Should she tell the police? What would she say? And if she did report it, she'd have to admit the truth. She'd have to say what happened. That she hit Bruce Craven with a stone on the beach and honestly believed he was dead at the time. She'd left him for dead, but he must have recovered well enough to be able to leave the camp the next day. Could she be prosecuted for something like that after all these years?

But he'd tried to rape her. He was the guilty party, not her. If Will had given her one great gift in her life, it was to make her understand that Bruce Craven's actions were not her fault. So why did she feel that she was to blame at that moment?

'Miss Weir was supervising the pupils as per our school procedures, Mrs Grayson. Girls of your daughter's age have very active imaginations. Is it possible she might have made up that scenario?'

He was trying to blame her daughter. Was he daring to suggest like mother, like daughter? That Lucia might be as crazy as she was?

'I saw a man approach my daughter...'

'He was simply asking the time Mrs Grayson. I do believe that is still permitted in our modern-day society. And I'm sure that I don't need to remind you Mrs Grayson, your daughter is a young adult now. She is old enough to think about work or taking up an apprenticeship. Interactions with other adults are how she will learn to navigate this world.'

Charlotte realised she was beaten. She'd have to take the medicine and force it down. In any scenario, she'd come over as completely crazy. She thought that the man was Bruce Craven, a man who she hadn't seen for well over thirty years. A man who she tried to kill. It sounded crazy even to her - yet there it was, the anonymous Facebook contact and a photograph of the necklace. Who else could it be?

Charlotte said nothing. If she'd learned anything about male head teachers of a certain age, it was that they generally liked the sound of their own voice and they were very unaccustomed to being challenged. Her quickest route out of Mr Hyland's office was humility and compliance. She allowed him to deliver his pronouncement and made no further challenges. Besides, Lucia and Olli were already horrified enough with her behaviour at the school gates, and it was unlikely that they'd forgive her for some time.

'Mrs Grayson, I can appreciate that you're probably very anxious about your children changing schools and moving to a new area. Any concerned parent would feel that way...'

Charlotte felt a shit sandwich heading her way.

'...but however concerned you feel, it is always inappropriate to bring violence and confrontation to the school gates, in front of children who are sometimes as young as eleven and twelve years old ...'

Charlotte felt indignation at the use of the word *violence* but made a tactical decision to let it ride. He was reaching his crescendo now - it was almost over.

'I will not inform the police of your behaviour on this occasion, but I must caution you from taking this type of direct action again in the future. Please come and see me in the first instance if there is any concern on your part. Violence and confrontation are never acceptable Mrs Grayson, under any circumstances.'

She wanted to punch him on the nose. *Pompous oaf!*

Instead, Charlotte nodded, acknowledged what he'd said and began to make movements towards the door. Her eyes flickered towards the large clock above the door in his office. She was late for checking in their guests.

'Please don't take this out on Olli and Lucia,' Charlotte said, making a positive movement towards the door now. 'They'd be horrified. It won't happen again, I promise.'

Charlotte was accompanied to the school gates by Mr Hyland's secretary who insisted on making empty pleasantries throughout. Charlotte couldn't help but feel that she was being escorted off the premises.

'Oh, we saw your article in the local paper,' she said, as Charlotte crossed the threshold of school property onto the public pavement. 'How lovely to see that you've taken one of the guest houses. God knows, this town needs it!'

With that, she was gone. Was there anybody who hadn't seen that damned newspaper article? Charlotte had thought papers were struggling to maintain a healthy circulation, but everybody in the resort seemed to have seen a copy.

Charlotte rushed towards the car, but a white van had replaced the vehicle that had been there before. She was wedged in. There was no way she could squeeze out of a spot that small.

She looked around, searching for signs of workmen in a nearby house. There was nothing, no sign of who the van might belong to.

She felt in her pocket for her phone, then cursed when she remembered that she'd left it at the holiday camp.

Charlotte felt a wave of panic wash over her. Lucia had stormed off in a huff. Olli had been horrified seeing his mother being escorted into the school. And she was too late to check in the first guests. She had one thing to do - to be there when the first guests arrived to welcome them into their brand-new business venture - and she'd failed completely.

She felt herself beginning to spiral. The guests would be furious, and they'd leave bad reviews online. Seeing the reviews, nobody would book a holiday and the business would flounder. The local paper would run the story and they'd become laughing stocks. And, quite understandably, Will would be furious with her. How much patience could she expect the poor man to show?

She scanned the area for a phone box. There wasn't one. She wasn't even certain she had any change even if there was; it was years since she'd used a phone box. The last one she'd made a call from had stunk of urine and vomit and she'd resolved never to use one ever again. It seemed that everybody else had made the same decision, as there appeared to be very few phone boxes left in the world.

There was only one thing for it. She'd have to walk back. It wasn't so far that she couldn't cover the ground in twenty minutes or so. Besides, Lucia and Olli were walking back after school.

Charlotte attempted a slow jog but settled instead for a fast walk. There was a time when she'd have thought nothing of running that distance, but life had overtaken her, and exercise was now a thing that other people did. She committed to taking it up again at some as yet unspecified time in the future.

It took Charlotte half an hour to get back to the guest house. She paused outside the front door before entering. Would it be a scene of carnage?

To her relief, Will and Isla had it under control. As she walked into the hallway, she could hear the hubbub of relaxed chatter from the dining room and Will's voice as he organised things with Isla in the kitchen.

'I'll take the mixed grills out to the couple by the window, then we've got it sorted...'

Charlotte walked into the kitchen. She could tell by Will's sour expression that he wasn't happy, but hopefully he'd save the inquisition for later.

'Oh, hello dear,' Isla said, 'I was worried about you. Is everything alright?'

'I'm so sorry!' Charlotte said, 'I got caught up in something...'

'I heard!' Will interrupted, letting his patience slip for just a moment. 'Olli told me.'

He was using that terse voice that he used when furious. If Charlotte could just solve the immediate problem - of getting the first guests sorted - they could save the row for later.

Will picked up the two mixed grills and headed out of the kitchen.

'Well, everything is fine here,' Isla reassured her. 'I know what I'm doing. And the guests think your refurbishment is delightful.'

Charlotte praised the gods for sending them the gift of Isla.

'I'm just going to take this bin bag out to the back,' Isla continued, picking up a trade waste bag and heading into the corridor.

Will returned. Seeing Isla was no longer present, he

could contain himself no longer. He tore into Charlotte, keeping his voice low, to avoid being heard by the guests.

'For Christ's sake Charlotte, what were you thinking? Olli said you'd been hauled in to see the head teacher because of some disturbance at the school gates. I get back from my first day in a new job to find our first two guests standing on the doorstep, ringing the doorbell and trying to check-in. And to top it all, Lucia's not home yet; she's an hour overdue. And you just swan off and leave us to it! I'm beginning to wonder if we should ever have bought this place, it's already turning into a nightmare...'

Will and Charlotte turned, hearing a small cough behind them. It was one of the guests.

'Sorry to disturb you. You don't have any ketchup, do you?'

CHAPTER TWENTY

Present Day - Morecambe

Will paused a moment before rushing after Charlotte. They'd been here before; this had all the hallmarks of another breakdown. He wasn't sure the family could weather this again.

'Olli, take care of the guests if anyone needs assistance,' he called up the stairs. There was a grumble from Olli's bedroom.

Charlotte was clearly horrified that the guest had heard their altercation in the kitchen. Will had stayed calm, reaching out for a bottle of ketchup on the worktop, handing it over and smiling, as if nothing had happened. But it was too much for her right now.

'I'm sorry Will, I can't do this tonight...'

She walked out of the kitchen, through the hallway, then out of the front door.

Will knew his wife's sanity was balanced on a knife-edge. And he was feeling guilty about pushing her back into work so fast. He'd thought she was ready for it, but it looked like he'd been wrong.

'Olli!' he called.

'Okay, okay!' came the begrudging acknowledgement from behind his door.

'And try and raise Lucia on her mobile phone. Tell her I want her back here straight away!'

Isla was returning from the back yard as Will made for the front door.

'I'm so sorry Isla, I just need to make sure that Charlotte's alright. Olli will be down to help; can you cope on your own?'

'Go and make sure Charlotte is alright. Olli and I will be fine here.' She smiled, looking at Olli as he made his way down the stairs. 'Won't we Olli?'

'I'll be back shortly,' Will said, then headed out the door to locate his wife.

The traffic along the sea front had calmed, now the back from school and work rush was over, so it didn't take him long to cross over to the other side of the road. Standing on the long promenade, he looked up and down, trying to pick out Charlotte among the dog walkers, joggers and hardy tourists. He couldn't see her anywhere.

Will took a chance. He guessed that Charlotte would walk towards the town, rather than away from it. She wouldn't have gone far; he knew that much. She'd take half an hour on her own, then it would all be over. Until the next time.

It was beginning to get dark now. Will checked his phone to see if there was any news from Lucia. Maybe she'd made a new friend, headed off into the town and forgotten to let them know where she was. It was great if she was making friends, but they'd told her about checking in at home before. She was old enough now; she should know better.

He jogged along the sea front, checking each bench, hopeful that Charlotte had found somewhere to get her head in order.

It wasn't long before he found her. He should have known. The pier wasn't there any more - it had been demolished several years previously - but she was sitting on a bench at the place where they'd been dropped off on their first day out together. Where the pier had once stood. The day when everything started.

Will sat next to her, saying nothing. He loved her for coming to this spot, and he loved that she remembered, just as he did.

'I'm sorry,' she said. 'I've just had a hell of a day.'

Will waited, saying nothing. It was best coming from her; he'd learned that much, at least.

'Do you remember that first day in Morecambe?' Charlotte asked. 'We had such a brilliant day, I never wanted it to end...'

'It wasn't all fun...' Will began, stopping himself. 'But yes, it was a great day.'

'How long has this pier been gone?'

'It burned down; don't you remember? Years ago now. It's a real shame. They knocked it down after the fire damage.'

'Yes, nothing stays the same, does it?'

'We do,' Will chanced.

'Not really,' Charlotte replied. 'We've changed too. I'm sorry I've put everybody through all this, Will. I just wish I could get my head straight. Every time I think I'm close, something comes up and I'm back where I started.'

'Olli told me what happened at the school. Well, he told me part of it. What on earth were you thinking?'

'I thought I saw somebody... Lucia told me something at breakfast. It was troubling me. I had to make sure...'

'Olli's horrified,' Will said gently. 'He reckons they'll never live it down. He said he was walking out with some girl he's met, and there's his mum, in trouble with the head teacher...'

Charlotte laughed.

'Damn it, Charlotte, what's going on? We've been through this before. You're away from teaching now - it's over, and you never have to go back. I thought you were getting better. Now, all of a sudden, when we're hundreds of miles away from where it all happened, we get this. What's going on?'

'I thought Lucia was in danger. I just did what any concerned parent would do.'

'But how is Lucia in danger?' Will pushed. 'She's perfectly safe at school; this town is completely safe. She's at less risk here than she was in Bristol, and Bristol was perfectly safe too. You're getting paranoid again.'

'Why did you go back to the holiday camp?' Charlotte asked, suddenly on the offensive. 'Why didn't you tell me that's where the mud came from on your shoes?'

'I - I...' Will was on the defensive now, he hadn't expected an attack. 'I just felt like I wasn't done after you rushed off the other day. I wanted to take a proper look around. For old times' sake.'

'And why couldn't you tell me that? Why did you lie?'

'I didn't lie about it...'

'You said you'd picked up the mud going to the cash and carry. Why did you lie to me, Will? Do you think I'm too fragile?'

'I didn't say that. But you have been behaving...'

'How, Will? How have I been behaving?'

'Well, erratically.'

'Erratically? You mean like a mad woman, that's what you mean!'

Charlotte was raising her voice now. A jogger looked at them as he passed, clearly wondering if an intervention would be required.

'No, I don't mean that.'

Will did his best to calm things down. This wasn't the way he'd meant it to go.

They sat in silence a few moments.

'Coming back here has brought it all back, hasn't it?' Will ventured.

'What do you mean?'

Charlotte was calm again now.

'Me bringing you back here. I thought we'd moved on from all that. I thought coming back would be good for us. It's over, Charlotte. Bruce Craven pissed off years ago. He can't touch you anymore.'

He felt her tense the moment he mentioned Bruce. They hadn't talked about him for years. It was like a silent pact, a place they never went.

'He's back.'

'Who is?'

'Bruce. He's back.'

'Is that what that scene was all about at the school gates today?'

Charlotte gave a small nod.

'You think that Bruce Craven is back?'

Will was raising his voice now. He was exasperated.

'How can Bruce Craven be back? In this place and after all these years? We were done with Bruce Craven in 1984.

He walked away, he left you alone. He's gone, Charlotte. How can that man still have a hold on you after all these years?'

'He's back, I'm telling you. I don't care what happened at the school gates today. It wasn't Bruce Craven that time, but he's come back for our daughter. And he's come back for me. I know it's true. I know you think I'm crazy. But I know it. It's him!'

Their voices were getting louder now.

'Is everything alright here?' a dog walker asked.

'It's fine!' Will snapped.

'Are you sure, luv?' the man checked.

'Yes, it's fine, honestly,' Charlotte reassured him.

The main hovered a while, trying to decide whether to stay or not. He could see that they had calmed down, so he moved on.

'Why do you think Bruce is back?' Will asked after a long period of silence. 'How can he be back after all these years? Why would he even care about you after all this time?'

'Because he tried to rape me, Will!' Charlotte exclaimed. 'He tried to rape me, and I hit him on the head with a stone from the beach. I thought he was dead! But the next morning I found out he was alive, and he just left the holiday camp. I thought he was gone forever...'

'He was,' Will replied. 'How can he possibly be back? It's years ago now.'

'He's connected with me on Facebook. He has the necklace that I lost on the beach.'

'What necklace?' Will asked.

'You know - the one I used to wear when we first met. I told you I lost it. I lied. I left it on the beach that night when Bruce tried to attack me. And now it's back. Bruce is the only one who could possibly have that necklace. I'm telling you Will, Bruce Craven is back in this town ...'

'He can't be back in Morecambe!' Will shouted. 'Listen to me, Charlotte. It's a physical impossibility for Bruce Craven to be back in this town. Listen to me, will you?'

'How then?' Charlotte screamed back at him. 'How does somebody have a necklace that I lost on a beach three decades ago? Why are they messaging me now?'

'Bruce Craven can't possibly have sent you that message.'

'Why, Will? Why can't it be him? How can you be so sure?'

'Because I had a terrible fight with Bruce after you left the pub. If he's really come back for revenge, he would have tried to make contact with me too. I was the last person to see him before he left the holiday camp. I left him there, thinking he was dead. I had to Charlotte, he was trying to kill me.'

CHAPTER TWENTY-ONE

1984 - Sandy Beaches Holiday Camp

The toasties were long cold by the time they were ready to think about eating them.

'He hasn't hit me.'

Charlotte was doing her best to reassure Will, but it didn't look like she'd convinced him.

'But he's working up to it, isn't he? He's treating you roughly, pushing you around. It's not normal, Charlotte. People don't do that. If he does anything which leaves any kind of a mark on you, that's not normal.'

'I know,' she replied, looking down, ashamed of the corner she'd painted herself into. 'He was charming at first. I was flattered. The guys I mix with normally, in sixth form and university, they're so damn... well, polite. I don't mean that nastily. It's just that sometimes they're so careful with not pushing their luck and behaving like gentlemen that... I'm embarrassed to say it. Sometimes you just want to know that someone fancies you. I've never met people like the staff who work here. Not the students, they're just like they are back at college. I'm talking about the people who haven't gone through the whole 'O' levels, 'A' levels and university thing. I feel like I've been living in a bubble all my life. Bruce was so confident, so flirty. He made it very clear what he wanted from the moment I met him. And he kept telling me how gorgeous I am and what a stunning body I've got. The men I mix with don't talk like that. I know it's all a lot of nonsense, but I fell for it. It made me feel great about myself. And I just thought, it's a summer fling - I'll never see him again when I leave this place. It seemed harmless at first.'

She liked the way Will didn't judge. He just listened. He didn't offer any solutions. He allowed her to get it off her chest. It felt like a massive relief to be able to articulate it at last. The tears wouldn't stop. It had been bottled up inside her for weeks, an impending sense of something nearing crisis point. She didn't know how to get away from it.

'Can I get you more tea?' the waitress asked. 'You look like you need it.'

Charlotte smiled, wiping her tears.

'It's okay, honestly. I'm just getting a bit emotional about something.'

'If it's a bloke - and I'll bet it is - give him a swift kick in the bollocks and send him on his way. Don't take any nonsense!'

'If only it was as simple as that,' Charlotte replied. 'I will have that second pot of tea, if that's alright. Thank you.'

The waitress headed for the small kitchen at the back of the tea shop and Will played with a small leakage of molten cheese that was solidifying at the edge of his toastie.

'You see, we're so polite and scared of everything,' Charlotte said, once she was gone. 'We live in this educated cocoon; I'm not sure that it helps us in the real world.'

'Has he ever threatened you?' Will asked. 'I mean directly. Has he ever said he'd hit you?'

'No. It's just the way he talks and the things he says. And how he pushes me when he's angry. It wasn't like that at the beginning. After we slept together...'

Charlotte stopped. She was moving into new territory with Will, treating him like a friend or confidant. She hesitated before committing to that course of action.

'He was sweet and polite until that first night. But after then, it crept up on me, bit by bit. He was rougher with me, less gentle. He wasn't violent or anything. It's just that it was different. It felt like he cherished me at first. Then suddenly it was like he resented me. But he wouldn't end it. He never spoke about ending it. It was like he felt caught in a relationship with me, and he hated me for it. But it's just a summer fling Will - he can walk away any time. I can walk...'

'I told you, a kick in the bollocks and a punch in the face. It's sorted out a lot of my exes.'

The waitress was back, dropping off two new pots of tea and a topped-up jug of milk.

'Don't leave those toasties too long, they're disgusting when the cheese gets all rubbery!'

She was gone, having dispensed her wisdom like a fairy godmother who knew how to throw a punch.

'You know, she's partly right,' Will said, picking off the blob of cheese and popping it in his mouth. 'People like me and you tend to be the ones who suffer at the hands of bullies. I'll bet you were bullied at school, weren't you?'

'Yes, for a short time.'

'Did you ever confront the bully? Did you ever resort to violence?'

'No, that's not how people like us do things. We use the official channels. We try to sort it out by talking.'

'Exactly!' Will said, filling his empty mug with the newly arrived tea. 'Why can't they make these things so they don't dribble all over the tablecloth?'

'Yes, I spoke to my teacher, who did nothing. She just suggested we shake hands and make up. That made the bullying worse. Eventually they moved onto someone else. And I was relieved. Can you believe it, I actually rejoiced the day they found somebody else to torment? How scummy is that?'

'I hit a bully once,' Will said, trying to absorb some of the spilt tea with a serviette. It was going to leave a stain on the white tablecloth.

'Really?' Charlotte asked, taking another serviette and helping with the clean-up operation. Their hands touched on the table. Neither was in a rush to move away.

'Yes, he just kept hassling me. He didn't even have a gang; it was just him. He pushed me so far that I just decided, one day, sod it! So I started a fight with him. It wasn't really a fight, it looked more like an epileptic fit I think. I don't think I even landed a blow on him. It looks so easy on the telly, but nobody ever teaches you how to fight. Anyhow, he was so shocked that I'd done anything, he never bothered me again. He just ignored me.'

'So what are you saying? I should hit him?'

'No, no, don't do that, not with Bruce. I think perhaps you just need to stand up to him. Maybe even in public. Let him know what is and isn't acceptable.'

'But that's just it, Will. It creeps up on you. It erodes normality bit by bit.'

'Do you want to stay with him?'

'No, of course I don't. I want to end it. I want to end it now. But somehow the words never come out. I feel paralysed when he's there.'

'Should we tell the police?' Will suggested.

'But that's just it, isn't it? What do I tell them - Bruce makes me feel bad? He's not very nice to me. There's nothing to tell, that's just the point. And he's got me caught in a place where I don't feel like I can walk away. I'm just... stuck.'

'I'll come with you,' Will blurted out. 'I'll come with you for support. I'll make sure he doesn't threaten you or hurt you. And if he does, at least you'll have a witness.'

'What if he goes for you?' Charlotte asked. 'He's already hurt you once.'

She reached out to touch Will's hand, examining what was left of the scald marks.

'We should do it in a public place. He won't try anything then. But he needs to be told, Charlotte. You have to break it off with him. Don't humiliate him, but do it quietly, in a public place.'

'And if he gets difficult? What then?'

'We'll have to report it then. To the holiday camp management and to the police if we have to. But you can't carry on like this. You should be free to leave a relationship at the time of your choosing. Nobody has a right to force you to stay.'

They sat in silence for a few minutes, both thinking over the strategy they were about to commit to. It seemed brave and audacious, an easy plan to sign up to in the comfort of a tearoom like Julian's Pantry. They both played it out in their minds, thinking through all the ways in which Bruce might react.

'I think these toasties have seen better days,' Will said. 'Shall we order some more or grab a burger further along the promenade?'

'I don't fancy mine any more, it looks a bit rubbery now. Shall we drink up our tea and move on?'

'Are you going to do it, Charlotte? Are we going to try to free you from Bruce?'

Charlotte blew on her hot tea and took a gulp before answering.

'I think I have to. It makes me feel sick just thinking about it, but I'm going to have to bite the bullet sometime. He must know it's coming. I've been distant and cold, trying to send signals for days now, but he just doesn't get the message.'

'He gets the message alright,' Will said. 'He just refuses to accept it. So we're on, yes? When we get back to the camp tonight, you'll tell him. I'll come with you; I'll stand nearby so he knows I'm there. That way he can't hurt you or threaten you. And we'll do it in one of the bars too. Yes?'

Charlotte looked at him and saw his defiance. It gave her courage, a courage which she'd lacked so far. She had an ally now - Will made her feel stronger, made it sound as if their strategy might actually work.

It seemed so simple in that tearoom, forging a battle plan over two cold toasties and a weak pot of tea. But it was there that Charlotte resolved to be rid of Bruce Craven. Forever.

CHAPTER TWENTY-TWO

Present Day - Morecambe

Charlotte looked into Will's face. She couldn't believe what he was telling her.

'That can't be true. It's ridiculous. Why are you saying that?'

'It's true, Charlotte. I've lived with it all these years. I can't even begin to explain what happened. But Bruce was gone and nobody was looking for him. I just kept my mouth shut. You didn't say anything and the police never came. I've lived in this no man's land for so many years. It's become a dull sensation now, but it's always there, it never leaves me.

Charlotte could see from his face that he was telling the truth. But none of it made sense. Why had he never spoken about it in all those years that had passed?

'How can that have possibly happened? I mean, I thought I'd killed him that night. Where were you? Why didn't you help me?'

'It's so long ago now, but I remember every detail. Do you remember after you left the pub? It was last orders and you were cross with me and Abi. Bruce had been much quieter, so we thought it was over, even though he was playing pool in the next room at the time. I'll always regret letting you walk back to your chalet on your own. It was such a stupid row to have.'

Charlotte was getting cold now. She zipped up her jacket. The sea front tended to catch the wind whatever the weather. But she didn't want to move on just yet. She needed to hear everything that Will had to tell her about that night.

'Well, we were much younger then and we'd only just started going out together. How long had we been a couple, two weeks? It can't have been more than three.'

'I was always convinced Abi was after you. She seemed so predatory and sexually confident. She wouldn't leave you alone.'

'It was only because I was helping her with her maths. And she was feeling more confident with her singing. I think she wasn't used to men helping her without any expectation of sexual favours in return. She couldn't compute it; I think she almost expected to have sex with me just because I was trying to help her. She had low self-esteem, I think. I wonder what happened to her. I hope she got that 'O' level. And I hope she did something with her singing; she was amazing.'

'So what happened after Bruce followed me out? Did you see him?'

'Well, it was all a bit emotionally charged that night, wasn't it? We'd all had too much to drink. When you and I had our row, I stewed for a couple of minutes after you left the pub. And I had to sort out Abi, who was a bit worse for wear. I felt terrible letting you walk back on your own like that. But I was cross with you - you were really pissing me off with your constant accusations about Abi...'

'They weren't unfounded though.'

'No, but you should have trusted me. It's water under the bridge anyway. I was sitting in the bar, simmering in my own juices, when I caught a glimpse of Bruce moving towards the exit. At first I just assumed he'd finished his game of pool and his drink and he was calling it a night like everybody else. But after a short time I got a bad feeling. It seemed like a coincidence that you'd just left the pub and he'd followed shortly after. It didn't seem right to me.'

A phone rang.

'It's not me,' Charlotte said. 'I lost my mobile earlier today. Well, I didn't lose it. I know where it is, I just haven't got it right now.'

Will felt in his pocket, took out his phone and activated the keypad.

'It's Olli. He says Lucia isn't home yet and he can't raise her on her phone. Do you think we need to call the police?'

'What time is it?'

'Five past six,' Will replied. 'School finished quite some time ago, that's two over hours...'

'She was really fed up with me at the school gates. She's done this before, going off in a huff. Granted, not in Morecambe. She's probably just gone to a Costa coffee shop to calm down a bit. Shall we leave it until seven? She's sixteen now, I don't want her to think we're breathing down her neck.'

Will texted Olli.

Let us know the moment you hear from her, thx, dad x

He moved his fingers over the keyboard, opening up his messages and sending a second text, this time to Lucia.

Where are you? Let us know you're ok pls, dad x

'We should start to walk back,' he said. 'I might need to go out in the car looking for her. What have we told her about checking in with us? I thought she'd have got the hang of that by now.'

Charlotte stood up, and Will followed her lead. They began to walk slowly, back towards the guest house. Charlotte didn't want to arrive too soon; she was desperate to hear Will's story.

'So what happened after Bruce left?'

'Well, he had a head start on me. I assumed you'd gone back to your room, so I ran back there first of all. I knocked on your door, but you weren't there and neither was Jenna. So I ran back to my chalet to see if you'd let yourself in there, but you hadn't. And that's when I started to panic.'

'He'd followed me out. He headed me off before I got to the chalets and I stupidly took a turn to avoid him. It meant I was heading for the beach. When I think back to it, I reckon that's why he moved to that area of the holiday camp. He knew I'd have to head towards the beach to avoid him. He was isolating me.'

Will squeezed Charlotte's hand.

'You know, Julian's Pantry must have been around here somewhere? I can't recall exactly where it was, but it was around here somewhere, on the other side of the road. I remember us having a rather long conversation about Bruce Craven in there, many years ago. And here we are - what is it, thirty-five years later? And we're still discussing him.'

They walked in silence for a while, looking out over the bay at the lights shining from the Cumbrian side. The sea was rough, but nowhere near as ferocious as it could get in a high wind.

'As I said, I think I know what happened.' Will said, out of the blue.

'What?' Charlotte asked, but she knew what he was talking about.

'I saw Bruce lying on the beach, out cold. He came round when I walked up to him.'

'Then you knew all about it? And you never told me?'

'I didn't know what to do,' Will replied. 'Remember, we were both just kids then.

'I didn't see you that night, not after I stormed out of the bar,' Charlotte continued. 'I was still angry with you in spite of what happened with Bruce. But I know that when I was walking through the camp, I thought that someone else was there. I was by the gas canister storage area; do you remember that? We always used to joke about it exploding and improving the look of the place.'

'That wasn't me,' Will said. 'I took the other route.'

'You don't think there was someone else out there that night, do you?' A fourth person who saw what happened?'

Will stopped walking, turned and looked at her.

'Maybe,' he said, 'Maybe. If there was somebody else out there, then they might have seen what happened.'

'What did happen, Will? What did you do that night?'

'I got there too late. I didn't see you again. By the time I got to the beach, Bruce was out cold on the shingle.'

They walked in silence, recalling the events of that night. She felt better for having someone to share it with, after all that time. It had been agonising holding on to that terrible secret, yet Will had known all long.

'So what happened when you checked on Bruce?' Charlotte asked.

'He was lying completely still,' Will continued, 'and the

tide was getting too close for my liking. I checked that he was breathing, but I couldn't tell.'

'So what did you do?' Charlotte asked. They were directly in front of the guest house now. They'd just need to cross the road and they'd be home. She didn't want to leave it like that - she wasn't ready to enter the house yet.

'I didn't want to leave him close to the water like that. I didn't even know how he'd got there at the time. As I was checking on him, he just jumped up and started attacking me...'

'So you saw him alive after I hit him?'

Charlotte felt an immediate gush of relief as she was released from a burden that had tormented her for more than three decades.

'Yes, he was alive after you hit him. He was only unconscious. But he was trying to kill me, accusing me of destroying your relationship. He was so strong and I couldn't do anything to protect myself. I was terrified.'

'So what did you do?'

'I did everything I could to stop him from killing me. What else could I do?'

CHAPTER TWENTY-THREE

Present Day - Morecambe

The guest house was full of activity when they walked through the door into the hallway. George was there, standing in the kitchen with Isla and Olli, all three of them laughing at something or other. And in the lounge was the gentle hubbub of happy guests. They'd found the board games that Charlotte had suggested placing in there. Two couples had paired up to play Scrabble, and the other single guest was reading quietly with her child.

'Any sign of Lucia?' Will asked.

'Nothing yet,' Olli replied. 'But she's alive, at least. She's read her Facebook messages; she just isn't answering.'

'I brought your phone over,' George interjected, holding it up for Charlotte. 'You dropped it earlier. You've got yourself a fine young man here. I always liked you two - I hoped you'd stay together. You've done well; Olli here is a lovely lad.'

Olli's face reddened. He could withstand anything but a well-meant compliment.

Charlotte took the phone and activated the screen.

'You want to get yourself a PIN number put on that,' George suggested. 'A less honest person might have been tempted to pry. I didn't of course,' he reassured her.

'Have you been back to the holiday camp?' Will asked.

'Yes,' Charlotte replied. She wasn't ready to go into the details yet. They still had a lot to talk about. They'd curtailed their conversation, but only in the interests of finding Lucia.

'Well, thanks for coming round, George,' Charlotte said, moving the conversation to safer ground. 'I take it you got the address from the newspaper article?'

'I certainly did!' George smiled. 'It's a good little local paper you know. Nobody seems to buy it, but everybody knows what's in it. I still buy my weekly copy, have done for years.'

'Can I get you a cup of tea?' Isla asked.

'That would be delightful,' George replied.

Bearing in mind how they'd abandoned Isla to take care of everything at the guest house, and the fact that she'd done it so ably, it seemed the least they could do to encourage a bit of age-appropriate male company for her.

'Go through to the lounge with the guests,' Charlotte suggested. 'I'll make the tea, you relax. You deserve it!'

'What are we going to do about Lucia?' Will asked when the others had moved out of the kitchen. Olli had made his exit, keen to get back to his homework.

'Of all the days she has to storm off in a huff, she chooses to do it today,' Charlotte grumbled.

'Well, she's not the only one to spring surprises today, is

she?' Will replied. 'I mean, let's face it, we've done a pretty good job of it on our own, haven't we?'

'It's nearly seven o'clock. We said we'd call the police at seven...'

'I can go in the car and look for her. She's probably just walking it off.'

'About the car. I had to leave it at the school gates. It's why I was so late. I got wedged in by a white van man.'

Will checked his phone again, as Charlotte finished making the tea.

'Olli's right,' said Will, 'She's reading her Facebook messages but she's not replying. Little devil, she's getting a punishment for this.'

'And how are we going to punish her?' Charlotte asked. 'Any more than tearing her away from her school friends in Bristol, moving her to the other end of the country and dropping her into a school she doesn't like very much? With a head teacher who's a bit of a dick, if truth be told.'

'Yeah, maybe we should cut her some slack on that, you're right. I think perhaps one of us had better try for a day out with her somewhere. Find out how she's doing. We've been a bit caught up with the guest house - it's not been fair on her.'

Charlotte took the teas through to the lounge and apologised to the guests for her absence, blaming it on new business teething problems. None of them appeared to care. They were comfortable, well-fed and settled in for the evening.

'Isla is a godsend,' Charlotte whispered to Will as she rejoined him in the kitchen. 'I also reckon she and George have taken a bit of a shine to each other. It'd be nice for both of them if they hit it off. It must get a bit lonely if you've been married for all those years and your partner dies.'

'What are we going to do about Lucia?' Will asked. 'Tell me where you left the car, and I'll go and look for her. Should we call the police?'

'Do you think we should yet?' Charlotte asked. 'I mean, until we've finished our conversation?' She dropped her voice further. 'It turns out I thought I'd murdered a man, and now I discover my husband thought he'd done the same thing. Do you really think we should be getting the police round here before we've had a chance to think things through?'

'But Bruce Craven left the holiday camp the following morning. He was alive, even if I couldn't understand it – I thought I'd killed him!' Will protested, louder than he'd meant to. There was a brief lull in the conversation in the lounge, but it picked up again soon after.

He lowered his voice.

'Bruce Craven left the holiday camp, and nobody was looking for him. You thought you'd killed him. I thought I'd killed him. But we both found out the next day that he walked out of that place and nobody even cared. But nobody saw him, did they? He just left a note saying he'd quit.'

'Look at my phone,' Charlotte said. She held it up with the Facebook message on the screen. Will took it from her and studied it closely.

'That's your necklace,' he said after some time. 'Or, at least, one that looks exactly like it. Who do you think sent this?'

'I don't know!' Charlotte replied, exasperated. 'I just don't know, Will. But if you want to know why I've been so scatty this week and why I did what I did at the school gate, that's why. It's driving me slowly mad. It's just like Bruce is back. He's got his arms around me and he's squeezing the life out of me.'

Will thought for a moment. 'One of us should talk to Nigel Davies.'

'What on earth about?'

'He's a journalist - he'll know how to trace Bruce Craven. He was from Newcastle, wasn't he? He should be easy enough to find, what with the internet and all that now. We'd never have found him back in the eighties. But it should be easy enough now.'

'You know, that's not a bad idea,' Charlotte said. 'At least we'd be closer to knowing who's sending us all these messages. Maybe I can do it while you're at work. Somebody knows what happened that night. You're sure you never saw my necklace on the beach?'

'I don't remember seeing it. After our fight, I did the same as you, I panicked, went back to my room and waited for a knock at the door. The next day, I was going to hand myself in, but I didn't have to. Bruce had gone. I thought I'd killed him that day, but I can't have. Not if he resigned and left the holiday camp.'

Charlotte made a start on wiping down the kitchen, thinking it was about time she made some effort towards the upkeep of the guest house. After a moment, she turned to Will and took the car key out of her pocket.

'It's parked just to the side of the White Swan pub, opposite the school gates - just walk along a bit. You'll see it. Hopefully that van has gone by now; you'll never get it out if it hasn't. I'll call you if I hear from her. But we'll contact the police at nine o'clock, if she hasn't got in touch by then - yes? Are we agreed?'

'Yes, agreed,' Will confirmed. 'I'll text you if I find her.

But no longer than nine o'clock. That's too late for her to be out on her own without checking in with us.'

He looked like he was about to move forward to kiss her goodbye but thought better of it. Will popped his head around the lounge door, thanked Isla for her help and wished George well, then he was on his way. George took it as his cue not to overstay his welcome and made his own exit, exchanging phone numbers with Isla and suggesting that they meet up for a coffee sometime.

'I'll need to be getting back to poor old Una,' he said, 'I don't like to leave her on her own for too long; she likes the company.'

It was nearing eight o'clock by the time Isla put on her coat and came into the kitchen to check out for the day. Charlotte had been watching the clock, urging Lucia to get in touch and cursing that she hadn't.

'Oh, by the way, we got a new booking this evening,' Isla said, putting on her gloves. 'It came in by email, while you were out. I managed to get into the laptop to check. He reckons he knows you - he put a little message in the *Special Requirements* section.'

'Oh yes, who's that then?' Charlotte asked. 'It must be someone we used to know when we were students. Somebody else has spotted us in the local paper, no doubt.'

'It's a Mr Craven,' Isla replied, trying to recall the details of the booking. 'A Mr Bryce Craven. No sorry, it wasn't Bryce. His name is Bruce, Bruce Craven. Do you know him?'

CHAPTER TWENTY-FOUR

1984 - Sandy Beaches Holiday Camp

Charlotte wished that day could have lasted forever. Will provided a complete release from the pressure she'd felt being around Bruce. He was easy company, fun and he made her laugh. The day passed in no time, moving through the arcades, stopping for candy floss and spending most of the afternoon in the amusement park.

Charlotte was clutching the cuddly toy that Will had won on the bingo. Charlotte had never played before, but Will seemed to be an expert on the quiet.

'Come on, it's great fun!' he said as the amplified voice of a bingo caller grabbed their attention when they strolled past another arcade.

'Legs eleven, number 11,' came the caller's voice. 'We have a house call from the lady in the end seat. We'll just come and check your numbers darling. Playing again for a line or full house - a full house wins any prize that you see...'

'I'll show you what to do,' Will reassured her, gently taking her arm and encouraging her over to the arcade.

They got carried away and played several games in a row. When Will shouted 'House!' Charlotte could barely believe it.

'Choose anything you want,' he said to her.

'I'll forgo the bow and arrow toy and the roman gladiator armour set... how about that sinister teddy over there? The one with the rainbow fur and the piercing eyes? It looks like it's about to murder somebody.'

They laughed their way along the street, and for a moment - just for a few seconds - Charlotte forgot what they would be returning to in the evening. She'd have to lose the toy before she even spoke to Bruce. He had a habit of homing in on things like that straight away.

'Doesn't that chap over there work in the kitchens?' Will said, stopping suddenly on the pavement. 'Don't make it too obvious, but he's on the promenade side of the road, underneath the Danger Mouse figurine that's attached to the lampstand.

Charlotte tried not to make it too obvious that she was looking, but she caught his eyes and couldn't pretend to have missed him. She held up her hand to wave.

'Hell, that's one of Bruce's pals from the kitchens.'

'Do you know him?'

'Not well, but he knows me and Bruce are supposed to be an item. He's not coming over to talk. But I'm going to have to speak to Bruce tonight. I can't put it off in case he mentions he spotted me with you. I'd forgotten all about him too, I was enjoying myself.'

Charlotte could feel her stomach knotting again. It was unusual for it not to feel like that lately. She was dreading the confrontation, certain that Bruce would not let it slip without some challenge.

'Look, forget about Bruce, Will began, 'we can deal with him later. Let's finish the afternoon in the amusement park, it'll be fun.'

Charlotte and Will stood at the entrance gate which was styled as a Wild West Fort. She listened to the screams of fear and joy as youngsters and their parents enjoyed the log flume, big dipper, mouse ride and spinning top.

'I've never been anywhere like this!' Charlotte exclaimed, brimming with enthusiasm for the thrills ahead. 'Where I live, you're lucky if the travelling fair comes with dodgems.'

She rushed ahead, eager to secure their passes and try out some of the rides.

It was on the ghost train that they first kissed. It had been hanging in the air all afternoon. But the moment one of the ride attendants stepped out of the darkness of the ride, a ghostly mask on his face and his hand touching Charlotte's shoulder, she screamed with shock and it felt like the most natural thing on earth to put her arms around Will's neck.

As their wagon twisted and turned along the tracks, the roar of zombies and the laughs of vampires punctuating their journey, Will turned to meet her as she moved in close and their lips touched for the first time. By the time the kiss was over, as they burst out of the final wooden doors back out into the sunlight, Charlotte was crying.

'I'm not that bad a kisser, am I?' Will smiled.

'I can't believe how foolish I was to get caught up with Bruce,' Charlotte sniffed. 'I'm just so cross with myself for getting in a fix like this. I'm so stupid!'

Will took the teddy bear toy from Charlotte's hand as he helped her out of the wagon, which was inching slowly towards two very excited youngsters who couldn't wait to begin their ride.

'It'll be over soon,' Will tried to reassure her. 'One day you'll look back at this and laugh. It won't matter at all in the grand scheme of things.'

They moved over to one of the wooden benches scattered throughout the amusement park. Charlotte did her best to stop crying, but she felt frustrated with herself for showing such poor judgement and going against her better instincts, dismissing Bruce as a brief summer fling, a man she could brush off when she felt like it. She'd never done anything like that before and she would never be doing anything like it again. With men like Will, she knew she was in safe hands.

The day drew on and the evening was announced by a chill in the air and the slow disappearance of the sunshine. After another round of bingo in the warmth of the arcades, Will suggested finding a place to eat and to have a drink, so that they were close to where the last bus would leave. They found a restaurant called The Old Galleon which served good, basic food and they were soon tucking into a plate of scampi and chips, washed down by a couple of ice-cold drinks.

As they sat there eating and chatting, Charlotte was so comfortable in Will's company that it felt like they'd been doing this forever. They hadn't kissed again since the ghost train. It had sent a thrilling spark through the whole of her body, but she wanted to finish with Bruce first. However much she needed to break free from him, it was only fair to bring the relationship to an end first. She was old fashioned enough for that to matter.

Occasionally they would bump gently into each other or their hands would touch. Charlotte could tell that Will wanted this as much as she did. But he was content to wait, knowing that Charlotte had to walk out of Bruce's oppressive shadow first.

The last bus was on time, with barely any passengers. They had to make a request stop from the village at Middleton to the holiday camp at Middleton Sands. The bus driver was graceless about receiving the news. He'd thought the last stop would be at Overton, and now he found himself with a twenty-minute loop to make along the narrow, country road.

Charlotte and Will kept out of his way, sitting on the top deck again. It was dark now; there was very little to look at as the streetlights petered out beyond the outskirts of Morecambe.

'What's the plan then?' Will asked. 'Will you tell him tonight? You should.'

'Yes, I'll need to catch him on his bar break. In fact, he'll be taking it at half-past ten. I'll head straight up there when we get back. There's no time like the present.'

'I'll come with you; it'll be alright. It'll be over within the hour. You can do this, Charlotte.'

The bus drew up outside of the camp and dropped them at a different bus stop to the one they'd been picked up at, just beyond the holiday camp gates. They thanked the driver, but all he could muster was a begrudging grunt.

'Ready?' Will asked.

Charlotte nodded.

They walked toward the porter's lodge. The lighting within the boundaries of the holiday camp was good, better than the municipal bus stop where there was only a dim lamp inside the inadequate shelter. As they strolled through the gate, they saw a figure standing to the side of the first lamp post. It was a thickset man; he was smoking. He turned to look at them as he heard their footsteps.

Charlotte knew who it was immediately. If Bruce was waiting for them during his evening break from the bar, his pal from the kitchens must have headed back to the camp on the afternoon holidaymakers' bus to tell him Charlotte had been spotted with another man in Morecambe. Bruce would know who it was.

They'd been caught unawares. It was an ambush, the last thing they were expecting.

Bruce rushed at them with some momentum.

'You bloody slag!' he shouted at Charlotte, forming his hand into a fist and punching Will in the face. Will dropped to the floor. Not only had he never experienced violence like this before, but he was also no match for Bruce's hostility.

'Leave him alone!' Charlotte shouted, letting the teddy bear fall to the floor.

Bruce flew at her, pushing her to the ground with such force that it left her stunned for a few moments.

'This relationship ends when I say it does!' he seethed at her, as she held out both hands to shield herself from any further assault.

'And if this dickhead comes anywhere near you, I'll...'

'You'll do what?' came a voice from the darkness.

Bruce looked up to see who it was. It was one of the security guards from the holiday camp, returning from his rounds of the site.

The man was slighter than Bruce and dressed in black trousers and a well-pressed blue shirt with lapels showing the corporate branding of the holiday camp.

Bruce looked him up and down, as if assessing whether this man was a match for him.

'I'm going to kick this little prick's head in,' Bruce began.

CHAPTER TWENTY-FIVE

Present Day - Morecambe

Will cursed Lucia as he jogged along the path in the direction of the school. Of all the times to go AWOL. He'd considered calling a taxi, but by the time it finally arrived, he'd have got there already. Uber hadn't made it to resorts like Morecambe yet.

The temperature was beginning to drop and a white mist was starting to form where his breath emerged into the cold, night-time air. He picked up his pace but was getting a stitch. He was out of shape; if he didn't do something about it soon, it would get ahead of him and he'd sink into old age far too easily.

Will knew where the school was, because they'd visited on an open day prior to making the move. He couldn't recall the White Swan pub being nearby though.

After twenty minutes, cold and more out of breath than he'd like to admit, Will found the car, parked exactly as Charlotte had described it. He stopped a moment, to think through their conversation. She knew what he'd done now. He'd held onto that secret for all those years and they'd both stayed silent about it, fearful about what the other might say or do. There had been no fuss about Bruce, he wasn't missed, he wasn't reported missing. Like Charlotte, Will just assumed that he was mistaken about how badly he'd hurt his attacker.

He'd been so relieved the next day to find out he hadn't killed Bruce. Even better, Bruce had thrown in the towel, handed in his notice and left. Will had spent the night imagining what jail would be like for a man like him. Full of men like Bruce, no doubt.

Charlotte and he had much more talking to do. He knew it had to come, that night probably, as long as they found Lucia. Where was she?

The car was still wedged into the parking spot, but no longer by a white van. A red 4-wheel drive had packed itself into the tiny slot, its huge bumper only millimetres away from the boot of their car. Will looked through the windscreen for clues. There was no parking permit on display, suggesting it wasn't one of the local householders. Will looked around and saw there was a one-hour waiting time restriction. Charlotte was lucky she hadn't been spotted by a warden; she should have got a ticket for parking there so long.

The sound of laughter and lively conversation could be heard in the pub. That's probably where the driver was. He needed the car - a search for Lucia would be pointless on foot.

Will took out his phone and sent a Facebook message to Charlotte.

The car is still blocked in. Going to see if anybody in the pub owns it. Don't call the police just yet. Give me half an hour to look for her first.

He lurked in the doorway as he waited for Charlotte's reply, the three dots hanging in the message window for a long time. When it came, it was brief.

Okay. We need to discuss something when you get back.

That was the understatement of the year. Will headed for the lounge area, experience telling him it was generally a bit more welcoming on that side of a pub. He walked up to the bar.

'Good evening fella,' the barman greeted him. 'What can I get you?'

'I'm trying to find the driver of a red 4x4 that's parked outside. It's blocking me in.'

'That'll be Tony. He's running the pub quiz in the public bar. He'll be finished in ten minutes. Alright if I interrupt him then?'

Will was tempted to say no, but when he heard raucous, predominately male laughter from the other side of the bar, he decided against it. It was ten minutes; he could wait.

'I'll have a half pint while I'm waiting,' he replied. 'Can you just let him know when you can get his attention without messing up their game?'

'Will do, fella,' the barman replied.

Will took his beer, found a table by the open fire and took a long sup. It tasted good; he couldn't remember the last time he'd been in a pub. It was a nice pub too, with traditional wooden beams and a newly refurbished lounge. Bar meals were served every night and they appeared to have a full programme of entertainment.

Will read down the chalkboard, impressed by how hard the pub was working to stay relevant - and open.

He could see that Quiz Night was that week's main

attraction. There was a hypnotist in the night after and a female vocalist on the Friday. Will did a double-take at the name.

Abi Smithson, Morecambe's Vocal Sensation

Surely not?

Will stood up and walked over to the bar.

'Five more minutes fella,' the barman said, seemingly annoyed that Will had come over to ask again.

'No, it's not to do with the car,' Will reassured him. 'That singer you have here on a Friday night. Abi Smithson. How old would you say she is?'

The barman relaxed, no longer thinking he was going to have to deal with a pushy customer.

'Oh, Abi's been singing around these parts for years. We're lucky to have got her on a Friday - she's rushed off her feet at weekends. She's a big star in this part of the world. She was on Opportunity Knocks several years ago. Not the good one, with Hughie Green. The rip-off version with Bob Monkhouse. She got beaten by an acrobatic monkey. Can you believe that?'

'Would you say she's around fifty years old, with very striking grey eyes?'

'Sounds like her,' the barman replied. 'Why, do you know her?'

'Maybe,' Will replied. 'Maybe.'

He returned to his table and activated his phone. The pub had free Wi-Fi, so rather than burn up his data, he connected to it. As his finger moved to locate the Wi-Fi settings, he spotted the security app that he'd placed on the family's phones to try and prevent them from getting any viruses or malware. He opened it up, on a hunch.

He was right. The software package had a tracker on it. In theory, he could see where connected phones were located. He'd forgotten all about it. He'd only used it once, ages ago, when Charlotte thought she'd lost her phone in Bristol. It turned out she'd just left it on the windowsill in the downstairs toilet.

Will navigated to the tracker menu and opened it up. There was a list of the family's devices. Olli was on his laptop and his phone. Charlotte's phone was active too, he could see the icon on the map placing them on the sea front. His own icon placed him further along the promenade, towards the end, directly in the pub. If Charlotte was looking right now she'd want to know why he was sitting in a pub when he should have been searching for his daughter.

Lucia's phone was offline, but it showed that she'd been in the town centre only ten minutes previously.

He stood up, abandoned his drink and headed back to the bar.

'They're into a tie-breaker,' the barman said, pre-empting what Will was about to ask him. 'Probably another ten minutes.'

'It can't wait until then,' Will said, pushing now. 'I need to move my car. I'm trying to find my daughter...'

The barman wasn't keen on interrupting Tony, who sounded like he was in full quiz master flow on the other side of the bar.

'I'll be waiting outside,' Will said, 'I'd appreciate it if you could catch his attention.'

Will made his exit, unlocked the car with the remote and made a start clearing the windscreen which had become misted up in the cold. The car started on the second turn of the key and he switched the fan onto a full blow. He waited while a half-drunk Tony staggered toward the 4x4 and got into the driver's seat.

Will was examining his phone again when Tony's

glaring headlamps shocked him away from looking at his screen. Tony messed up his gears and the massive 4-wheel drive crunched into his boot, shunting the vehicle forwards slightly.

'Oh shit!' Will said aloud. His phone fell on the floor and he scrambled to pick it up. Tony's engine roared behind him as the requested car shuffling manoeuvre was poorly executed at Will's rear. As the device came back into view, Will saw that Lucia's phone had found a connection once again. She was at the railway station. He'd found her.

Tony had reversed his vehicle fully now and was staggering out of the driver's door to assess the damage that he'd done to Will's car. But Will didn't care about that. He moved the gear stick and screeched away at speed, eager to catch up with Lucia before she moved on. Tony was left calling after him.

'Hey, mate, we need to talk about insurance!'

The railway station was ten minutes away. The traffic was light now, so he made good progress. He almost made a wrong turn, forgetting the station had been relocated since he and Charlotte had first come to the resort. As he came off a roundabout, with the new station just ahead in the distance, Will saw a blue flashing light coming up behind him. He didn't care - he had to find Lucia. He pulled up in a bus stop just ahead of the railway station, put his hazard lights on and ran towards the platforms, ignoring the police car that was slowing just behind him.

There she was, standing on the platform, looking like she was awaiting the arrival of the next train to Lancaster.

'Lucia!' Will called, holding up his hand to get her attention. He ran up to her, aware that he was now being pursued by two police officers on foot.

Lucia dropped her backpack onto the floor and rushed

at Will, burrowing into him as she used to when she was young, her arms around his neck and sobbing.

'Oh Dad, I'm sorry! I just want to go back to Bristol. I hate it here! I'm just so unhappy at the school.'

The two police officers caught up with them, out of breath from trying to catch up with him.

'We need to have a word with you about your car, sir. Did you know that your rear brake light is out?'

CHAPTER TWENTY-SIX

Present Day - Morecambe

It was an unusual start to the morning, even though they hadn't had a chance to establish a new routine yet. Charlotte felt unwell from the moment she woke up. She was so exhausted that she had to think through the events of the previous night to figure out who was still in the house. They'd given Lucia the day off school, with the head teacher's blessing. They all needed to talk, but they were just so relieved to have her back home, safe, after the fright of the day before.

She'd had to go and pick up Lucia from the police station. They'd wanted to check Will's car paperwork and, having smelled beer on his breath, he had to go through a breathalyser test. They also wanted to be certain that Lucia was in no danger from Will. Under any other circumstances, Will and Charlotte would have been grateful for the care the police had taken over their daughter's wellbeing, but it just made a bigger mess of the evening than it had already been.

Will ended up in a taxi anyway, in spite of his earlier reluctance. The police had insisted that the car was taken to a garage, so Charlotte had to collect him and Lucia, but they didn't get back to the guest house until after eleven o'clock. By the time Charlotte had stayed with Lucia in her bedroom until she dropped off to sleep, Will was out cold in their own bed, mentally exhausted by everything that had happened.

The next day, Olli was out to school and Will was up for work. Charlotte came around to the sound of Isla downstairs, capably dealing with the guests. There was a man's voice too, but she couldn't quite place it.

Charlotte desperately wanted Will there, to talk about what he'd done at the holiday camp and where that left them. She needed to tell him about the room booking by Bruce Craven. And he'd mumbled something the previous night about Abi - that she was still living locally. It was becoming too much. Whatever else happened that day, they needed to sit down together and thrash it all out later on.

She got out of bed and made her way to the family kitchen. Will had left a hand-written note on her placemat.

Go easy on Lucia today. We need to talk. Tonight, I promise. Will x

She walked across the hallway to Lucia's room. The door was slightly ajar, enough to see her daughter was fast asleep.

Charlotte gently pulled the door shut, showered and dressed and made her way down to the kitchen. Isla was working there.

'I'm so sorry to abandon you once again...' she began.

'Oh, it's no trouble my dear. Besides, Will told me you'd be up late today, so I planned around it.'

'Thanks for helping out again. I assume Will updated you on what's been going on here since we saw you last?'

'I'm just pleased that you found Lucia safe and sound,' Isla said. 'After I left last night, George and I exchanged mobile phone information. We were chatting away until the small hours on our phones. I can see now why you youngsters never have them out of your hands! It turns out George and I have quite a lot in common. We were at the same school - well, there was only one upper school in town at that time - but I was in the year above him. How much of a coincidence is that?'

'That's amazing,' Charlotte replied, distracted. 'I suppose if you spend all your life in a small resort like this, you're bound to bump into people you know.'

She looked at the clock in the kitchen. It was past nine o'clock; the local newspaper office would be open by now.

'Are you alright to check the guests out Isla? They've all pre-paid, so there's no money to collect. We're quiet again tonight.'

'What about that Mr Craven I told you about yesterday? Did he cancel?'

'I don't think he'll be arriving tonight Isla. I think it might have been kids messing around.'

Charlotte wanted to speak to Nigel Davies at the paper, anxious to see what became of Bruce Craven after he left the holiday camp. Nigel would know. A journalist always had ways of finding someone.

She left a note on the table for Lucia.

Get Isla to serve you up breakfast in the downstairs kitchen. I'm heading into Morecambe - we can talk when I get back. You're NOT in trouble. Love you, Mum. xxx

The home phone rang as she was about to leave. It was the garage, wanting the go-ahead to make a start on the car repairs.

'I think we're going to have to sort out the insurance first,' Charlotte said. 'Can you work up a quotation? I'll try and make a start with the insurance later.'

With that done, she headed into town on foot. Her phone dinged as she walked along the sea front, the cool air waking her up at last.

It was Jenna.

Enjoyed seeing you again. Want to do it again sometime soon?

Love to! Charlotte replied. *Same place at midday?*

Jenna sent a thumb icon back. With a few texts, a coffee date was set up and confirmed.

The newspaper office of The Bay View Weekly was located in the town centre. Charlotte wasn't entirely sure where, but she knew it wouldn't take long to find. She was right - the old-fashioned shopfront was central, making it easier to get there on foot than it would have been to drive and pay for parking.

A bored receptionist sat on a chair behind a desk. Behind her was a wall of previous newspaper headlines.

Sea Defence Proposals To Be Discussed By Council

Death Of Stalwart Councillor, Aged 92

Popular Author To Visit Resort On Latest Book Tour

Photo Exclusive! Fat Cat Rescued From Heysham Tree

The receptionist didn't look up immediately. When she did, Charlotte saw that she was chewing gum. Her nails were immaculately manicured, her eyebrows sculpted to within an inch of her life.

'Can I 'elp yer?' she asked.

'May I speak to Nigel Davies please? Is he in?'

'Not sure, 'ave yer got an appointment?'

'No, I'm sorry, I didn't think to call ahead. It's about a news story he covered last week. He'll know who I am. It's Charlotte Grayson.'

The receptionist made no acknowledgement of the information. She picked up her phone and pressed some buttons. Charlotte caught a glimpse of her name badge. Her name was Reagan and she was, apparently, a Customer Service Executive.

'Is Nigel up there?'

Reagan spoke into the mouthpiece.

'Nah. Nah. Yeah. Alright.'

She put the phone down.

'Yeah, Nigel's in. E'll be down in a mo. Take a seat!'

Charlotte was dismissed. She looked behind her for the aforementioned seat. There were two of them, constructed from metal with orange padded vinyl for comfort. She sat in the one that looked cleanest and a gush of air shot out of the side as she placed her weight on it. Reagan looked up with a disgusted look on her face, as if Charlotte had just passed wind.

It was an old building and Charlotte could hear muffled voices and creaking floorboards above her. Then, she heard a door slam upstairs, rapid footsteps down the stairs, and Nigel Davies appeared, a photographer trailing behind him, two cameras on straps around his neck.

'Hello, Mrs Grayson,' he said, recognising her straight away. 'I'm so sorry, I won't be able to see you right now. We've just received a tip-off for a big story. In fact, you'll probably be interested in it - I'm sure you mentioned that you and your husband used to work there years ago.'

'Oh yes?' Charlotte asked, disappointed not to be able to

speak to him about Bruce but intrigued by what Nigel had said.

'Yes,' he continued, 'You know the old holiday camp at Middleton? They started digging out there first thing this morning. Apparently, when the contractors moved in, they found the security guard had been bludgeoned in the grounds overnight.'

CHAPTER TWENTY-SEVEN

1984 - Sandy Beaches Holiday Camp

Ignoring the voice from the shadows, Bruce Craven darted at speed towards Will, who was clutching his face, still in shock at the violence that had been directed at him.

'Leave him alone!' Charlotte screamed, pulling herself up off the ground and rushing over to help Will.

Bruce drew back his right foot, goading her to stop him, ready to deliver a violent kick to Will's ribs. He sneered at Charlotte, but before he could deliver the blow with his booted foot, he was taken down to the ground, completely oblivious to the man who'd come to Will's defence.

The man was nowhere near as well built as Bruce but made up for that with a well-targeted tackle which brought him crashing onto the grass.

Bruce was only stunned for a moment. Charlotte was making a lot of noise, shouting at him to stop, imploring him to back off. But the man in the blue shirt was calm and steady, waiting to see how this would play out.

Charlotte studied him in the semi-light, his face now partly illuminated by the first streetlamp at the entrance to the camp. It was George, the friendly porter. At least they had someone in authority on their side; Bruce would have to back down now.

'Walk away,' George said, his eyes fixed on Bruce. They were opposite each other now, hands clenched, ready to fight if the wind blew that way. Will was still nursing the blow to his face. Charlotte was desperate to end the confrontation but had placed herself in the middle of the standoff. Bruce pushed her out of the way once again and she fell at Will's side.

Before George could move to help her, Bruce took advantage, charging at him and sending him flying into a bed of roses.

Charlotte winced as he landed on two of the bushes, imagining the thorns scratching his skin as he landed.

Bruce didn't give him time to pause. Running towards him and picking him up by the front of his shirt, he lifted him effortlessly and spat into his face.

'We walk away when I say it's time,' he seethed at George, throwing him to the ground just beyond the planted bed. He was moving in to deliver a kick, when George thrust out his leg, tripping his assailant and sending him to the ground for a second time. George moved fast, wasting no time. He flipped himself to his side, stood up and jumped on Bruce while he was still on the grass, pinning down his arms.

Bruce struggled with the fury of a caged beast, spitting at George and subjecting him to a tirade of swearing and abuse. George held firm, using his position of advantage to pin Bruce to the ground. However much Bruce struggled, he couldn't release himself from George's grasp. Eventually he stopped struggling. Will and Charlotte recovered themselves and walked over.

'You've got a simple choice,' George spoke calmly. 'You can walk away from this and there won't be a problem. Leave this couple alone, stay out of their way, and we can all get on with our lives. But if you insist on escalating this, you're going to force me to report you to the management. You'll lose your job and you may even end up in trouble with the law. All you have to do is walk away.'

'It's over, Bruce,' Charlotte pleaded. 'You must see that we can't carry on now. Not after this. Especially after this.'

Bruce was silent. Charlotte looked at the thorns stuck in George's leg. He must be in some considerable pain, but he wasn't letting on.

'Can I release my hands?' George asked.

Bruce said nothing but nodded. Slowly George released his grip, expecting Bruce to strike back at any moment, but nothing happened.

Cautiously, George stood up, offering his hand to help Bruce get up off the ground. Bruce didn't take it, choosing instead to get back on his feet unaided.

George was clearly still alert, expecting the fight to continue. Bruce stood up fully, puffing out his chest and flexing his arms, fists fully formed.

'It's over... for now,' he said menacingly. 'If you want to shag this student slag, that's up to you,' he seethed at Charlotte. 'But what you need is a real man. I'll bide my time. But it's not over until I say we're done.'

Bruce jumped at them, making George tense immediately. Will and Charlotte stepped back, praying for it to be over now. But Bruce was just re-asserting his power, and didn't strike. Instead, he began to move as if he were heading off back into the camp. As he skimmed past Charlotte, he suddenly made a turn, lunged forward and spat in her face.

'Slag!' he shouted. 'You were a lousy lay anyway.'

At last, he walked off up the main drive of the holiday camp, leaving the three of them in silence, stunned by what had just happened.

Charlotte wiped her face and Will placed his hand on her shoulder.

'Is everybody alright?' George asked.

'I think so,' Will said. 'He's a strong bloke.'

'Yes, he is. Are you okay?' George continued, looking at Charlotte with concern.

'Yes, I think so,' she replied, struggling to fight back the tears. It was a combination of fear and relief, combined with elation that she might finally be free of Bruce.

'Come into the porter's lodge,' George said. 'Let's get everybody patched up and have a drink. I think we all need to calm ourselves down a bit.'

He guided them towards the lodge and unlocked the door.

'Well, he's a nasty piece of work, isn't he?' George said, flicking the switch on the kettle.

'I'm so sorry I caused all this trouble,' Charlotte began. 'I didn't know Bruce was like that. He was nice to me when we met... I'm sorry he hurt you. Thank you for helping me.'

George put his hand up. 'That's all on him,' he reassured her. 'It's nothing to do with you. He chose to behave like that, that's just the way he's wired.'

'Should we report it to the police?' Will asked.

There was silence. George moved over to him to study his face.

'Has he broken your nose?'

'No, he skimmed my nose and struck my chin. It's sore,

but there's no lasting damage. If you've got some paraceta-mol, that will help.'

'What about the police?' Charlotte asked. 'I mean, that was assault wasn't it? He's crazy. Would the police do anything?'

'I'd appreciate it if we could keep the police out of it,' George said, searching his drawer and locating the drugs Will had just asked for. 'It's a bit difficult for me.'

Will and Charlotte looked at each other.

'What's the problem?' Will asked.

'This job means a lot to me,' George explained. 'I've had some trouble of my own with the law in the past. Nothing serious, but when I left the armed forces, it was hard to find work. Let's just say I did some things that I shouldn't have. I'm determined to put that right though - this job gives me a chance to put my life back on track. They're used to working with all sorts of people in these places; they overlooked my police record for petty theft. I'd just like to keep my nose clean and my head down if I can. If I can get by without landing in any scrapes, I might just make something of this job. It would mean a lot to me.'

Charlotte looked at Will, searching his face to try and read his thoughts.

'Do you think he'll attack us like that again?' Charlotte asked.

'I certainly hope not,' George answered. 'Once he calms down, I'm sure he'll see the sense of backing down. After all, we all need the work here. If he causes a fuss, he knows the police will get involved and then he'll be booted off the premises. I reckon most of the people working here - with the exception of the students - most of them will have some sort of past. If you can steer clear of him, I think the situation might resolve itself. If it doesn't, you have my word, we'll all report him to the management.'

George handed Will the glass of water he'd poured for him while they'd been talking. Will washed down two paracetamol tablets.

'How will I explain my face?' he asked. 'People will ask questions, won't they?'

'It'll calm down overnight,' George reassured him. 'If he'd broken your nose, it would have bruised, and you'd have had to go to A&E to get it fixed. I'm going to need to buy a new pair of trousers and get a tetanus shot after my fall in those roses, but apart from that, I think we'll survive.'

'How about you, Charlotte?' Will asked. 'You're the most important person in all this. What do you want?'

'I want Bruce Craven out of my life. I knew it was going to be difficult, but he knows it's over now. I've got witnesses too; we've all seen what he's like. If it helps you, George, I'm happy to leave it at that now. But if he tries it again, if he threatens us once more, we have to make a complaint about him. Together. If we stick together, we can sort him out.'

'Okay,' said George, 'We're agreed. I won't write this up in the incident book, we'll keep it to ourselves. Thank you, it means a lot to me. This job means a lot to me.'

'Thank *you*,' Charlotte said. 'I mean that, George. I don't know what he'd have done if you hadn't stepped in.'

Will backed her up on that.

'We'd better get back George, we're up for the early shift tomorrow. I'm going to see what I can do to calm this soreness on my face. I'll walk you back to your room Charlotte, just to make sure you're okay.'

CHAPTER TWENTY-EIGHT

Present Day - Morecambe

'Oh my God, have you got a name for the security guard?' Charlotte asked, following Nigel out of the building.

She couldn't believe what he'd just told her - a security guard bludgeoned at the former holiday camp. It seemed unbelievable in such a quiet area.

'No, there's no name - it's a breaking news story. Apparently, it was lucky he didn't get crushed in the demolition. Why, do you know someone out there?'

'Yes, George has been working shifts there. We've known him for years. He's an old man now. What on earth are they doing attacking a man of his age? I only saw him last night, at the guest house.'

Charlotte struggled to keep her voice steady. The thought of something like that happening to her friend was inconceivable.

'It's a screwed-up world, and I'm pleased to say things like that don't happen very often around these parts. Which means we just got our front-page story for this week's paper. Do you want to tag along, see if we can find out any information about George?'

'Yes, if that's alright,' Charlotte asked. 'If I won't be in the way?'

'So long as you let us get on with our job, you're welcome. Hop in!'

Nigel opened up the passenger door to the heavily branded car. The photographer was holding the keys, so claimed the driving seat. Nigel climbed in and took the seat at his side.

'All buckled up?' he asked.

He must have kids, Charlotte thought to herself.

'This is Chris, by the way,' Nigel said. 'He's our staff photographer. He comes out with me to cover the serious news stories. He's also available for weddings, bar mitzvahs, family occasions and so on.'

Charlotte laughed, distracted for a moment.

'What were you coming to see me about?' Nigel asked. 'Sorry to rush you off like that, but as a journalist in Morecambe, stories like this are few and far between.'

'It's okay, I'm anxious to see if George was hurt,' Charlotte replied from the back seat, speaking more loudly to be heard over the sound of the diesel engine. 'I was just after some advice, really. I'm trying to find somebody who used to work at the holiday camp. It was a long time ago, 1984 or thereabouts. I just thought you might know how to find him, as a journalist.'

'Yes, I can give you a bit of guidance on that,' Nigel said, turning back to speak to her. A police car came tearing past them as they turned onto the promenade.

'I wonder if he's heading where we are?' Chris remarked.

'I'll bet he is,' Nigel laughed. 'A news story like this gets the cops and the journalists salivating.'

'Was your guy local?' Nigel said, returning to Charlotte's question.

'No, from Newcastle I think. It's so long ago now...'

'Yes, no internet, no social media, it makes you wonder how we ever coped. Your best bet is old newspapers or telephone directories - what used to be our internet in the dark ages. You'll find those on microfiche at the local library. Also, try a website like 192.com or ancestry.co.uk - if you pay a small amount of money, you'll be able to search the electoral roll on one of these online websites. That's where I'd start if it was a news story I was researching. Does he have a family or any other connections? Do you have a place of work, anything like that?'

Charlotte shook her head, then realised she'd have to answer aloud - Nigel couldn't see her in the rear-view mirror.

'I know very little about him,' Charlotte said. 'It's so long ago and nobody used computers back then. The holiday camp company doesn't even exist any more. It's like searching for a needle in a haystack. We were once part of a feature about the holiday camp in summer 1984 though - it might have even been in your paper, come to think about it.'

'Morecambe Library will have the local back editions of the newspaper. Otherwise, try my suggestions,' Nigel replied, 'And let me know if you hit a dead end. I'll see what I can do.'

'Thanks,' Charlotte said.

They were nearing Middleton and Charlotte's stomach was beginning to feel unsettled in the back of the car. She always forgot what it was like to be a back seat passenger, since most of the time she was either driving herself or sitting in the front passenger seat. She considered mentioning it to Nigel, but she didn't want to hinder them in their work. She'd be able to hang on until they reached the holiday camp - it wouldn't be long until they arrived.

'We've had a great response to that story we ran on the guest house.'

Nigel's words distracted her from asking Chris to stop the car for five minutes while her stomach settled.

'Oh yes?' Charlotte replied. 'All positive, I hope?'

'Yes, it seems that quite a few people around here remember you. I've spoken to a couple of locals in the past week who were asking after you.'

'Really?' Charlotte asked, surprised at his answer. 'We haven't lived around here for years. We may know some people still - from college and university, I suppose. I guess some people from the holiday camp might have settled around here too. But I'm quite surprised to hear that. What have they been saying?'

She shuffled in her seat, trying to make her stomach feel more comfortable. It wasn't working.

'Oh, just the usual sort of thing. Nosey locals, just trying to find out what you're up to. How many kids you've got, that sort of thing. One guy was very interested in making contact. Not the sort of person I'd expect you to know. I don't mean to be snobby, but - you know - he was a bit rough to say the least.'

Charlotte was feeling nauseous to the point of throwing up now. She reckoned in two more minutes they'd be at the gates to the camp. The moment she was out in the fresh air, she'd be fine. She opened the rear window a little and breathed in the air from the breeze.

'Did he give a name?' Charlotte asked, struggling to think of who he might be. 'What did he look like?'

'No name,' Nigel said, 'He was a thin, wiry guy. One of those men with what I call *the look*. Just looks like he's up to no good. He's probably perfectly alright, I may be doing him a disservice.'

Charlotte could see the entrance to the holiday camp now. The diggers had moved in already, the old porter's lodge was half gone, and they'd begun to take down some of the administration block. History was about to be erased. There were four police cars and an ambulance parked just beyond the wire safety fencing. It was bustling with activity.

'Stop the car!' Charlotte said.

'What?' Chris asked.

'Please, just pull up now!' she said.

Chris slowed immediately and rode the car up the verge. Charlotte opened the door, got out as fast as her legs would carry her, and threw up just beyond the group of police officers and contractors.

'I'd have given you my hard hat if you'd asked, luv!' a contractor shouted over, his fluorescent jacket flapping in the breeze. The police officers looked over to her and, seeing that Nigel was rushing over to attend to her, continued with their work.

'Well, you know how to make an entrance,' Nigel said. 'Are you alright? You should have said. We could have swapped seats if you get travel sick. Chris throws the car around quite a bit when we're in a rush.'

Chris had parked the car in a more suitable place and had already locked it up and begun to take photographs.

'I'm fine, honestly,' Charlotte said. 'You don't have a bottle of water in the car do you, so I can rinse my mouth out?'

She felt stupid and humiliated. It hadn't been the first

time she'd experienced that same emotion outside the porter's lodge. She felt ridiculous throwing up in front of those people.

After a few moments, she was steady on her feet again, her mouth rinsed thanks to a half-finished bottle offered by one of the contractors. She was anxious to see if George was alright after the incident.

'Don't go anywhere the police tell you not to,' Nigel advised. 'And remember, this is an active building site, it's a dangerous place.'

Nigel checked in with the police and the foreman, showing his ID. Charlotte observed the nods coming from the group ahead of her. She was impressed by how fast Chris was working, taking pictures of everything, moving on the periphery while Nigel worked at close quarters. Nigel gave her a wave.

'You're here on a work exchange if anyone asks,' he smiled at her. 'Here, take a hard hat and fluorescent jacket from the table over there. We're allowed in - the DCI is on site, she'll answer my questions. The ambulance crew are still attending to the security guard over there too. Come on, follow me and look like it's all in a day's work.'

They made their way along the drive and took a turn towards the staff accommodation. It seemed remarkable to Charlotte that she'd only recently been there, looking around, walking with George and Una. The place had changed already, becoming a building site in no time at all. They'd have the place levelled soon and there would be no evidence of it ever being a holiday camp.

'Follow my lead,' Nigel said. 'I know a lot of these cops - we see them all the time... DCI Summers? It must be serious if you're here!'

At last, another woman, Charlotte thought.

'Hi Nigel, good to see that the vultures are here already. We haven't even moved the victim off-site yet; did you get a tip-off?'

'Now you know I can't reveal my sources,' Nigel smiled. 'This is Charlotte Grayson, by the way. She's on a work exchange.'

'From a guest house?' DCI Summers asked, not allowing him to finish.

'You saw the newspaper article too?' Charlotte said, extending her hand. The DCI took the prompt and shook her hand.

'DCI Kate Summers. Yes, I'm a local copper. I read the paper every week - it's surprising what you pick up in there. It's what counts as light reading in my job. So why are you really here?'

'Oh, I just tagged along with Nigel. I'm anxious to know who was hurt. We used to work here many years ago. I know the security guard.'

'Well you might be able to help us with some identification,' the DCI remarked. 'His ID was gone when we found him, so we're still waiting for his security firm to come down and identify him.'

As she spoke, she saw two uniformed ambulance workers walking down the staircase to the chalet with a stretcher.

'He's not... he's not dead, is he?' Charlotte asked. 'Please tell me George isn't dead!'

CHAPTER TWENTY-NINE

Present Day - Morecambe

Charlotte hardly dared look as the medics reached the bottom step and turned to walk in front of them. As they levelled up, she could see that whoever was on that stretcher had a breathing mask over their face. That meant they were alive, surely?

'Do you know him?' DCI Summers asked, hopeful of a quick resolution.

Charlotte braced herself and took a proper look. The person on the stretcher had a heavily bandaged head.

'That's definitely not George,' Charlotte said, relieved. 'He's much younger than George. He can't have been working last night after we saw him.'

'You're sure?' DCI Summers asked.

Charlotte nodded, a feeling of relief washing over her.

'Okay, we'll pick up from here,' she said to the medics. 'Go and take care of him.'

'Do you have any idea what happened up there?' Nigel asked.

'Not really,' DCI Summers replied. 'It was probably just someone scouting around, seeing what they could steal. It's an occupational hazard on building sites - it goes with the territory. Whoever it was used more violence than was strictly necessary. That guard took a bad blow to his head. It's at least a concussion, I'd say. But what's more worrying is the way they left him up there in one of the rooms. If it wasn't for the foreman running a tight ship here, they might have assumed those buildings were empty. He'd have died if they'd bulldozed them.'

'Are we on or off the record now, Kate?' Nigel asked.

'Are we ever really off the record, Nigel?' she replied.

Charlotte sensed they liked each other, in spite of the professional rivalry.

'This is on the record, nobody died here, we need to get to the bottom of it. My gut tells me it's just a case of security guard disturbs thieves who beat him up for doing their job.'

'Thieves? Or a thief?' Nigel challenged.

'We're not certain yet,' DCI Summers continued. 'We'll get this area fingerprinted and check the tyre treads in the parking area just outside the gates. I'm not holding out much hope though, not unless the guard can identify his attackers.'

'CCTV?'

'No, not this far out from the town. You can only just get a mobile phone signal out here. It's a bit of a dead zone on the beach side. I don't suppose the owners thought it was much of a risk. Besides, they're levelling the place - I reckon they'll have it all flattened and cleared in two weeks.'

Nigel was taking notes in a notepad all the time she was talking. Charlotte noticed his shorthand; she'd seen loops and squiggles like that before. The school secretary used to use it.

'Anything you want me to place in the article?' Nigel asked. 'Or is it a Crimestoppers job?'

'Let's leave it at Crimestoppers for now,' DCI Summers said. 'But put my name to it as well. If this turns out to be something different, I wouldn't mind the calls coming directly into my office.'

'I got your good side!' came Chris's voice from behind. Charlotte hadn't even realised he was there, cataloguing and recording everything that might make the paper.

'Do I have a good side?' DCI Summers smiled. 'I'd only just dropped the kids off to school when this call came in. I haven't even brushed my teeth yet!'

Charlotte smiled and walked over towards the chalet block.

'Don't go up the stairs please,' DCI Summers shouted over. 'We're not finished up there yet.'

In the distance, Charlotte's eye was drawn by the flashing blue lights of the ambulance. They'd save the siren until they hit the traffic, closer to Morecambe. She didn't envy the security guard the winding journey along the road to Middleton. If the beating didn't finish him off, the ride might. She was relieved that it wasn't George. Her mind went back to that night with Bruce, the fight that they'd had. George had been able to handle himself back then. She wasn't so sure how he'd fare nowadays. Thank heavens it wasn't him.

As Nigel finished off his questions and Chris ravaged the area with his camera, like a locust feeding off images, Charlotte surveyed the scene. The diggers were positioned like predators, ready to reduce their prey down to nothing. DCI Summers was right; they'd have it levelled and cleared in a short time. Good riddance to the place. She had many happy memories from there, but she was pleased to see many of them buried for good, in the past, where they belonged.

'Okay, we're done here!' Nigel said. 'We need to get back to file the story online.'

'Bloody signals are so bad I can't even send pictures back to the office,' Chris moaned.

'It's an internet-enabled camera,' Nigel remarked. 'Unfortunately, much of our area isn't covered, so it's not a lot of use. How about you take the front seat this time, and I'll take the back? It might be safer for the upholstery.'

There was little conversation on the return journey. Nigel was scribbling in the back seat writing out his news copy to file on the website and Chris was letting him get on with it.

Before long, they were back in Morecambe and Charlotte had been spared a repeat of her earlier humiliation with travel sickness.

'Just let me know if you need any more help,' Nigel said, keen to get back to the office. 'But the library is the place to look. That's where I'd go first.'

Charlotte checked the time. The library was only a few streets away, so she decided to act on Nigel's advice immediately. It was modern and airy, set out over one level. She couldn't recall having gone there on their day visits to Morecambe. Why was that? It seemed to be an obvious place to kill time.

The library staff were almost too eager to assist her. They assigned her to the local history expert, a man called Jon, who looked as crusty and dusty as the archives he presided over.

'I don't know if you can help me?' Charlotte began. 'I'm

trying to find a story from the local papers. It'll be June, July or August of 1984 - I can't quite recall the date. I also need to go out of area, to Newcastle for a second query. Do you keep records from that far afield? I'm looking for a family name of Craven.'

'I can certainly help you with that,' Jon began. 'The local papers won't be a problem, but I may have to access my network of contacts to help with the Newcastle information.

It occurred to Charlotte that Jon's *network of contacts* was probably as exciting as it ever got in local history.

'Of course, you're looking at an area that encompasses Ashington, Blyth, North Tyneside, Newcastle, South Tyneside and Gateshead. It has a combined population of around 700,000 or thereabouts,' he began.

Charlotte wondered if he'd seen the immediate horror in her eyes. The look of fear that screamed *history bore!* Whatever it was, Jon immediately checked himself and got busy in the records area, asking her to take a seat before he did so.

'Write down what you know regarding the Newcastle query, and I'll make some calls for you. Are you around for the next half hour?'

Charlotte nodded and watched as Jon disappeared into the stacks to track down the microfiche files. She scribbled everything she could think of about Bruce, which amounted to his name, a city and a rough period in time.

Jon returned soon after with a series of files and some faded papers.

'Bingo!' he said, delighted at the find. 'It turns out we have more than I thought. In the good old days when we were properly funded, we used to hang onto all this stuff. Not these days though - we don't even stock the local newspaper, the funding cuts are so bad. Here are the local papers, everything from June to August 1984 on microfiche, plus a few microfiche files of special events from that time.'

Charlotte held out her hands to take the items and asked Jon to walk her through the microfiche a little more abruptly than she would have wished. If she'd given him any encouragement, she feared that she might be stuck until the next person came in wanting to trace their great aunt thrice removed. History had never really been her thing.

Before long, she was immersed in her search, poring over newspapers which probably hadn't been looked at in years. People like Nigel were recording this stuff every day for posterity, as they had done for years. Jon had gone off to access his network of contacts.

Charlotte winced as she thought how little she'd known about Bruce at the time they'd started dating. There was no way of checking him out, no Tinder profiles, Google searches or social media. She spent her life warning Lucia about the dangers of living her life out on the web, but was it really any more dangerous now? She'd been careless and foolish back then; no wonder she'd landed herself in such trouble.

She didn't really know what she was looking for. Neither had she come up with a game plan or any sort of strategy. All she knew is that somehow, she had to get a trace on Bruce Craven. She had to find out where he lived and what had become of him. Even though that might place both she and Will in real danger once again.

CHAPTER THIRTY

1984 - Sandy Beaches Holiday Camp

It was easy to avoid Bruce for the following week because he'd earned himself a promotion from the kitchens to the bars. That meant he worked bars all the time, rather than just picking up extra shifts in the evenings. Had things worked out better in their brief relationship, it's the sort of event that Charlotte would have congratulated him on. She knew he was trying to get out of the kitchens and move into work that might allow him to make a living abroad.

It was a huge relief to Will and Charlotte that they could now go in and out of the kitchens without fear of encountering him at the dishwashing machine. They'd replaced him with a young guy from Middleton, who was friendly and humorous and made a tray packed with dirty crockery and cutlery about as much fun as it could ever be.

All they had to do in the evenings was to steer clear of whichever bar Bruce had been assigned to work at, and it was possible to completely avoid him. They were like passing ships in the night - the bar staff were generally sleeping while the waiting staff were up at the crack of dawn, so their shifts barely coincided, with the exception of lunchtimes.

'Your face is looking much better now,' Charlotte remarked one morning at breakfast, using the harsh lighting of the restaurant to take a close look.

It was seven o'clock and the tables were set and ready. They were standing around chatting, awaiting the arrival of the first early risers.

'It was better than I'd expected: no bruising and no damage to my nose,' Will said, touching his face as if to check.

'It looks like it's all calmed down now. I haven't seen Bruce and I'm not going to go back to collect the few things I had in his room. It was just a toothbrush, spare knickers, a bra and a brush. With any luck he threw them in the bin. I'm so pleased it's over. I feel like I ought to buy George a gift to say thank you.'

Jenna walked over to join in the conversation.

'Watch out, watch out, there's a Mickey about!' She smiled.

'What's he up to now? Please tell me he's not messing about with the rotas again?' Charlotte replied.

'No, word is he's looking for volunteers. Here he comes now, make sure your cutlery is straight.'

It was always easy to tell if Mickey was in asking or telling mode - his body language was that predictable. Charlotte decided he was in asking mode this time around, which put them on the offensive. At least it meant he probably wasn't going to screw up their day off that week.

'Hi, top team,' he began.

It was a big ask by the sound of it.

'Good morning Mickey, what's up?' Will said.

'I could do with your help, truth be told.' Mickey grimaced. He was playing it up, which potentially meant a deal could be struck.

'How can we help?' Jenna asked.

'I've been dropped in it from a great height by management. The local paper is coming around today. They're doing a feature on *Holiday Hot Spots* and they want to feature Sandy Beaches Holiday Camp.'

'Sounds interesting,' Will replied. 'How have they dropped you in it?'

'Well,' Mickey replied, readying himself to drop the grenade. 'They want to photograph and feature some members of the staff. You know the drill, they'll do a little fact file about who you are, where you come from, what your job is... that sort of thing. We need a couple of students to help. As my top team, will you do it?'

'Not me!' Charlotte answered straight away. 'Sorry Mickey, it's not my sort of thing.'

'I'll do it,' Jenna volunteered.

'Yes, I don't mind either,' Will said. 'It'll be a bit of fun. What's in it for us, Mickey? How about you make sure me and Charlotte get the same day off for the next two weeks? You can manage that, can't you?'

'Deal,' Mickey said, clearly expecting to have had a much harder time of it. 'The next two Tuesdays are yours and Charlotte's. The reporter is coming at 10 o'clock, at the end of the breakfast shift.'

'I'll finish off your tables if you've got any late stragglers.' Charlotte offered. 'It seems only fair if I'm getting the days off with Will.'

The deal was struck and there was excitement in the air; it was a rarity to get a photograph in the local paper.

They spent the morning joking about how many copies they'd buy when it was published and how proud their parents might be at their achievement.

The reporter turned up promptly, as Mickey had suggested. He came with a notepad, pen and a photographer.

'Hi, Eddy Edwards,' he said, holding out his hand.

Will saw Jenna's smile and tried to ignore it. What a name to be saddled with.

'Hi Eddy, I'm Will, this is Jenna, and we're your student subjects.'

Eddy worked fast and with the sure touch of an old hand. He took a photo of Jenna serving one of the customers with prunes, much to her delight.

'Their constipation will be immortalised in the newspaper forevermore!' they'd laughed afterwards.

When it came to Will, Eddy quickly sensed that he and Charlotte were a couple.

'Did you meet here?' he asked. 'That's a great angle. Can I picture you together?'

It took some cajoling to convince Charlotte.

'Go on Charlotte, nobody ever reads the local paper anyway. It's a laugh, it can't do any harm.'

Jenna worked on her until she agreed. Eddy the photographer took a staged shot of Will serving a breakfast to Charlotte. She winced at the thought, but Jenna and Will seemed to think it all hilarious.

'Just move your necklace around slightly,' the photographer said before taking the snap. 'It's just got a little twisted, we want you looking your best, don't we?'

Eddy asked the type of question that Mickey had suggested would be used for the feature, and after Will and Jenna had divulged every detail of what they were studying, where their home town was, what they did at the holiday camp and what their favourite attraction was on site, he moved on to the next subjects for his article.

'I'm heading over to the bars next,' he said. 'I think the staff start clocking in at about half-past-ten. Is that right?'

Will gave him directions to his next designated location.

'By the way, I don't know if Mickey told you. We want to take a group photo of everybody we've interviewed at half-past eleven, before we leave. We're taking it in front of the new paddling pool - we're keen to show it as a brand-new feature, boost the local tourism and all that.'

Mickey hadn't mentioned that bit. It wasn't so bad, but it meant squeezing the short time they had in between shifts.

'Do you think he meant me too?' Charlotte asked. 'Seeing as I was just a hanger-on?'

At the designated time, Will called round at Charlotte's chalet to pick up Jenna.

'I've convinced her to tag along,' Jenna said.

As they approached the new pool area, Eddy was already in full flow, getting everybody organised.

'Oh hell, Bruce is there!' Charlotte said, stopping dead on the pavement.

'It's okay,' Will reassured her. 'He's not going to play up while management are here. Just stand away from him. It'll all be over in five minutes.'

Bruce had clocked them too and seemed just as intent on giving them a wide berth. The photo was taken, and Eddy mopped up with final questions and fact checks before taking his leave.

'They'll be putting in the concrete base for this new pool any day now,' Will remarked. 'I wonder if it'll be open in time for us to use it before we leave?'

'Bruce got out of here fast enough,' Charlotte commented, scanning the area.

'That's a good sign,' Will replied. 'Maybe he's decided to cool it down now. Hopefully, that's the end of it.'

Abi Smithson walked up to them. Charlotte bristled, still unsure about whether she had her eyes on Will. She wasn't secure enough in their fledgeling relationship yet to know how things stood.

'Hi Will... hi Charlotte. Are we still on to do some maths tonight, Will? My roommate has gone home for two days, so I have the place to myself. We'll be able to concentrate and have a good session.'

Charlotte hoped he'd say no, but Will was too nice for that. He'd picked a social cause in Abi and, so far as she could tell, he was sticking with it.

'Yes, that's fine - isn't it Charlotte? We're meeting up to go to the Old Codger's Bar at nine o'clock. That'll give us at least an hour.'

'That's plenty of time,' Abi teased. 'We might even have time for some maths too!'

Will's face reddened, and Charlotte shot him a stern glance. Abi seemed oblivious to the tension she'd just caused.

'See you later!' she waved, heading off to start her shift.

'We'd better go too,' Will said. 'I'm sure Mickey's goodwill won't extend to being late for our lunch shift.'

'Can we go via my chalet first?' Charlotte asked. 'I just need to get my headpiece; I didn't want to wear it for the photo. I hate that thing!'

Will turned and they made their way back towards the staff chalets. It was a beautiful summer's day, so they took their time, enjoying the shrieks of excited children and the hum of chatting adults. They seldom got to experience the camp like this; to them it was mainly a place of work or an environment which they stepped into at night.

As they walked up the staircase towards Charlotte's room, their hands touched. It was good to be a normal couple, without the fear and worry of Bruce's erratic moods. For the first time in weeks, walking in the glorious sunshine, Charlotte felt her life was finally in control. Things were great with Will; he'd come like a rush of fresh air in a fetid room.

As they approached Charlotte's room, they saw it immediately, but it took a moment or two to work out what they were looking out. Taped to the door of Charlotte's apartment were the bra and knickers that she'd left in Bruce's room. And, on a sticky note attached to the crotch area, the word *Slag*.

CHAPTER THIRTY-ONE

Present Day - Morecambe

There it was, the picture taken a lifetime ago. Her and Will, aged nineteen years, in a black and white photograph. For a moment she wanted to cry. She felt the pain of the years slipping by, the yearning for youth, the loss of the intoxicating spark of a new love.

They'd forgotten all about the newspaper article. It had been such a big deal at the time and then they all forgot to go out and buy the paper. They hadn't even read the papers in those days; they had no interest in the news whatsoever. So it was the first time she'd ever seen it.

Working her way through the archived editions, she'd hardly dared to expect that it would still be there. It was irrational, she knew. Jon's newspaper archive could stop time. And there they were. Thursday 26th July 1984, captured in a moment for eternity.

She laughed at the staged photograph. *Love on the menu,* the subheadline read. There was Will, just a skinny boy, with an elasticated bow tie that looked like it didn't belong and a pair of black, crimplene trousers that had more than a hint of a flare in the leg. Or maybe it was just that Will's legs were so skinny at the time.

And there it was, her mum's necklace. The photo was taken before that night when everything turned on its head. The picture was poor quality, indistinctive, the necklace a rough blur of dots. But she knew what it was.

Charlotte wished that she could step into the picture and warn herself. *Leave while you're happy. Leave before it all goes wrong.*

She couldn't believe how young she looked. Young and naïve. Her hair was short; she hadn't worn it in a bob like that for years. Princess Diana, that's who was responsible for that haircut. Lucia looked much more worldly-wise, and she was three years younger.

'Have you found anything?' Jon asked.

His voice shook Charlotte out of her distraction.

'Yes, I have actually. Look, would you believe that's me?'

Jon studied the photograph.

'So you worked at the old holiday camp, did you? We've got some wonderful old photographs of that, if you ever want a look. It was splendid in its heyday.'

Charlotte turned the page to read more. There was Bruce. She knew he'd have to be there, but it still shook her. He'd been an image in her mind for so long, captured in time, her memory never ageing him.

'Are you alright?' Jon asked. 'Your face just went white; you look like you saw a ghost.'

'I did, kind of.'

'I'm heading down to the fax machine - my friend at Newcastle Library thinks he's found your man on the electoral register. I'll be back in five minutes. Don't go anywhere, will you?'

Charlotte gave a nod and turned back to the image. They were all there: Will and Charlotte, at the end of the row, and Abi too. There were several people in the picture who she couldn't even remember. And there was Bruce, well away from her, but standing close to Jenna. She hated him; her stomach knotted immediately as soon as she saw that smirk. *You bastard.*

Charlotte moved on to Bruce's article to see if it held any gems about where he lived or where he might be tracked down to. The article was all about his promotion to bar staff, making a big deal of the employment opportunities available at the holiday camp. There was little of interest in there, just a superficial interview. But there was one clue. Bruce lived in Newcastle. At least she had a location now.

Her phone pinged. One of the library staff walked over to her.

'Excuse me, please would you turn your notifications off. They can be very distracting to other readers. Thanks.'

Damn!

It was Jenna asking where she'd got to. The clock on her phone said it was past midday, when they'd arranged to meet up. She'd got carried away in the excitement. Charlotte tapped out a message.

On my way! Sorry! 10 mins.

She reckoned she could run it in that time. Charlotte took out her phone and swiftly photographed the pages that Jon had handed to her. She then folded up the newspaper and slotted it back in the July folder. On the folder was a date record. She noticed that the same file had been looked at in the past week. She thought nothing of it; the library was crawling with local history bores.

Jon walked up with a handful of faxed papers.

'I'm so sorry, I've got to rush!' Charlotte said.

'He's got you a couple of names and addresses and something else he thought you might be interested in. Reckoned it might be something, or it could be nothing.

'I really appreciate your help, Jon; I didn't know we had such a brilliant library on our doorstep. Thank you - I'll buy you a coffee some time. What do you drink?'

'Cappuccino, always.' Jon smiled.

Charlotte took the pile of curled papers and made her exit. Who even used faxes still? The local library, apparently. She wasn't sure why the Newcastle Library hadn't just emailed it over.

The moment she stepped out from among the library doors, Charlotte began jogging. She couldn't believe she'd forgotten her date with Jenna; the morning had flown by in a whirl of activity. She'd been so busy, she'd barely had time to get her teeth into running the guest house. Thank goodness they'd taken on Isla; she'd been a blessing already.

Charlotte was hot and sweaty by the time she reached the coffee shop. She almost didn't recognise Jenna at first. She had dark rings under her eyes and her hair looked like it needed a wash.

'I'm so sorry I'm late,' Charlotte said, pulling up a chair and struggling to catch her breath. 'I got caught up in something. You'll be interested to see it, I think.'

'I'm so pleased you're here. I forgot my purse,' Jenna said. 'I've ordered a coffee and a panini. I couldn't ask you to pick up the bill for me, could I? I'll pay next time.'

'Of course, of course,' Charlotte replied. After all, she did owe her one for being late. Though she had paid last time. Jenna had made some fuss about her card being flagged or something like that.

Charlotte ordered lunch and a drink and settled in to catch up with her old friend.

'So, how are you?' she asked.

'Oh, you know. Same old shit,' Jenna laughed.

'Yes, I know the feeling. Lucia's at home and off school. Will and I had a bit of a fall out last night. And Olli is embarrassed by me. As you said, same old shit. Did you say you're seeing somebody at the moment? Surely you've got some fun in your life?'

'Yes, on and off, I suppose. A local chap. It's only a casual thing, you know how it is. Or maybe you don't. What's it like being married to someone for so long?'

'Me and Will were living together for years. We've been married for twenty-four years - it's our big anniversary next year. Did you ever think we'd make it that far?'

'Yes, you and Will were destined for each other. I was always jealous of you both. You met, you fell in love and that was it. I wish it had been that easy for me.'

For the first time since they'd got in contact again, Charlotte could put her finger on what wasn't quite right with Jenna. Everything she said was tinged with sadness and regret.

Charlotte had enjoyed her morning and had no desire to get mired in anything negative. She took out her phone and opened up her images folder.

'Take a look at this, Jenna. How gorgeous were we then?'

Jenna took the phone and expanded the pictures on the screen.

'These are amazing!' she said. 'Where did you get them?'

'They're from old newspapers at the library. They're all

on microfiche and old, curled up newspapers. It's brilliant, isn't it?'

'Look how skinny we both were. And look at your Princess Di haircut! What happened to us?'

'Life and babies happened. Oh, I'm sorry Jenna. I just assumed...'

'It's fine, honestly,' Jenna said. The sadness was back again. 'Pies and lager, that's where my weight come from.'

Charlotte's food arrived, a timely distraction from her clumsiness.

'I have to ask you - tell me to buzz off if I'm prying,' Charlotte began.

'Go on, I'm an open book.' Jenna replied.

'You and Bruce Craven are standing very close together in that photograph. What made you go with him after he and I split up? You knew what he was like.'

Bruce's name almost stuck in her throat. But she wanted to know.

'It's so long ago now, isn't it?' Jenna replied. She seemed to be stalling. 'Look, it was years ago, I think it's safe to tell you now... please don't hate me for this. But we were kids, right? We were young and stupid. It's all water under the bridge, yes?'

Charlotte postponed her bite of toastie and looked closely at Jenna's face.

Jenna kept her head down. 'Me and Bruce had a thing going on for a short time before you and he split up. I'm sorry. Our relationship overlapped with when you were with him. It was a shitty thing to do. But God, he was so well built. I couldn't resist a try on that.'

CHAPTER THIRTY-TWO

Present Day - Morecambe

For the second time that day, Charlotte felt like throwing up. Jenna was talking about events that occurred thirty-five years ago. So why did it feel like such a betrayal?

'As you say, we were young and daft back then,' was all Charlotte could think to say to fill the silence.

'Aren't you going to finish that toastie?' Jenna asked.

'No, it turns out I'm not that hungry,' Charlotte replied. 'You have it if you want.'

'I see Abi is in that photo too. Did you know she still lives locally? It's amazing how many of us settled around here.'

'Will said something about it, yes. Do you still see her?'

'No, not really. She sings in local pubs and clubs these days. She had a daughter, you know, when we were all working at the camp. She never mentioned that, did she?'

'I knew,' Charlotte said. 'Well, Will knew and he asked me to keep it to myself. So I did.'

'She was a funny one. Remember all those love bites she had? What was it they used to call it? Chalet rash? God, that's funny. We were so young, weren't we?'

'What made you go with Bruce when you knew how he'd behaved with me?' Charlotte asked. She needed to know.

'You're forgetting how good looking he was,' Jenna answered. 'Don't you remember that six-pack he had? I guess I thought that you and he were as good as over, and it was just a bit of fun over summer. Besides, he just dumped me unceremoniously, don't you remember? He just quit his job and pissed off back to Newcastle or wherever it was he came from.'

Charlotte felt in her back pocket. She'd had no time to check the faxes from the library yet. She didn't want to do it with Jenna there, not now she knew about her and Bruce. She and Jenna had grown apart after they went back to college. She'd always put it down to Will being on the scene. She'd spent so much time over in Will's room, she had all but dropped Jenna and left her to her own devices. She had no idea what was going on in her life towards the end of that summer.

'I always wonder if it's how you were back then.'

'What do you mean?'

Jenna looked agitated, her right leg shaking up and down. Charlotte found it distracting.

'Well look, you can see it in that photo. Your body language. You were so timid in those days. I wonder if he could sense it. Maybe it brought the worst out in him?'

Jenna's amateur psychology had hit the nail directly on the head. Charlotte had been asking herself that very question for more than three decades. *Was it my fault? Was I asking for it? Was it something that I did?*

'Do you believe that, Jenna? That a woman encourages it by her behaviour? Have all these years of equal rights been lost on you?'

She could feel the anger rising. There was probably a good reason why she and Jenna had drifted apart by their second year at college. And perhaps it had been foolhardy returning to the past.

'No, a woman never encourages it,' Jenna was quick to backpedal. 'I just wonder if sometimes men and women bring out the worst in each other. I've had my fair share of idiots; don't think I'm crowing. Besides, I was always jealous of you. Girls like me and Abi always had to try so hard. You had all the guys drooling over you.'

'I didn't!' Charlotte protested.

'You did,' Jenna answered. 'You just never knew it. Every guy in the place was jealous of Bruce when he was going out with you. And when you and Will got together - well, I think Bruce's image took a bit of a knock among the staff. I think he was pissed, that's all. And by taking your place for a short time... well, it made me feel like I was you for a little while.'

There it was again. That sadness.

'I never saw it that way,' Charlotte said, thinking back to how things were. 'That's never how it looked to me. I had no confidence at that age. I'm not so sure things are better now.'

Jenna had become increasingly fidgety while they'd been talking.

'I need to go, sorry, I have to be someplace.'

'That's okay, I'll pick up the bill,' Charlotte replied.

'We must do this again sometime... soon?'

'Yes, yes, let's.' Charlotte replied. She had no intention of setting a date. It was time to cut Jenna loose; there was nothing good that was likely to come out of the re-acquaintance.

Charlotte watched as Jenna left the coffee shop and poured herself a second cup of tea from the pot. She felt in her back pocket and drew out the fax sheets.

They were now even more tightly curled than when Jon handed them to her. She rolled them the opposite way and flattened them on the table. There were two entries from the electoral register. Jon had also handed her a newspaper cutting on which he'd scribbled *Same Craven?*

She examined the Electoral Register first. Jon's colleague at Newcastle had found two possibilities. There was a B.A. Craven and a J.T. Craven in Gateshead. It wasn't that one. The other listing looked promising. It was family listing based in Jesmond, which is what the local paper had said. P.L. Craven, A.S. Craven and B. Craven. No middle name. She tried to recollect. Hadn't that been one of Bruce's first-date facts? No middle name, just Bruce. And named after Bruce Forsyth too. His mum loved Bruce Forsyth, she remembered that. He'd been so funny on that first night out. Bastard.

That was Bruce alright, with his address in Newcastle. She turned to the final piece of paper which had rolled itself up again. She flattened it on the table, holding the far end down with the teapot. It was a newspaper cutting. The date had been scribbled on it, beneath the comment. The cutting was from The Newcastle Herald, an article from 1982.

Tragic Death of Jesmond Couple the headline read.

Jesmond residents turned out in their hundreds today to pay their final respects to much-loved local couple Paul and Alison Craven, who died tragically in their terraced home on Tuesday 6th April. The couple died from carbon monoxide

*poisoning resulting from a faulty gas fitting in their front
room. The couple were much respected for their work in the
local community. They are survived by their only son, Bruce
Craven.*

This was two years before working at the holiday camp.
Bruce had no family; his parents were dead. They'd died
just after he'd started his first stint working at the holiday
camp. Three years' worth of summers he'd been there in
1984, that's what he'd said. Charlotte looked up the 1982
calendar online. The holiday camp always opened up the
week before Easter. Tuesday 6th April was Easter week;
Bruce would have been killed alongside his parents if he
hadn't started working at the holiday camp. Then the
thought struck her, but she dismissed it immediately. Had
Bruce just got lucky with his timing? Surely not – he
wouldn't murder his parents?

Charlotte wanted to speak to Will and she was in no
mood to wait. She looked at her phone, knowing he was in
work until four o'clock. She wanted to have that conversation right now. She had to know what happened after Will
fought with Bruce on the beach. Was Bruce back for some
sort of revenge? Was he going to threaten them? She sent
Will a Facebook message. *Come home straight away tonight
please. We need to talk. x*

She scanned her phone. If the email booking that Isla
had mentioned was genuine, a Bruce Craven was due to
check into the guest house at three o'clock that afternoon, or
thereabouts. If by some miracle he did turn up, at least she'd
be able to confront him then. They were all adults now;
she'd threaten him with the police. There would be no
keeping silent this time around. It was probably just some
sick joke. If it was him, he was trying to intimidate them
again.

As she pressed Send on her note to Will, Charlotte noticed that she'd missed a couple of messages while she'd been in the library. She'd switched off her notifications at the request of the librarian. That was annoying.

Lucia had got in contact.

I'm up and fine. I want to talk about school. I'm not happy Mum. Can we chat when you're back?

Will got straight back to her too.

Coming back now. I've only got admin time this afternoon, see you asap.

Finally, there was a new message from her mystery connection. As soon as she read it, she stood up, gathered her papers and left the shop, forgetting to pay the bill.

Just about to check-in at the guest house. Hope there's somebody at home. BC

CHAPTER THIRTY-THREE

1984 - Sandy Beaches Holiday Camp

Will hated it when there was tension in the air. He and Charlotte were still getting used to each other, but he could tell that she was furious with him. And it all centred on Abi.

'Look, I can't let Abi down now. I promised her I'd help her with her maths. That was before you and I got together. If I fancied Abi, I'd be going out with Abi. But I'm not - I'm going out with you!'

'She's so predatory, everything she says has some sexual overtone to it. And I can tell she likes you...'

'She's entitled to like me, Charlotte.'

'I don't mean in a platonic way! She's always making eyes at you. Can't you see that?'

'There's nothing going on and nothing's going to happen. She's doing well with her maths - that's all I'm interested in.'

'It's not all she's interested in.'

'I feel sorry for her, if you really want to know. People

like you and me have all the advantages - well-off parents, a good start in education, a supportive home environment. Abi's had people telling her how useless she is her whole life. And you saw how she sang in that bar. I just want to give her some confidence, that's all.'

He knew Charlotte had to concede at that point, but she obviously begrudged it. She was at risk of becoming like Bruce if she was going to become possessive and controlling in the relationship. But he knew not to say that - it wouldn't go down well.

'Did Mickey let you see the rotas for the week? You'll be able to steer clear of Bruce if you go out. You can avoid whichever bar he's working in.'

'I don't think I'll be out tonight - not until you and Abi are done. Jenna seems to have got friendly with somebody else; she's never around these days. I'll just get some washing done in the sink and maybe read my book.'

'Why not use the launderette?'

'It's faster in the sink. Besides, those machines are always busy.'

'Did you mention the underwear incident to Mickey?'

'No, because...'

'Charlotte! You promised you would.'

'When I started talking about it, it just seemed ridiculous. Besides, we can't prove it was Bruce.'

'Who else do you think it was?' Will asked.

Charlotte was silent.

'If I told Mickey about the underwear, I'd have to go into all the details about the relationship. I don't want to discuss all that with him. Do you trust him not to go gossiping to everybody else?'

This time it was Will's turn to concede defeat. Mickey was hardly what you'd call a personnel professional, but he was their first line of contact for any queries or issues. And, as such, he was lacking in skills, discretion or training. Only that morning he'd sidled up to them at their workstations to let them know why Lydia Fellowes had had to leave at short notice.

'Pregnant,' he revealed. 'And not by her husband back home! Cast your eye over to the kitchen porters and you'll find the culprit there.'

Although Will had been as interested as everybody else in the news, he'd felt sorry for Lydia, even though he was only on nodding terms with her. After all, the chances were they all knew about her pregnancy before her husband did. So he understood why Charlotte was reluctant to pour her heart out to Mickey.

'Okay, look, we can chat more later. I'm going around to Abi's, but I'll be no more than an hour. We'll both have had enough of quadratic equations and algebraic formulae by that time.

He moved to give Charlotte a kiss, but it was reluctantly received, and she clearly had no intention of returning it.

Will made his exit. Charlotte and Jenna's shared chalet was in a different block to his own, so it took him five minutes to make his way along the long balcony that ran on the exterior of her floor, walk down the steps then repeat the process up the stairs to Abi's and back to his own chalet. He wondered if it might help matters if Charlotte moved in with him. If she was in the opposite room to Abi, she'd see for herself that nothing was going on.

The lock on the bathroom door slid across and Abi stepped out into the recess around which the doors to their chalets were located. She had a towel wrapped around her head and a very small one wrapped around her body. It barely covered her crotch area.

'Oh hi Will, I'm running late, sorry. Do you want to come in? I'm sure you've seen it all before. Just avert your eyes. I was just thinking, it's funny that we've shared a bath together. Not at the same time of course. Yet!'

She smiled at him, a twinkle in her eyes.

He liked Abi, but in his mind, nothing was going to happen. He wanted to help her - he had no ulterior motive. From his point of view, it was as simple as that.

'I'm going to be a gentleman and let you get changed first,' he smiled back at her. 'Just tap at my door when you're ready - there's no hurry.'

Abi's smile dropped a little. Will noticed how she'd got a couple of new love bites, but he hadn't been aware of any men going in and out of the room. Her Liverpudlian chalet mate had all but moved out to shack up with another one of the bar staff, so she was just back every now and then to grab some clothes or make-up. It wasn't that Will was running any kind of surveillance operation on her, but there didn't seem to be any time for Abi to be out pulling men in the bar and taking them back to her room.

He waited until she tapped on his door before going over to start the lesson. She was dressed in a pair of tight shorts and a vest top; she hadn't bothered to put on a bra. Will noticed straight away; he was probably supposed to. He kept his eyes firmly on Abi's face, not wanting to give her any hint that he might be interested.

There was very little furniture in the rooms, so they had to work sitting side by side on the single bed. Abi had her revision guide and an A4 pad at the ready.

'So, what are we looking at this evening?' Will asked. 'More algebra, or shall we give that a rest for a bit?'

As he looked at Abi for her reply, he noticed a new love bite just above her left breast. It was fresh and raw. At the side of Abi's bed was an empty, plastic coke bottle. The sides were semi-compressed.

'Abi,' he began, uncertain whether to raise the topic. He'd had his suspicions, but he wanted to help. 'You know those marks on your skin? Is everything alright? You don't need to disinfect them, do you? That one looks sore.'

Abi was immediately on the defensive.

'Oh these? They're hickeys. You know what it's like in this place. Everybody's all over each other.'

'You don't need to pretend with me, Abi.'

She studied his face, obviously searching for signs of mockery or derision. She clearly found none, because tears began to well up.

'I'm sorry Will, I was lying. You've got to promise me you won't tell. Not even Charlotte?'

'I promise. You can talk to me Abi, trust me. You don't have to pretend when I'm around.'

Abi leaned over and picked up the plastic bottle.

'I make them with this. It does a good job, don't you think?'

'Why Abi? You're a lovely person, why do feel that you need to do that?'

Will chose his words carefully. He wanted to encourage her without giving any indication that it might be a come on.

'Because that's how it works around here. Maybe not for the students, but for the staff who are here all season, it's like a pecking order. A way of survival.'

'I don't know what you mean?'

'Everybody here is sleeping with somebody else. If you haven't got chalet rash - or a hickey - you don't fit in. I learnt that the hard way, with Bruce. In my first year, I thought I'd better get it together with someone, seeing as all the girls were discussing who they were sleeping with. I was young and a bit daft. Bruce was a good-looking guy, so I slept with him. It's what I did to fit in. But I fell pregnant. I have a daughter. She's called Louise.'

'So why the love bites?' Will asked. 'They look sore.'

'I fake them because it allows me to fit in. Getting pregnant with Louise gave me a shock. Nobody ever knew. I had her after the season ended and I had to come back here because nobody else would give me a job.'

'Surely somebody would have?' Will began.

'Look, we don't all have bright futures laid out ahead of us, right? I come from a horrible housing estate in the North-East, where nobody goes to university and most girls are pregnant by the age of fifteen. This is the only place that will take me. I can earn enough over summer to pay my mum for the rent and clothes and feed me and Louise for a year. She takes care of the baby. That's how I survive. While I'm lying about who I'm shagging and what I'm getting up to, nobody asks me any questions. They see the hickeys and they give me a knowing smile. Everybody thinks I'm a slapper, but I'm doing it for my little girl. I want her to have it better than I did.'

Abi had tears in her eyes now.

'It's okay Abi. I get why you feel you have to do that. I can see what it's like here. It's easier being a student, we just come and go. It's a seven-month season for you guys.'

'You mustn't tell anybody Will, please promise.'

He nodded.

'The baby is Bruce's. Nobody knows I have a child, but if they ever do find out, I can't let on who the father is. I don't want him anywhere near her.'

'Why did you decide to keep it from him? I mean, I kind

of know from his behaviour. But he was alright with you, wasn't he?'

'At the start, yes, he was a perfect gentleman. But he got more and more possessive. I was pleased to get away from him in the end. And I don't want that nasty bastard getting anywhere near my precious daughter.'

CHAPTER THIRTY-FOUR

Present Day - Morecambe

Charlotte cursed the car for still being out of action, though it was still a close-run thing as to whether she could run home faster than she'd be able to drive. She messaged Lucia.

Lock the doors. Do not let anybody in. I'll explain later. Back in 10.

There was no point calling; she'd ignore it anyway. She hated phones herself, but it was ironic that they were called phones when no teenager - as far as she could tell - actually used them to speak into.

Even as Charlotte was running, she knew that there would be no Bruce Craven turning up at the guest house. Someone was trying to intimidate her, to prod a wound that been open since 1984. But she was taking no risks with her daughter. She ran from the town centre and out onto the promenade, crossing the road because it was wider on the sea side. She was out of condition and they'd need to sort out a hire vehicle if the car was going to be off the road for any length of time.

As she passed the RNLI building, she pulled out her phone to check that Lucia had received the message.

OK, she'd typed.

At least she was home and safe. Five more minutes and Charlotte would be there herself. She slowed to a walk, a brisk wind off the bay making it hard to catch her breath. Soon, she reached the guest house. From the opposite side of the road, she could see there was something on the door, but she'd worked up such a sweat it was difficult to make it out. She squinted, but it was no use.

Charlotte walked over to the edge of the road and spent another five frustrating minutes waiting for the heavy prom traffic to allow her a gap to cross over. She'd figured out what was on the door even as she began walking up the path to the double doors. It was underwear, bra and knickers. And stuck to the crotch of the pants, a sticky note.

Slag.

Charlotte activated her phone and took several photographs of the scene. She hadn't had that luxury in 1984, but she sure as hell wasn't missing out on it now.

The door was locked, just as she'd instructed Lucia. She felt in her pockets for the keys and couldn't open the door fast enough. Tearing the underwear off the door, she threw it on the floor just inside the entrance hall.

'Lucia! Lucia!' she called, running for the stairs.

'I'm here, Mum, I'm here.'

They met on the second landing, Lucia looking bemused by her mum's obvious concern.

'Did anybody come to the guest house?' Charlotte asked, still struggling for breath after her run along the promenade. 'Was it a man? What did he look like?'

'Mum, calm down. Nobody came to check-in. I'm fine, I locked the doors like you asked. The only person I've seen all day is Isla. She popped in to check on me before she left. You've had a last-minute cancellation for tonight, she asked me to tell you.'

'Who was it? What was the name? Was it Craven?'

'Mum, calm down! No, it was Turner. It was Mr & Mrs Turner. She's ill, apparently. Isla said they've re-booked for next week and sent their apologies.'

'Nothing from Mr Craven?'

'Mum, what is it with this Mr Craven? There's no Mr Craven.'

Charlotte exhaled.

'I'm sorry, Lucia, I didn't mean to panic you. Has anybody been here? Did you hear anybody downstairs?'

'No, it's been quiet since Isla went. She was picked up by that old guy, George. He seems like a nice bloke; they were going for a walk around Happy Mount Park. Oh, and the laundry people came - Isla and George took care of that. And the postman. That's it.'

'You're sure? No phone calls? No other visitors?'

'Mum, you're spooking me. What's up?'

'Just tell me Lucia, I need to know.'

'Oh, there was one thing. The phone rang, but it was a wrong number. And some local woman called in to ask about prices. She has some friends visiting, but there's not enough room in her house, so she was checking to see if she can put them up here.'

'Did she give you a name?'

'No mum, it was just an enquiry. She was just some woman who'd read about you and dad in the paper and asked if you were in, to say hello to. I told her you were out, but that you'd be back later.'

Charlotte sat down on the staircase, as happy as she could be that she'd covered all angles.

'Did the woman have anything with her? A bag or anything like that?'

'Mum, she was just a woman. She was only here for two minutes. That's all that happened. Oh, and I checked the telephone number with 1471 but it was withheld, so I couldn't ring them back and see what they wanted.'

The door opened noisily on the ground floor.

'I'm back!'

It was Will.

'Charlotte? Lucia?'

'We're up here!' Charlotte replied.

Will joined them on the landing, taking a seat on the step at Charlotte's feet.

'Everything alright?' he asked.

'Yes, we're good here,' Charlotte lied. It didn't look like he'd seen the discarded underwear at the door; she was grateful for that.

'Are you feeling better?' he asked Lucia.

'Yes, much better for a day off,' she replied. 'I think things just got out of proportion. I'm sorry about yesterday. Everything has just happened so fast; I've barely had time to think. I reckon it might have been better if I'd missed this term at school and started at the beginning of next term. I feel like I'm trying to jump on a moving roundabout.'

Charlotte held out her hand and Lucia slapped it. It was as close to a hug as she got, all physical contact with her daughter having been banned since she was fourteen. Will got a hug occasionally, but only on very special occasions.

'Oh, I forgot to tell you. Olli's not coming home for tea tonight. Apparently he's got a hot date with a sixth former from school. He said he'll be back by ten.'

'Seems like I didn't queer his pitch with my performance at school then,' Charlotte smiled. 'I hope it's the girl he was with when I saw him the other day. She looked nice.'

'Can I go now?' Lucia asked, as if they'd been detaining her for questioning.

'Yes, thanks, I'm sorry if I worried you.' Charlotte did her best to dispel any concern she may have conveyed.

Will waited until she'd gone into her bedroom, then signalled to Charlotte that they should speak downstairs.

'What's this?' he asked, spotting the bundled underwear just inside the door. He picked it up and looked at the note.

'You're kidding me?'

Charlotte shook her head.

'It was there when I got back. Lucia says she's seen or heard nothing. Somebody knows what happened at the camp, Will. I'm really scared now. This brings it to our door. We need to tell the police.'

Will was silent as he walked into the kitchen. He rummaged in the drawers for a bin bag and placed the collection of underwear in there along with the note.

'I thought I'd killed him that night,' he said. 'I honestly thought I'd murdered him. It was him or me, Charlotte - he was trying to kill me. I've never seen such anger in someone's eyes. I wish I had killed him. He's still hounding us after all these years, trying to ruin our lives. I know you still think about him.'

'I tracked him down today. I know where he lives. At least, I know where he was living in 1984. His parents died, you know.'

Charlotte felt in her pockets and handed him the fax papers. They were damp from her sweat.

'We should report this to the police,' Will said. 'We can

show them who he is, they'll be able to trace him even from an old address. Did you take pictures of the underwear?'

'Yes, I did,' Charlotte replied. 'The bastard isn't getting away with it again. I'm recording everything this time.'

'Oh, I asked one of the computer guys at work about that email. Bruce's booking. It was sent through a disposable email address. You send the email and it self-destructs after an hour, a day, whatever it is you want. As far as he could tell, it was sent from a server in the North of England.'

Well, that's no help, is it?' Charlotte snapped, more forcefully than she would have liked.

'No, I'm sorry. But it's not a real booking - there's no Bruce Craven turning up today. It's been sent to intimidate us. Just like your Facebook messages.'

Charlotte hung her head in her hands and sighed.

'What are we going to do, Will? If we go to the police, we'll have to admit what we did that night. We both thought we'd killed him. It's a miracle we didn't. Is going to the police the right thing? Maybe we could meet him and pay him off, apologise perhaps. We're all older and wiser now. He'll see sense, surely he will?'

'Come on Charlotte, you remember what he was like; do you really think a man like Bruce Craven would see reason? Anyway, I'd like to go to see Abi sing at the pub tonight. I can also find out who that guy was who pranged the car, so we can get the insurance sorted out. How about we catch up with Abi first, and see if she can throw any light on Bruce's whereabouts? He was the father of her child after all, so she must at least have an idea where he is.'

'I'm coming with you,' Charlotte said. 'We don't have any guests this evening, so we're both free. Lucia can lock the doors; I'll give her strict instructions. The police station isn't far from the pub. Let's see what Abi has to say first, then we'll go to the police if we have to. But if we can sort this out directly with Bruce... well, I think that might be better for all of us, don't you?'

CHAPTER THIRTY-FIVE

Present Day - Morecambe

'Now, you swear to me you open this door for nobody, alright? Nobody. Am I clear?'

'Yes, Mum. I've got my phone notifications on, I've got the number for Morecambe Police Station, I've got the telephone number of the pub. I'm fine. What do you think is going to happen?'

'Nothing, but you can never be too sure,' Charlotte answered.

'Here's Isla's number too,' Will said, copying it down from his mobile phone onto a piece of paper. 'She's only around the corner, so if you see or hear anything, give her a call, okay?'

'Yes, dad!'

Lucia rolled her eyes.

'Taxi's here,' Charlotte said, seeing the car draw up outside. 'We won't be late - as soon as Abi's done her musical turn and we've had time to chat, we'll be back. Be good!'

Charlotte checked the front door twice before she joined Will in the vehicle.

'Do you think we should have left her?' she asked, as the taxi drew off along the sea front.

'She's old enough and sensible enough,' Will reassured her. 'Besides, she's safely locked in and she can call somebody if she's worried. We're only ten minutes away. If I ran fast enough, I could be back there in no time.'

'Okay. Let's hope Abi can help us.'

Charlotte's hand tightened around the plastic bag that she was holding. If they had to go to the police, they'd go to the police. But only after they'd spoken to Abi.

The force of the booming music in the pub could be heard from the street. There were flashing lights inside too, their reflections bursting out from the windows onto the road in front. Will paid the driver and they headed inside. There was a chalkboard on the pavement: Abi was on at nine o'clock. The band performing as they walked in was Davy Vegas and the Street Smarts, playing a medley of Elvis, The Eagles and Oasis tunes, like they were the evil spawn of the world's most eclectic record collection.

The barman recognised Will immediately and came over to serve him.

'I'll have a pint please and a half cider for my wife. Also, is Tony in? I need to speak to him about our little prang the other day.'

Yes, Tony's in the other bar. I think he's quite keen to talk to you too. I'll let him know you're here.'

He disappeared to the other side of the bar, then returned with Will's order.

'He'll nip round in a moment, when the band stops. It can get a bit noisy in here.'

Will saw that Charlotte had managed to find a seat.

'I thought nobody was drinking out these days. This place is packed,' he said.

They sat through the final number from Davy and the guys - an interesting medley of Hotel California, Wonderwall and Viva Las Vegas - in complete silence. It was too loud to hear anything else, yet many of the people in the room persisted in speaking.

At a quarter to nine, Davy announced that Abi Smithson would be making her appearance at nine o'clock prompt. They began to unplug their instruments, stripping the performance area back to a single microphone.

'Here's Abi now.'

Charlotte was pointing to a lady in a sequined dress, looking like Shirley Bassey had taken a wrong turn and wound up there by mistake, a bigger star than the pub deserved.

Charlotte leapt up from her seat, almost knocking over the drinks. Abi was checking in with the barman; if she was quick she'd catch her.

'Abi Smithson?' Charlotte said.

Abi turned and looked at her.

'Charlotte Grayson!' A delighted smile appeared on her face. 'I saw from the local paper that you were back in town. And still with Will. Is he here?'

Will joined them and Abi gave him a huge hug.

'I can't believe you're here; I'm so pleased to see you. You know Will, I got my 'O' level maths after we all went our separate ways that summer. I can't thank you enough. I even do my own accounts these days - I studied at night class, and it's saved me a fortune over the years. You both look amazing.'

'I'm so glad you got your singing career too,' Will said. Charlotte could see he was choked up to see how a little kindness several decades ago had helped her so much. She felt like a bitch when she remembered what a hard time she'd given him.

'Yes, it could have been a lot more glamorous than this. I'm sure it will be again one day. I was on Opportunity Knocks you know, I got to the finals. Not the good one with Hughie Green, it was the remake. I got to play cruise ships and big clubs for a time after that, it was amazing.'

'What happened?' Will asked. 'What brought you back here?'

'My daughter, Louise. Do you remember? My big secret back in those days. It seems so trivial now. She's a troubled girl, I'm afraid. I came back to be with her, to make sure she's okay. Things are fine though, I'm not complaining. Can we talk after my set? I'm on in five minutes and I have to fix my make-up.'

'It's great to see you!' Will said.

Charlotte felt like they'd just peeled away thirty-five years. They were older, greyer and weighed considerably more than they had last time they were together. But they were still the same people, Charlotte could see how delighted Will was to have discovered how well Abi had done.

'Your little protégé did well, didn't she? Do you feel like Professor Harry Higgins to her Eliza Dolittle now? I've been feeling guilty about how I was on at you all the time over Abi. You did a good thing - well done.'

'Yes, it's great to see. A bit worrying to hear about her

daughter though. Kids eh? They might grow up, but they're always yours.'

'Are you the bloke who backed into my car the other night?'

Will looked up. Charlotte gave him a questioning look.

'This is Tony, the driver of the car I told you about. Hi Tony, I think it was a little bit different though. I was stationary at the time - you reversed into me.'

'Ladies and gentlemen, put your hands together for the amazing - the fabulous - the glamorous Miss Morecambe herself ... let's hear in for Abiii Smithsonnnnn ...'

There was an enthusiastic round of applause as Abi was introduced by the barman. A backing track started up and Abi began to sing Adele's *Hello*. Perfectly.

'That's not how I saw it mate. I'm gonna need your details for my insurance.'

'Shhhh!' came an admonishment from the table opposite.

Tony lowered his voice.

'It's gonna cost me over a thousand pounds to get that fixed. I've got witnesses too!'

'Who are your witnesses?' Will asked. 'It was just you and me out there. I was waiting for you to move your car because you'd pinned me in too...'

'Shhhh!'

Abi persisted with her song, even though it was beginning to get uncomfortable in the lounge area.

'Steady Tony,' the barman said, as he pulled a pint for another customer.

'Well how would you know who was out there? If you'd been looking, you wouldn't have run your car into me!'

Charlotte flinched as Tony's body language suddenly became more confrontational.

'Will,' she cautioned.

'Look Tony, you were pissed when you moved your car. I was going to overlook that fact in my insurance claim, but you're lucky you don't lose your licence for drunk driving.'

'Are you accusing me of lying?'

Tony darted out a punch, which sent Will, the table and the drinks flying. Abi carried on singing, like the true professional she'd become, but it was a small lounge and Charlotte could see that if the barman didn't intervene quickly, it was going to be game over for that night's entertainment.

The punch had caught Will completely unawares. Charlotte was torn, but he was managing to get to his feet, so she decided to try to calm the situation by pleading with the barman to intervene. The barman leapt over the bar to pull Tony off, but he was too slow. Tony grabbed Will by the side of his shirt and launched a second punch at him. Charlotte shrieked as Will staggered across the room, crashing into Abi mid-chorus and pushing her to the ground.

As the backing track to *Hello* continued to play, Abi's microphone rolled across the floor and the lounge fell silent at the sight of Will lying out cold on top of a struggling Abi.

CHAPTER THIRTY-SIX

1984 - Sandy Beaches Holiday Camp

Charlotte was prickly with Will before the evening even began. Not only was he spending more time with Abi and her ever-increasing love bites, he completely refused to acknowledge that there was any possibility she might fancy him. She had nothing against Abi personally, but she viewed her like a stray dog - show it a bit of love and it'll follow you home.

She despised herself for even thinking it, but Bruce had made her feel that way. She was insecure and on edge still, unable to believe he was out of her life and that she was with Will, when quite clearly so many other women at the holiday camp fancied him, guests included, at times.

She was also angry with Mickey Lucas, since she'd tried to speak to him about what Bruce had done earlier that day. Although she'd brushed it off when Will asked her about it, in reality, she was embarrassed and furious with how silly Mickey had made her feel. And what she'd said to Will about Mickey spreading rumours - she meant that too. She didn't trust him to keep his mouth shut and treat the information in confidence.

At the end of her evening shift, she'd sent Will back to his chalet to get changed, promising to follow him over in ten minutes. Mickey was on the prowl, checking that the tables had been set up properly for breakfast the next day. They'd had a spate of complaints from the holiday-makers that the cutlery and plates weren't coming out of the washers clean enough. One old lady had had to pick a leaf of a Brussels sprout off a plate crammed with a fried breakfast that morning. The complaint had come back to Mickey and it had ruffled his perfectly sprayed hair enough to agitate him into action. Charlotte walked up to him as he was straightening place settings on Jenna's table and using a clean white tea towel to polish up the cutlery.

'Can I have a quiet word?' Charlotte asked.

'When you see Jenna next, tell her I want to speak to her will you?'

'I don't see that much of her.'

'This table setting is really quite sloppy. Look at that, there's still egg encrusted on this knife.'

'They're coming out of the kitchens like that. I think Jenna was in a rush.'

Mickey moved over to Will's cluster of three tables, and began walking around, checking everything that had been set out for the next day.

'This is better... what did you want to ask me about? If it's this week's rotas, I'm not moving anything around. It's too busy and I had two waitresses walk out on me this week. You students, the slightest thing and you're off.'

'No, it's not about the rotas. And from what I heard, one of them had to go back because her dad had had an accident and the other had exams to re-take. They're hardly being flaky!'

Charlotte surprised herself at challenging Mickey, but it was always 'us and them' with the other staff. They were always so quick to have a go at the students.

'It's about a member of staff. I want to know what I should do if I need to make a complaint.'

'You see?' Mickey said. 'That's exactly what I meant. You students don't have any sticking power. One small problem and you're complaining.'

'This is hardly a small problem - it's about Bruce Craven. He used to work for you in the kitchens.'

'Oh yes, Bruce. He's a bit of a lad. He's working in the bars now, isn't he?'

'Yes, and we were seeing each other for a while....'

'He's seeing your mate Jenna now, isn't he? I've seen them all over each other.'

Charlotte's stomach turned. She didn't know that. Jenna had been more distant since the break-up with Bruce. But they were together now? That was a lot to deal with.

'Yes, that's right. He returned some of my clothes - some underwear - and stuck it to my door. I want to complain about it.'

'Well, he was probably just giving it back to you. Maybe Jenna wanted to use a drawer for her own underwear. Come on Charlotte, you know what this place is like. People are jumping into bed with each other left, right and centre. It was probably just a silly joke.'

'It didn't feel like that.'

'You're being oversensitive, Charlotte, take it from me. Bruce is a good lad. Maybe you're just a bit jealous that your friend is seeing him now?'

Charlotte's face reddened. He'd made her feel stupid

and neurotic. She knew what Bruce doing, there was no doubt about it in her mind. But if any small part of her had expected a serious response from Mickey, she'd been wrong. He was the dickhead she'd thought him to be.

'Was that it?' Mickey asked, polishing a glass on one of Will's tables.

'Yes, thanks,' Charlotte replied. She couldn't believe she'd just thanked him for dismissing her.

It was no wonder Will took the brunt of it that night. Not only did she give him a hard time about seeing Abi, but she was also cold with him when he came back to her room to pick her up.

'You stink of Abi's perfume!' was the first thing she said to him.

'Yes, she'd just come out of the bath when I arrived.'

'That old trick! And she had a towel wrapped around her too, I'll bet!'

'Well, actually...' Will stumbled.

'Yes, I thought so. She's totally predictable, that one.'

'I invited her out to join us for a drink. I'm sorry, I know you'll be cross. But she's actually quite lonely, you know.'

'I was hoping we could spend an evening alone for once. You really don't get it with Abi, do you?'

In spite of her current mood, Charlotte did not want to pass the evening stewing in the chalet. She was ready for a drink, and at least in the bars they could pretend they weren't stuck on a crappy holiday camp for the entire summer vacation.

Abi was waiting for them when they arrived, wearing another revealing outfit.

In the bar, the abrasive tune of the Kids' Holiday Club anthem was playing. It had been a source of amusement when they'd first arrived, but the Holiday Hippopotamus song got a little wearing after the first few weeks. It did, at least, announce the arrival of nine o'clock, when the kids were packed off to their beds for the night, and adult time began.

They watched in silence as the music boomed through the room.

Horace the Holiday Hippopotamus says good-night ...

At least Abi offered to buy the first round of drinks. While she was gone, Charlotte listened while Will did his best to repair the uneasy atmosphere he'd created.

'I know you're a bit nervous about Abi, but she's really nice, honestly. She's a lot a shyer than you'd think. A lot of it is a show.'

Charlotte looked over towards the bar. The skirt Abi was wearing was riding up the cheeks of her behind, not leaving a lot to the imagination.

'Jenna's in, look. She's chatting to Abi. Unusual to see those two together.'

'Well, don't get even angrier with me, but Bruce is playing pool at the far end of the other bar. I didn't want to tell you, but we may need to move on and give him a wide berth. It must be his day off if he's not working the bars.'

Abi came back with the drinks. As she placed them on the table, she bent over, giving Will a full view of her cleavage. Jenna walked over and joined them.

'Hi Charlotte, hi Will. I feel like we haven't chatted for ages. How're things?'

She joined them at the table, placing her drink in the middle as if to claim her territory.

Charlotte followed Will's gaze as he looked over to the pool table. Bruce had obviously been keeping an eye on Jenna, clocking where she was sitting. After what Mickey had said, she knew all about Bruce's interest in Jenna now.

She'd kept that quiet. No wonder she was never sleeping in the room they were supposed to be sharing.

It seemed everybody was on a night out. Even Sally was there with her boyfriend Zachary, the Purple Coat.

'Zach's got a night off; can you believe it?' Sally said. 'Mind if we join you for a bit? I'd love you to meet him.'

Zach walked over with their drinks, pulled up a chair, and before Charlotte knew it, she'd forgotten all about Mickey, Abi and Bruce. As a Purple Coat it was Zach's job to be the life and soul of the party. And he was just that, even on his night off. The moment his rear touched the bar stool, he was not only making them laugh, but he also brought them together as a group, so that - for a few hours at least - none of the tensions mattered.

By the time last orders were called in the bar, it was past eleven o'clock. Charlotte had had too much to drink and was feeling tipsy. Will was giggling at a level commensurate with the number of beers he'd drunk, and Abi looked as if she'd almost lost control of her body. Only Jenna seemed to be watching the amount she was drinking. She looked more serious than usual, and in between the howls of laughter at one of Zach's stories, Charlotte had observed momentarily that her make-up was very heavily applied that night. Jenna didn't usually bother too much with make-up.

Midway through the evening, Jenna had left the table to re-join Bruce, who appeared to have claimed the pool table as his own for the night. She'd thought they'd all go their separate ways at that point, after the lull of her leaving, but Zach sensed that his audience wanted more and he soon had them laughing their heads off again at the table.

As the bell rang to announce that there were no more drinks being served, the evening turned on a pinhead.

Abi leaned over and began kissing Will's neck. She was

completely drunk, but she caught Charlotte at precisely the wrong moment. Bruce was playing pool with Mickey Lucas.

She stood up, instantly incensed.

'For Christ's sake Abi, keep your bloody hands off my boyfriend. And you, Will - you might think about discouraging her every once in a while!'

'Hang on Charlotte...' Will began.

But she was out of her mind now. As she shouted at Will and Abi, she looked over to see Bruce smirking.

'Screw you both!' she shouted, throwing the dregs of her glass over Will.

She stormed out of the pub, furious with Will and not caring in the slightest what Zach, Sally or anybody else thought about her.

CHAPTER THIRTY-SEVEN

Present Day - Morecambe

In all their years together, Charlotte had never felt quite so much embarrassment. One police officer was with Will by the bar and another was talking to Tony at a table by the fireplace. Abi had given up on any hope of completing her set and retreated into the back office of the pub.

Charlotte had seen an evening flip like that once before in her life. It was strange how much of the past was rearing its head again. She saw Will beckon her over.

'Did you have to wind him up like that?' Charlotte scolded.

'I didn't wind him up - he was spoiling for a fight when he came over to talk to me!' Will protested.

'You're a grown man, a local lecturer - you can't get involved in stuff like this. We need you to keep your job.'

'They're taking us over to the police station to cool off a bit and take statements. Tony put his foot in it by saying I'd accused him of drunk driving. The cops seem to think he doesn't have the moral high ground on that one.'

'I can't believe they're taking you to the station,' Charlotte said. 'I've never been in a police station in my life.'

'Look, it's only routine,' Will reassured her. 'I'm not in any trouble; they just want to get a statement about what happened the other night. I'll be out in no time - the copper said there's no need to detain me. He thinks Tony might be sleeping it off in the cells, though.'

'Okay, but I'm not staying around here. I'm getting back to Lucia. You'll have to find your own way home. Do you want to take the bag with the underwear in it? Maybe you can get some advice from one of the police officers after you've cleared up this business with Tony?'

'Yes, that's a good idea,' Will replied, taking the bag from her hand. 'I'm horrified about what I did to wreck Abi's show. Will you go back into the office and apologise to her for me? I'll make it up to her, I promise.'

'Yes, I'll clean up your mess for you,' Charlotte replied in her most grudging voice, annoyed with how the evening had worked out.

'I'd go myself, but that copper asked me to stay where I am for a few minutes. I'll see you later. I'm sorry Charlotte, really, I didn't mean it to go this way.'

Charlotte left him to it and headed over to the bar.

'I'm so sorry about all this,' she said to the barman.

'I hope your husband wasn't thinking of making this his local?' the barman replied.

'No, I don't think we'll be back after this.' Charlotte managed a small smile. 'Do you mind if I nip back to the office to see my friend? I want to apologise to her.'

'She's your friend?' the barman asked. 'I'd hate to see what you do when your enemies are around.'

He made a gesture, as if to say *be my guest*.

Abi was sitting in a high-backed office chair, drinking a whisky, which had been kindly provided by the bar staff to help calm her nerves.

'Are you okay, Abi?' Charlotte asked gently, pushing the door fully open.

'Oh Charlotte, hello. Is Will alright? It all seemed a bit heated out there.'

'He's fine, just a bit of wounded pride. How about you? I'm so sorry about what happened. Will is mortified too. The police are taking him back to the station. He says he'll apologise in person as soon as he can.'

'If he doesn't like Adele's songs, he only had to say.' Abi smiled. 'I'd have sung some Madonna, if that's what he prefers.'

Charlotte burst out laughing. She was relieved that Abi was taking it so well.

'Don't worry Charlotte, I've learnt a lot since that first night I stood up and sung in the Old Codger's bar at the holiday camp. I've seen it all - drunks, fights and swearing - and that's just the women!'

Charlotte laughed again. The release was welcome; she hadn't realised how tense she was.

'So, you're a superstar and you've been on the telly. Is that really true?'

'Yes, I had a period of semi-fame. I did the cruise ships for a while and even had a tour of smaller theatres around the UK. It's been good to me - I'm comfortably off and I still enjoy it, even though the audiences are smaller. I have Will to thank for that, you know.'

Charlotte felt a wave of guilt washing over her once again. Now was the chance to apologise.

'You know, if I was ever a bitch to you back then, I'm

really sorry. Me and Will had just got together, and I had no confidence in those days. I thought you were after him.'

'I *was* after him!' Abi laughed. 'Charlotte, you had the hottest, kindest man on the entire holiday camp. I didn't know that a man could just be nice before that. I thought they were only after one thing. I was in love with him, but not in that way. I owe him so much - he gave me my confidence.'

Charlotte felt her eyes filling with tears. Will had always been like that. Maybe she'd been too down on him recently.

'So why did you come back here?' Charlotte asked, steering the subject to less emotional ground.

She heard her phone ping but didn't want to seem rude by looking at it.

'I thought it would be a great place to raise my daughter. And it was where my career began. We live over at Hest Bank, in a lovely house. I'd love it if you and Will came over some time. You can introduce me to your family. So long as Will promises to behave, that is.'

Charlotte laughed, using it as an excuse to wipe away a tear.

'Are you married?'

'Yes, same bloke for twenty years. We met on a cruise ship. Funny thing is, he also began his career at a holiday camp elsewhere in the country. I know we used to curse that place, but I have a lot to thank it for.'

Charlotte was silent for a few moments, reflecting on how funny it was the way things worked out. She'd been so jealous of Abi, yet she'd really had nothing to fear.

'How old is your daughter now?' Charlotte asked. She counted the years.

'She was thirty-seven this year,' Abi smiled. 'She's the

light of my life. She came with me everywhere, on the cruise ships, around the theatres. We had a lovely time.'

'She must have children of her own now?'

Charlotte felt the mood change, as if Abi had suddenly tensed.

'Louise has Downs syndrome,' Abi said. 'She lives with us in Hest Bank. It's why I stopped the touring. She has dementia, and I wanted to care for her.'

'Oh...' Charlotte began. She couldn't open her mouth without putting her foot in it. The older she got, the more she realised that everybody had baggage. There was always some sadness, hidden and lurking.

Abi placed her hand on Charlotte's arm.

'Its fine Charlotte, really it is. It happens a lot with Downs adults. I always knew my life would be different because of it. I never told Will, you know. I think I was ashamed. I was so young, I used to be scared that I couldn't deal with it. Thank goodness for my mum, that's all I can say. And we had so many lovely years together. I would always look backstage while I was performing and Louise would be there smiling and dancing. Will gave me a wonderful gift when he encouraged me to sing that night. I'll always be grateful - even if he did wreck my stage show in a drunken brawl!'

'Maybe we can have a reunion night out, for old time's sake. Jenna is still in town; do you remember her?'

Charlotte felt like the grim reaper had just stepped into the room.

Her phone dinged a second time; she had to will herself not to look at it.

'Yes, I know Jenna Phillips, alright,' Abi replied, her tone changing in an instant. 'She's a con merchant if ever there was one. You and she used to be great friends, didn't you?'

'We were when we arrived at the camp in 1984,' Charlotte replied, now forgetting her phone. 'Things cooled that summer - I'm not entirely sure why.'

'She asked me for money, you know. Have you met that man of hers yet? She seems to fall into bed with one wrong 'un after another. And I'm sure he's got her into drugs. I'd give her a wide berth if I were you, Charlotte - she's bad news, that one.'

Charlotte had wondered about Jenna. What Abi was telling her explained a lot.

'She and that scally of hers were trying to con me, I'm absolutely certain of it. I reckon she saw me as a soft touch. You don't work in as many rough clubs as I have without being able to spot trouble when it's coming.'

Needing a distraction to let Abi's last words sink in, Charlotte reached into her pocket to take out her phone.

'Excuse me one moment,' she said, 'We've left my eldest daughter in the house on her own, I just want to check that she's okay.'

'What is it?' Abi asked, seeing the colour drain out of Charlotte's face as she read the screen.

'Oh my God!' Charlotte said.

There were two messages, both from Lucia.

Mum, I think there's somebody downstairs. I'm phoning Isla.

Then, sent ten minutes later *I'm scared Mum. Come home NOW please.*

CHAPTER THIRTY-EIGHT

Present Day - Morecambe

'Is there anything I can do?' Abi asked.

'It's probably alright - give me a moment...'

Charlotte peered around the door into the bar. The two police officers, as well as Will and Tony, had gone. Of course they had, just when she really needed to speak to Will. She returned to the office.

'Abi, find Will at the police station please. Tell him it's probably okay, but he needs to check in with me as soon as he can. I'm going back to the guest house.'

She barely waited to finish the sentence before she was back out of the door, through the bar and out onto the street.

Shit, no car!

Charlotte looked around. She couldn't see any taxis nearby; it was too residential for that. Across the road, a man with a full head of grey hair had just got off a moped and removed his helmet. She took her phone and sent Lucia a message.

Are you okay?

The message was read immediately.

She tried dialling, but it rang and rang until switching to voice mail. She left a short message.

'Answer your bloody phone will you, Lucia! Sorry, I didn't mean to swear like that.'

There was only one thing for it, other than running again. She crossed the road and walked towards the moped rider.

'This is going to sound really strange, but I need to get back to my daughter, can I borrow your moped please? I'll leave you with my purse, so you'll have my ID...'

'Piss off!' the man said, walking on.

A taxi passed by and Charlotte ran out into the road to hail it. The driver slammed on his brakes.

'You stupid cow!' he shouted out of the window.

'I need a taxi now!' she yelled back at him.

'You and the rest of Morecambe luv. I'm private hire only, I'll lose my licence if I pick you up off the street.'

He wound up his window and drove on.

The moped rider was about to enter his house across the road, but as he reached for his house keys he dropped the keys to the moped on the pavement.

Charlotte ran across the road, darted her hand out while he was still fumbling for his house keys, and launched herself towards the moped with as much speed as she could muster. She'd only driven a moped once - messing around with a friend's as a teenager - but she knew it was just a case of switching it on and pulling back the throttle.

'Hey, stop!' the man shouted.

Charlotte straddled the moped and inserted the key.

'Damn thief, get off my bike!'

She searched the controls. A red button - that had to

start it. She pressed it. Nothing happened. There was a button above it, marked with a circle and a cross. She rocked it over to the circle position.

'I told you to get off my damn bike.'

The man had grabbed the back seat now.

Charlotte pressed the red switch and the moped started. The rest was easy. She pulled back the throttle and the bike surged forward, leaving the old man staggering behind it. Charlotte lurched forward, too fast, killed the throttle and stopped almost dead in the road.

'I'm so sorry,' she called out. 'Here's my purse. I'll return the bike, I promise.'

She threw her purse at him and pulled back the throttle before he could catch her again.

She was off now, minus a helmet, the wind blowing her hair. She didn't much care about the bike - she just wanted to get to Lucia. She was no criminal; it would all get sorted out. It wasn't as if she was a teenager going for a joyride.

Charlotte made her way back to the promenade and forced as much speed as she could out of the vehicle. She was back to the guest house in five minutes. As she drew up outside, she could see that the front door was wide open and the lights on. She barely stopped the moped before getting off, jumping off the back of it and letting it run ahead on its own before crashing to the ground.

She ran up the path and burst into the entrance hall, not knowing where to look next.

'Lucia! Lucia!'

She was about to run up the stairs to their private accommodation when something caught her eye in the kitchen. A pile of tins had rolled across the floor. Charlotte stepped through the door and gasped.

On the floor, a pool of blood forming around her head, was Isla.

'Oh my God, Isla!' she screamed.

She ran over to where her still body lay, touching her neck and then reaching for her wrist to feel for a pulse.

'Isla! Isla!'

She couldn't raise any life from her. Then she remembered Lucia. Had the same thing happened to her? Where was she?

Charlotte didn't know what to do. She needed to call for an ambulance but was desperate to find her daughter.

She started to run up the stairs, stumbling as she began to dial 999 on her phone. She cursed. Was it 999 on a mobile phone or 112? She stopped at the second digit, deleted the numbers and typed in 112.

'Lucia! Where are you Lucia, it's Mum?'

She flung open all the doors on the landing. There was no sign of her daughter.

She ran to the third floor, then the second floor, even checking the rooms which were mid-way through being redecorated. Nothing.

As she stood on the top floor landing, she could hear a voice coming from somewhere.

Hello? Which emergency service do you require? If you're unable to speak, please tap the phone.

'Hello, I need an ambulance. It's an emergency.'

Charlotte walked into the kitchen. There was a printed page of A4 there, on which a message had been typed, in capital letters.

DON'T CALL THE POLICE IF YOU WANT TO SEE LUCHIA AGAIN

Even in her state of panic, Charlotte noticed the misspelling of her daughter's name. She ended the call to the ambulance. They'd notify the police. She *knew* who had Lucia - it was that bastard Bruce Craven. She should have hit him harder on the beach that night.

Charlotte could hear her own heart pounding. She ran down the staircase, taking three steps at a time, then made straight for the kitchen, searching for Isla's mobile phone. She looked around, but could see nothing. If it had been in her hand when she was struck, it might have fallen underneath the kitchen unit. It was worth a try. Charlotte took a spatula from a utensils holder and fished around under the unit, trying to catch the phone. Eventually she found it, flicking it out just enough to ease it out from the narrow space with her fingers. It was an old-fashioned Nokia model. Isla had neglected to lock it with a PIN.

Charlotte activated the screen and located the address book. There were only four numbers in there, George being one of them. She dialled his number, but it went to voicemail.

'Shit!' she shouted out loud.

George's voice mail prompted her to leave a message.

'George, it's Charlotte. Isla's had an accident at the guest house. She's badly hurt. George, I'm so sorry - I can't call the ambulance. Someone's got Lucia. I can't risk them harming her, not until I know she's safe. Call me when you get this. I'm sorry.'

Charlotte didn't know what to do. It was impossible to tell if Isla was alive or dead; all she could see was the pool of blood and it frightened her. She daren't call the ambulance - they'd bring the police. She couldn't risk Lucia getting hurt. What did that mad man want from her? He'd caused them enough pain in the past. Then she got an idea. Olli, she'd call Olli. He'd pick up the phone, even if it was her dialling.

She keyed in his number. It rang several times before he picked it up.

'Olli, I can't speak but you've got to get back home. Call an ambulance as soon as I put the phone down.'

'Mum, you're talking too fast.'

'Listen to me Olli... I need you to get an ambulance to the guest house the moment I end this call. Isla's had an accident.'

Her phone dinged.

'But Mum...'

'Shut up Olli, please just do as I tell you. I want you to come back home immediately. Right now! And when the police come, don't tell them you've seen me. Do you hear me, do not tell them I found Isla like this. Your sister's safety depends on it.'

She ended the call, praying that Olli would follow her instructions.

Her phone dinged again; she navigated to the Facebook messages and opened up the app.

It was from her anonymous connection. Or Bruce Craven, as she now knew it to be. She'd make sure her daughter was safe and this time she'd finish the job that she started in 1984.

The messages popped up one by one.

I've got Lucia and you're necklace.

Even now, the spelling errors jarred. Even with her daughter in so much danger.

If you want too see them both, go back to were it all began.

CHAPTER THIRTY-NINE

1984 - Sandy Beaches Holiday Camp

Will couldn't make up his mind. Was Charlotte better being left to cool off? Or should he go after her? His immediate problem was Abi, whose weight was pinning him down.

'We're going back to our chalet,' Zach said. 'If I were you, I'd head out after her. If you don't, you'll only pay for it tomorrow.'

'We'll help Abi back, Will.' Sally offered.

'I think you're right,' Will said, gently moving Abi's right arm away from his lap. 'I'd better make sure Charlotte's okay.'

Zach got up off his stool and between them, he and Will managed to rouse Abi and get her to stand, albeit unsteadily, on both feet.

'I've got this,' Zach said to him, 'Go.'

Will raced out of the door and headed directly for the staff accommodation. The camp was quiet now, except for the occasional drunken laugh far off in the distance. They'd been last out that night, and the holiday camp was getting settled down for the night.

He ran up the stairs of Charlotte's chalet block and tapped at the door. The lights weren't on and all was quiet inside.

'Charlotte? Are you in there? Let me in, it's Will.'

He tried to think what Jenna had done after she left their group. She still shared a room with Charlotte - in theory - but most of the time she was elsewhere.

'Jenna, are you in there? Jenna?'

He wondered if Charlotte had gone back to his chalet. That would make sense, maybe she'd thought better of it and returned to his room. She had the spare key, after all.

He ran down the stairs and along to his own chalet block and opened his door. No sign of Charlotte - she hadn't even left her things.

He heard voices coming up the steps. It was Sally and Zach, back with Abi.

'Have you seen Charlotte on the site?' he asked. 'I can't find her.'

'Maybe she went for some fresh air?' Zach suggested. 'She looked like she needed to cool off to me.'

'It's a bit of a wild night to be on the beach,' Will said. 'But maybe you're right. I'll see if I can find her. If you run into her, please ask her to go to her room or let herself into mine. I'll catch up with her as soon as I can.'

Will locked his door and ran down the stairs then towards the centre of the holiday camp. It was possible that Charlotte had gone to the beach, but it seemed unlikely. She'd had a fair bit to drink - perhaps she wasn't thinking straight. For the first time he felt a short burst of panic.

Where was she? It was unlike her. She would have returned to her room.

Will re-traced his steps back to the family pub and then past the site of the new paddling pool. A concrete mixer was parked on the narrow road in front of the new pool, where they'd begun concreting that day. It was a small thing, but the prospect of the new pool had created a frisson of excitement among the holidaymakers.

Will could see the distinctive outline of the old tower far up ahead of him now. He stopped by the new pool before running on, out of breath, needing to pause a moment. He heard footsteps to his side.

'Good evening Will. What are you doing out so late?'

It was George, running a circuit of the camp, making sure everybody was safe and secure.

'George, have you seen Charlotte?'

'No, is she alright?' George asked, concerned.

'We had a bit of a falling out. She's had quite a lot to drink. She isn't in her room; I'm worried about her.'

'I'm heading out on my rounds now,' George said. 'I'll keep a lookout for her. I'll tell her you're concerned.'

'If you see her, please ask her to go to her room or to my chalet. I'll meet her there. This camp is so big, we could be passing each other all night. But please tell her to go to one of our rooms and stay put when she gets there.'

'Will do. Don't worry, Will. She's perfectly safe on the campsite. There are only so many places she can go to.'

'Thanks, George,' Will said. He set off towards the beach and soon reached the stone wall separating the camp from the sea. Walking through the open gate, he looked out at the crashing waves.

There was enough light from the moon to see the shingly beach ahead and the waves crashing onto the stones and debris before retreating again. What a beach it was, but not quite a holiday-maker's paradise.

He spotted something ahead, motionless, just beyond the reach of the waves. At first, he thought it was a branch or part of a tree trunk, but then he realised it looked human.

Will ran out to investigate.

'Charlotte? Charlotte, is that you?'

As he got closer, he could see it wasn't her. It was a man, lying face down, a bloody gash at the side of his head. Bruce.

'Bruce, what the hell happened? Are you alright?'

Bruce was stirring now, putting his hand to his head, touching the wound to assess the damage. He looked up at Will and his face changed from confused to hostile.

'What happened, Bruce? Do you need help?'

Bruce began to stand up, slow and menacing.

'Your damn girlfriend, that's what's up,' he said. 'Stupid bitch hit me on the head. We were only fooling around. I wanted to remind her what fucking a real man is like.'

Will watched as Bruce clenched his fist, not making the connection fast enough. His arm came around and slammed Will in the stomach, completely winding him.

'Why did you have to stick your interfering student nose in where it isn't wanted? Me and Charlotte were getting along fine until you came along.'

'She was scared of you, it's your own fault,' Will began, struggling to snatch a breath after the shock of being punched.

'Shut up!' Bruce growled, pushing Will so that he stumbled onto the hard stones and worn, half bricks that lined the beach.

Will knew he was no match for Bruce. He couldn't fight; his best bet was to run and hope that he found

George. They'd have to report Bruce. With this level of violence, it was assault. They couldn't put it off anymore - Bruce had to be dealt with.

Will stood up and started to run towards the gated wall. If he made it that far, he'd be in the grounds of the camp, and George would help him.

Behind him, the sound of stones crunching underfoot told him that Bruce was coming after him. As Will reached the mudbank leading to the boundary wall, his ankle caught the ground at a bad angle, sending the sharp sting of a twist through his foot. He could sense Bruce getting closer. It was no good; he'd have to run through the pain, find a place to hide and get out of Bruce's way. And where was Charlotte? Where the hell was Charlotte?

He ran through the wooden gate, down the grassy bank and back onto the camp footpaths at last. He was into arcades and entertainments areas now, all locked up for the night and no sign of George on his rounds. He'd been heading out in the opposite direction when they ran into each other. Maybe he was back at the porter's lodge already.

Will was struggling for breath. He reached the fencing which enclosed the new pool, and decided he had to pause for a rest. He turned to look behind him, assessing how much of a lead he had on his pursuer, but Bruce had been faster than he thought, and was running directly at him. Will flinched as he braced himself for the impact.

In one deft move, Bruce flipped him over the fencing and he rolled down the bank, falling awkwardly on the rubble that had been set for the foundations. Bruce leapt over the fence, coming straight at him.

Will had no time to recover, only just getting back on his feet when Bruce crashed into him once again, sending him flying onto the hard rubble, landing on his back.

Bruce knelt over him, pinning him down, his weight squeezing the breath out of his lungs. His arms were securely held; all he could do was to thrash his feet around, but it made no difference. He was powerless - Bruce had him now.

Will looked into Bruce's eyes, terrified at what he was about to do. He'd never seen flames of anger like that. Assured of his complete power, Bruce moved his right hand to Will's throat. Bruce's fingers were strong and deadly around his neck, squeezing, crushing his windpipe, no air... Bruce was trying to kill him.

Will thrust his right arm towards Bruce's neck, pushing upwards, trying to get a grip under his chin, doing anything he could to end the vicious attack.

'Charlotte is done with me when I say so, you smart-arsed little prick!' Bruce seethed.

Will was fading now, dizziness overwhelming him, desperate for air as he thrashed about helplessly, trying to find any way to stop the assault, to stay alive. He made one final squeeze on Bruce's neck, pushing his fingers as hard as he could.

Then, suddenly, he found air as Bruce released him. Not for long - there was a crushing weight as Bruce collapsed on top of him. Gasping for breath, he manoeuvred himself from underneath his assailant's still body.

In shock, Will tried to roll him over, seeking signs of life, terrified that Bruce might rouse himself and attack again.

'Bruce? Bruce?'

His body was silent and still. In a panic, Will scrambled to his feet and stumbled over the pool foundations, climbing up the bank and over the fence to safety. What had he done? Had he killed Bruce? He'd been attacked - it wasn't his fault. Terrified at what might happen next, Will ran through the night back to his chalet, all thoughts now focused on his own crisis.

He sat in the corner of his room, shaking, scared out of his mind, until early morning when the first rays of sunshine from the new day broke through his window. He would have to tell someone. Before he did anything, he would go to the admin block and tell them what had happened.

CHAPTER FORTY

Present Day - Morecambe

'I'm sorry Isla, but I have to find Lucia,' Charlotte said, bending down to kiss her on her head. She checked Isla once again to see if there was anything she could do to make her more comfortable. The laundry had been returned tightly wrapped in cellophane covering and it was sitting on the far worktop. She tore it open, taking out a couple of pure white sheets and laying them over Isla.

In the distance she could hear the sound of a siren. It was time to leave; she couldn't risk getting caught up in all the questions and investigating, not until she knew that Lucia was safe.

Checking Isla one last time, tears of frustration flowing down her cheeks, Charlotte ran outside, leaving the doors wide open to give the ambulance crew easy access. The moped that she'd been using was still left abandoned on the pavement, its sides scraped, the key in the ignition. She ran over to it, pulling it upright and climbing onto its seat.

This time, she knew the routine to get it started. She paused for a moment, the engine idling, the flashes from the ambulance now visible behind her as the emergency vehicles hurtled up the promenade towards the guest house.

If you want too see them both, go back to were it all began.

It had to mean Sandy Beaches Holiday Camp. That's where it all began. The nightmare with Bruce, daring to think it was all over, then finding out Will was also involved. And now, after all these years, Bruce had come back to get his revenge. Who knew why? What could his motivation possibly be after all those years?

Charlotte revved the engine and took off along the promenade, in the opposite direction of the sirens, towards Heysham and the Sandy Beaches Holiday Camp. She thanked her luck that the local police presence had become so depleted in recent years that the chances of her being stopped for riding the vehicle like a maniac and without a helmet were minimal. Besides, even with the throttle full back, she reckoned she couldn't be too much over the speed limit. As the strong wind off the bay blew her hair all over her face, she cursed that she hadn't thought to secure it with a hairband. Soon, she was at the end of the promenade, heading into the West End, moving steadily towards Heysham.

What did Bruce want? Was he here to scare her? Did he want money? Justice? He'd attacked her, and she'd hurt him - not killed him. So why the hell had he now taken her daughter?

And how had he found them after those years? Was it the newspaper article, maybe popping up in some internet alert that he'd set up, hellbent on ruining their lives? How pleased he must have been to see that she and Will were still together, that he could still make both their lives hell.

But how dare he involve Lucia in this? If she had to finish what she'd started in 1984, if he dared lay a hand on Lucia, she'd kill him. This time she wouldn't leave him for dead. If he harmed her daughter, she'd finish him with her own hands and take the punishment if she had to. It was long overdue. Bruce Craven had haunted their lives for more than three decades. This had to end.

Charlotte was about to enter a stretch of road without streetlights. It would be complete darkness once she left Middleton and started making her way along the winding country road which led to the holiday camp. She fumbled with her left hand, trying to find the switches for the head-lamps. As she did so, she swerved across the road, narrowly missing a white car on the opposite side. The driver sounded the car horn, slamming on the brakes and winding down the window. Charlotte clipped the front bumper with the moped, bringing it to a dead stop and steadying herself on the car's bonnet to prevent herself from falling into the road.

The driver was furious, winding down his window and cursing her.

'You silly bitch!' he screamed. 'You're not even wearing a helmet. What the hell were you thinking?'

'Sorry!' Charlotte said, pulling up the moped from its tilted position and pulling back the throttle to make sure the engine was still running. 'I'll sort it out with you later, I promise!'

She pulled the moped fully across the front of the car, drove past it and veered out onto the correct side of the road. 'Sorry!' she shouted, as the thrashed engine buzzed like an insect on speed and she drove away into the distance.

Soon she was at Middleton, passing the turn to the Old Roof Tree Inn. So many fun nights had been spent there with Will. Could they rescue their relationship once again? Would it ever be the same after this?

The road to the camp was pitch black. She was suddenly fearful as the streetlights disappeared behind her and she drove into darkness, or whatever awaited her ahead. She focused on Lucia with her eyes half-closed, wincing as she saw the silhouettes of bats overhead, hunting insects around the coarse bushes which lined the narrow road.

There was no traffic now and no signs of life. As the light diminished, her sense of isolation and vulnerability increased. Why hadn't she taken a kitchen knife? Bruce used his hands to harm. If she'd brought a knife, she could save Lucia, make their escape and alert the police. She hadn't thought it through. It was too late now; she was almost at the holiday camp. This was it. She was saving her daughter, whatever it took.

The holiday camp had already been transformed since she'd last visited. The demolition vehicles and diggers had moved in. Portable cabins had been delivered already, an area cleared for contractor parking, and two of the nearest chalet blocks had been knocked down.

Charlotte pulled up the moped outside the ruin of the porter's lodge. The only light in the entire area came from a dual lamp unit powered by a generator. It had been left running within the boundary created by the perimeter fencing, throwing a startling light out into the small section of road which led to what had once been the entrance to the holiday camp.

Charlotte remembered her first day at the camp,

arriving with Jenna on the bus, nervous at what they'd find there, and not entirely sure how she'd cope with the work. She felt that same sense of trepidation now, but tenfold, as well as fury at the danger that her daughter had been placed in.

She stopped the moped, attempted to find its stand with her foot, gave up and let it drop to the ground. An old car was parked up on the grass in the darkness, well away from the beam of the lamps. Was this Bruce?

Her phone pinged.

Your here. I see you. I want to be certain nobody else is coming. Come inside the site, wait by the new pool.

The new pool. Only somebody who worked at the camp back then would call it that. It was almost forty years old now and hadn't been used for years. It was most likely about to become filled with rubble. Charlotte tried to avoid stereotypes as a general rule, but Bruce wasn't the sharpest tool in the box. He kept screwing up his spellings. It had to be him.

She made her way to the section of fence where she and Will had entered the site previously. Although it looked like the fencing had been fortified since her last visit, she was still able to negotiate her way through the gap that they'd found last time. There was a muddy puddle there now; there was no way of avoiding the wet mess that splashed over her jeans.

The camp was completely still. There was no light other than that given off by the generator-powered unit at the front. The sky was dark and grey, the moon concealed behind ominous clouds. She felt like she was entering a ghost town as she cautiously made her way over to the main road that ran through the centre of the camp. At least she'd be able to navigate by memory that way. With so much of the entrance area a demolition site now, she had to take care. The fencing surrounding the old camp warned of the dangers, but this was one night where health and safety would have to get stuffed.

Charlotte held her phone in her hand, its screen giving off some small amount of light to her immediate surrounding area. It gave her a sense of some safety and security, even though she knew that was ridiculous.

Her mind returned to that night, when she'd followed this road, knowing that Bruce was following her, trying to loop around him so that she could return to the safety of her room. Was this what he wanted? To scare her like he'd scared her that night? If that's what he wanted, he'd succeeded.

She continued walking and flinched as an owl flew overhead, a predator hunting for its prey in the stillness of the night. The symbolism was not lost on her.

Charlotte looked at her phone. At the far end of the camp, she'd lose her signal. It was patchy at best on the site - she'd found that out already. As she inched forward, she felt a sense of somebody being there, watching in the darkness. She couldn't see them; perhaps she was imagining it. Feeling more vulnerable now, she looked straight ahead.

She arrived at the pool. It was overgrown with shrubs which hadn't been tended for years. Once, this would have been a joyous place for hundreds of holiday-makers. Now it was a place of fear.

Her phone pinged again. It was the anonymous Facebook account. Bruce Craven.

Look towards the pool. Do not scream and do not cross the fence.

She did as she was told.

The pool had been drained; she'd seen that on her

previous visit. All that was left now was a filthy, concrete base, with a small pool of rainwater in its centre.

A bright beam appeared from the far end of the pool. She couldn't see who was controlling it, but it seemed to be a torch or something similar. Illuminated by the light, on her knees, with her hands tied behind her back was her daughter. Her mouth was bound with grey tape. Although she could only see the back of her head from where she was standing, Charlotte could see everything she needed to know. Lucia was terrified. She was scared for her life.

CHAPTER FORTY-ONE

Present Day - Morecambe

The torch beam was extinguished, plunging the pool into darkness once again. Charlotte began to shake, picturing Lucia there, alone, terrified, thinking that it was all over. Why had they come back to this cursed place? What had they been thinking of, believing they could patch things up by returning to the area where they'd once been happy?

She had to control her fear. If she didn't get a grip, she'd let Lucia down, and wouldn't be there to help her when the time came. If it came.

Charlotte looked at her phone, her hand now shaking. She typed in a message.

What do you want?

She saw the dots appear, letting her know that a reply was being written. It seemed to take an age to come. Should she message Will or Olli? She daren't, not until she knew the lay of the land. For all she knew, Bruce might be armed. She couldn't risk it, not until she knew.

Make your way back to your old room. There's an envelope in the sink. Read it. Tell me when you're ready. No false moves. No police or she gets it.

All Charlotte could focus on was the spelling. The use of you're and your three times in one message and no mistakes. Had Bruce suddenly learned to spell correctly?

She made her way around the far side of the pool, not the most direct route, but one that would give her another glimpse of Lucia. If she was able to, she had to let her know that she was not on her own.

Without the torch beam, it was almost impossible to make her out. Once upon a time this pool would have been frequented by hundreds of shrieking children splashing in the water, filling buckets and playing games. Now her own daughter was there somewhere, scared out of her mind, and she couldn't help her.

Her phone pinged.

Don't think about it. One wrong move and Lucia gets it.

Charlotte knew she was reaching the point at which her phone signal would be disappearing soon, as she got closer to the tower and the wall which separated the camp from the beach. This was just like that night. The fear, the tension, the sense that she'd somehow done something wrong.

This is not my fault.

She kept imagining movement, to her side, ahead, behind her. Was he watching her? Of course he was - he knew that she'd walked along the far edge of the pool, rather than going directly to the chalets. Then she realised. Bruce could see her phone. It was a complete giveaway. It was like waving at him in the darkness.

Charlotte turned off her screen and the sound on her device. There were messages from Will and Olli. She was desperate to speak to them, but she had to focus on Lucia. There would be time for them when her daughter was safe.

She waited for her eyes to fully adjust to the complete darkness. The kids always made fun of her about how bright she ran her phone screen.

'No wonder your battery is always running down!' Lucia would tease. 'Your phone screen has the brightness of a solar flare. Dim it, old lady, and then your battery will last all day!'

What she'd give to hear Lucia's dismissive teasing right now.

A cloud had moved away from the moon, and for a moment it was possible to get a better sense of her surroundings. She could see her daughter's figure in the middle of the concrete pool base, kneeling and still. When the breeze subsided momentarily, she heard her sobs. What kind of monster would do this to a teenage girl? Bruce Craven, that's who. He'd done it to her when she was only two years older than her daughter. And now it was happening again.

Charlotte followed the curve of the pool's fencing, to where the doubles gates had been at the far end. She activated her phone light and left it on for a few moments. On-off-on-off. It would catch Lucia's attention. She might even sense it was her mother. It was the best Charlotte could do. All she wanted to do was to run down there and release her daughter and tell her how much she loved her and that she never had to go to that school again if she didn't want to. She'd have given anything to reassure Lucia in that moment.

Instead, Charlotte switched off the screen on her phone and found the side path that she should have taken if she'd been heading for the old chalet. Was he watching her? She felt her every move was being scrutinised. What was he planning? She stopped dead as she thought back to that night. He'd tried to rape her back then. She'd pushed it to the back of her mind, but that's what his intention was. He'd have succeeded too, if she hadn't slammed him with that rock. Would he try it again now? She'd felt safe ever since that day, a threat like that never entering into her world again. Was that what he had planned now? To finish off what he started? She hadn't thought it through - she was too vulnerable out there. Anything could happen.

Charlotte ducked into the doorway to one of the chalets, nearly there now. She activated her phone screen. There was no signal in this part of the camp, so she couldn't sound the alert if she tried. Looking around for a weapon, Charlotte spotted a piece of wood that had come away from the fence at her side. She flexed it to test it for strength. It dissolved in her hand, rotted by years of driving seaside rain.

Making her way along the side of the chalet, she kept close to the wall, hoping that she might at least be able to confuse Bruce momentarily, and perhaps create some element of surprise. He'd be older now and slower. Maybe he'd respond better to words and reasoning; perhaps he wouldn't be quite so handy with his fists.

She was passing directly underneath the concrete balcony which led to Will's old room. This was her husband's chalet. What she'd do to see him now. Will meant safety for her. She longed for his smile.

Soon, she was at the foot of the concrete staircase which would take her to her old room. The chalet directly ahead had been flattened, throwing off her sense of direction. She had to check she was in the right place. Her memories were being demolished. If only Bruce Craven could be reduced to rubble, buried in the foundations of a new building development, out of their lives forever.

Charlotte activated her phone screen and read the message once again. Still no signal.

Make your way back to your old room. There's an envelope in the sink. Read it. Tell me when you're ready.

She walked slowly up the concrete stairs, taking each step deliberately, fearful of what would await her there. She walked past the window of Abi's old room. Poor Abi. She'd given Will such a hard time about her. Her only crime was fancying her then-boyfriend - it wasn't so bad as far as misdemeanours went.

Charlotte waited on the landing, just outside the recess which led to her room. The one that she'd shared with Jenna. How strange that they should all still be drawn to that area, all those years on.

The door was wide open. Of course it was - she'd broken it down on her last visit. But there was light inside, coming from a lit candle.

She stepped inside, the candlelight casting a long shadow across the floor. Her eyes were drawn towards the sink in the corner, where she could see the envelope. Above it was the mirror, now broken, where - years ago - she'd made sure she looked her best for her dates with Will.

Charlotte moved directly in front of the sink and reached down for the envelope. As her finger moved to the sealed flap to begin to tear it open, she became aware of a second shadow appearing on the floor at her side. As she looked up, she saw not only her own reflection there, but also the face of a man about to attack her.

CHAPTER FORTY-TWO

1984 - Sandy Beaches Holiday Camp

Jenna Phillips saw nearly everything that night. She and Bruce had problems of their own that evening. She didn't want to leave the crowd, but Bruce had caught her when she left them momentarily to visit the toilet.

'I don't want you around that bunch of dickheads - do you understand me?'

He had her alone in the corridor space between the male and female cubicles. Her wrist was sore where he was gripping it so hard.

'Yes, of course, I'll stay with you and the guys,' she agreed.

Jenna should have listened to Charlotte. Instead of stewing in the juices of her own jealousy, she should have heeded her best friend's warning and steered well away. She saw that now - how Charlotte had been seduced by his easy charm and good looks, which had soon turned to controlling behaviour and intimidation. He hadn't hit her yet, and to her knowledge he'd never hit Charlotte. There was just a constant feeling in the pit of her stomach that it was always lurking there somewhere on Bruce's agenda.

At first, she'd felt some distorted sense of pride that someone who was so into Charlotte would give her so much of his attention. But she became quickly embroiled by moving in too soon with Bruce, and even though all the escape routes remained open, she was too paralysed to take any one of them. And so, as she looked on from the public bar at her friends laughing and joking, she smiled at Bruce and placated him, pretending to be enthralled by the conversation with his male friends when she found it offensive.

It was quite clear where Bruce's priorities lay. He kept glancing across to Charlotte's group all through the evening. Every time there was a roar of laughter, Jenna watched him seethe and scowl. But she couldn't keep her eyes off them either. On the other room was the life she'd left - of her own volition - and one which she now longed to return to.

As the night drew on, Jenna's attention was caught by a sudden change in the atmosphere among the group in the lounge area. She saw how Bruce had clocked it too. When Charlotte stormed out of the front door of the pub, Bruce handed his pool cue to her.

'Take my place in the game Jens, will you, I'm just off for a pee.'

Jenna took the cue and watched him as he made a lame attempt to be seen heading for the toilets, then quickly doubled back to follow Charlotte out of the front door. As he glanced over to make sure he hadn't been seen, Jenna leaned across the pool table as if oblivious to his subterfuge.

The moment he'd exited, she handed the pool cue over to one of Bruce's mates who was watching the game.

'I'm feeling a bit sick - carry on this game, will you?'

She made her own exit, looking in all directions as she emerged into the cool night air, anxious not to lose Bruce. She'd seen the way he'd looked at Charlotte as she'd left, unaccompanied. At the moment, she wasn't entirely certain if she was going to look out for her friend or make sure Bruce wasn't cheating on her.

Bruce had a good lead on her already, but she spotted him turning a corner, heading towards the far end of the camp, towards the beach. She couldn't risk him seeing her - there'd be hell to pay - so she hung back, ducking into the shadows, staying well out of sight.

By the time she'd made her way to the beach and cautiously peered through the wooden door which sepa-rated the camp from the seashore, Bruce was already on top of Charlotte. She darted through the door and took cover behind a dense patch of gorse growing on the bank which led down to the beach. She looked ahead, trying to work out what was going on.

Was he cheating on her with Charlotte? Were they about to make love on the beach? As she watched, it became apparent that this was more of a fight than a sexual encounter. He forced his hand to push up Char-lotte's skirt. She was struggling; this was not consensual. Jenna froze for a moment, not sure what to do. She stood up, ready to go and help Charlotte, then watched as Bruce's body crashed down on her friend. Charlotte had struck him on the head with an object that she'd grabbed off the beach.

Jenna retreated back to the cover of the gorse bush, watching as Charlotte pulled herself out from under Bruce and made her way back to the camp. Tears were streaming down her face, her hair was wet with seawater, and even in the semi-darkness, Jenna could tell she looked gaunt and scared.

Jenna shivered, unsure whether to reach out to Charlotte or check on Bruce. Was he dead? Had she just witnessed a murder?

Charlotte staggered through the wooden door, back into the grounds of the camp. Jenna stood up, checking that the coast was clear. Bruce was still lying motionless on the sand.

Tentatively, she emerged from the gorse bush, slowly walking down the banking onto the debris-strewn beach. She got her nerve back and ran over to Bruce. Charlotte's necklace was on the sand at Bruce's side. She picked it up and put it in her pocket to return to Charlotte next time she saw her.

Bruce stirred. He was alive. She didn't know if she was pleased or upset by that. Quietly, before he woke, she stepped away, trying her best to avoid small stony areas so he wouldn't hear the crunching underfoot.

Jenna decided her best bet was to head back to her room, to pretend that nothing had happened. She would leave the camp the next day and go home to her parents, where Bruce couldn't find her.

As she was heading back towards the wooden gate, from the beach, she saw Will approaching up ahead. She didn't want to be seen there, or to get involved, so she ducked back behind the gorse bush once again until he'd passed the doorway to the beach. He would see that all was well with Bruce and head back to his chalet.

What happened next shocked her. She watched as Will checked on Bruce, his body language proving even from that distance that he was not the aggressor. She saw everything: Bruce's violent punch and then his powerful push. She saw Will trying his best to get away and she shrank deep into the prickly gorse, putting up with the scratches to ensure that neither of them saw her, as their fight continued at the newly constructed paddling pool.

Jenna trembled as she followed the fight from the shadows and saw Will struggling for his life in the foundations of the pool. He had no choice but to do what he did to Bruce; he was completely overpowered. For the second time that night, she watched on as one of her friends, without a violent bone in their body, managed to overcome Bruce Craven with enough force to make their escape.

Jenna was hiding in the darkness as Will staggered by, dishevelled, gasping, desperate for the sanctuary of his chalet.

Like a bird moving in to pick at the body of its friend which has just been struck dead by a car, Jenna climbed over the low fence and made her way down the bank to Bruce. She placed her ear to his mouth, then felt for a pulse. It was faint, but he was still alive.

For a moment, Jenna thought through her life choices. She was jealous of Charlotte, envious of Will and scared stiff of Bruce. And here he was, defenceless. Nobody knew she was out there. As far as Charlotte and Will knew, they'd be responsible for his death. So she placed her hands around his thick, ugly neck and squeezed until she was certain he was finished. Bruce Craven would no longer be a problem.

Now panicking, she raked loose rubble over Bruce's body to conceal him as best she could. He was heavy, a dead weight, but it was the best she could do. Then, scared witless at what she'd just done, she returned to the room that she'd shared with Bruce so that she could feign surprise when he hadn't returned the next day. She was free of him. They all were now.

CHAPTER FORTY-THREE

Present Day - Morecambe

He'd been waiting for her to open the envelope, but she saw
him too soon. It happened fast; she'd barely caught a glimpse
of him. Was that Bruce Craven? He looked like he was a
completely different build. He was wearing a black face mask,
only revealing his eyes and his nose, making it difficult to tell.

None of it mattered. As soon as he realised he'd been
seen, he grabbed Charlotte from behind and threw her to
the ground. Her head struck the concrete floor, dazing her.
She immediately stopped her struggle, willing herself to
retain consciousness.

She was only half aware of what happened next. The
man grabbed at her feet and legs, and lying there, stunned
by the blow to the head, she feared that he was going to
assault her.

'No! No...' she tried to scream, but the words wouldn't
come.

She heard the rip of tape and felt her feet being bound together. She was flipped over onto her front unceremoniously, then her hands were also taped. Finally, another tearing of tape, and a strip was placed across her mouth. She tried to struggle, but she needed more time to recover. The fall had shaken her.

'Now stop struggling, bitch,' he screamed at her. 'Do as you're told, and this will work out well for everybody.'

Charlotte looked at him, hate in her eyes. There was no fear now, just a determined intent to save Lucia and get out alive.

'Here's how this is going to work. In August 1984, you and your now hubby murdered Bruce Craven.'

So this isn't Bruce? Who is he? How does he know?

'Bruce's body was concreted into the foundations of the pool the day after. Everybody thought he'd left, but you knew the truth. You'd killed him. First a blow to the head by you, then strangulation by your man...'

'I didn't kill him!' she tried to say, but her mouth was completely constricted by the tape.

'Even better, look what we found on the body - irrefutable evidence of who killed him.'

The man held up her necklace. Her precious necklace. Her last memento of her mum.

'So, here's how this works. You've got a lovely little set-up at your new guest house. Quite a little earner there, I'd say. Every month, you're going to pay me £500 in notes. I will tell you where to leave them. I know where the body is, and I have your necklace. If you ever fail to pay that money to me, the police will get an anonymous tip-off about the whereabouts of Bruce Craven's corpse. And when they do, they'll find a necklace with your mother's name on it. It'll be found there, because I'll bury it there before I call the police. Your lives will be over.'

It was probably a good job that Charlotte's mouth was taped up, since she was trying to scream every expletive that she knew at this man.

Had Will killed Bruce? Was this a con? Was Bruce's body really buried in the foundations of the pool? Was that why he'd put Lucia there? The thoughts raced through her mind: *Go to the police. No, Will killed Bruce, we both hurt him, either one of us might have contributed to his death. Pay the money. We can't! We can't afford to skim off £500 every month. Silence him. Kill him. I'm no killer. I have no choice. I have to agree.*

The man moved over to where the brown envelope had fallen onto the floor by the sink. He opened it up slowly, kneeling by her head. He showed her the page of A4 paper onto which some instructions had been printed. She read the words as he held them in front of her eyes. His hands were shaking - he was as nervous as she was.

Leave the money in a reusable coffee cup in the rafters of the boating club building at 5pm on the last Sunday of the month. Go home to your guest house straight away. We will be watching. No police, or we tell them about Bruce Craven.

The spellings had been bothering her, but she couldn't figure out why. As she read the note, she realised why there had been inconsistencies in the spellings. *There were two of them.* And it was Charlotte's guess that the person lurking in the darkness with Lucia had been working at the holiday camp with them back in 1984.

She nodded. She knew where he meant. The boating club building wasn't far from the guest house, on the sea front. It was an unusual building, built on iron stilts and suspended off the ground. It was a good place to leave the money - she or Will would easily be able to reach into the wooden rafters and conceal the reusable coffee cup.

She had to get to Lucia. Whatever reassurance she had to offer, she'd give it to this man. He and his accomplice had already shown what they were capable of. Poor Isla - she hoped that the ambulance got to her in time. She and Will could discuss the details later.

Charlotte indicated through her stifled mumbles that the man should remove the tape from her mouth. She needed to speak. He peeled it away without ceremony, ripping it off her skin. It stung.

'How do you know?' she asked. 'How can you possibly know about all this? It was years ago - there were no mobile phones, no videos ... even DNA testing was new back then. How do you know about all this? You weren't there, were you?'

Charlotte caught something out of the corner of her eye. It began with the flame of the candle flickering, as if it had just been caught by a light breeze. Then a partial shadow, just behind her assailant, away from his view. She looked towards the door.

It was Will. As he ran into the room, the draught of his movements extinguished the candle and the room was thrown into darkness.

CHAPTER FORTY-FOUR

Present Day - Morecambe

Charlotte closed her eyes as a body thumped to the ground beside her. A struggle was going on, but it was too dark to see what was happening. A piece of wood fell just by her head, and she could hear Will swearing and struggling. The man was giving as good as he got - it seemed to be an evenly matched fight.

There were two of them, she saw that now. And Lucia was still in danger. Charlotte moved her knees up towards her belly and stretched her arms down to her feet. With her fingers, she began picking at the tape, searching for the end so that she could begin to make her escape.

She heard the glass in the mirror over the sink shattering as somebody's head crashed against it. She could still hear Will's grunts and curses, unable to imagine what was going on. He knew nothing about fighting.

Every so often she flinched, trying to avoid the footsteps and crashing bodies as they blundered through the darkness. At last, she managed to free her legs, tearing off the tape so she could move.

Will and his adversary were in the far corner of the room now. She moved to where she knew the sink was, stepping gingerly in case of glass. It crunched under her shoes. Carefully, she reached down and found a piece large enough to saw at the tape around her wrists. Taking great care, she stood it up on the floor and pierced the tape with it, all by touch. Having made an incision in the tape, she flicked out the shard of glass and bit at the tape with her teeth. It followed the line of the cut and tore easily. She was free.

She still had her phone in her pocket, so she activated it straight away, pushing herself into the far corner of the room to avoid the fight. She turned on its torch.

Will and the man paused, just for a moment. It was almost comical. Both men noticed a broken chair leg on the floor and began to move towards the newly revealed weapon, but Charlotte shone her phone torch at the stranger's eyes. It gave Will the advantage he needed; he grabbed the chair leg and struck the man over the head. His knees crumpled and he fell to the ground.

'Please tell me I haven't killed him!' Will rushed over to the motionless body on the floor. Charlotte joined him, feeling his neck for a pulse.

'He's fine,' she said. 'Use this tape, get him secured. There are two of them!'

Charlotte was ready to rush off, anxious to get to Lucia.

'Wait!' Will said. 'Is this about Bruce Craven?'

'Yes,' Charlotte said, stopping dead.

'Take off his mask,' Will said. 'I've got him covered, if he moves, I'll hit him with this again.'

Charlotte removed the mask that was covering the

man's face, cautiously, expecting his hand to reach out and grab hers.

'There's no way that's Bruce Craven,' Will said, as Charlotte pointed her beam at the man. Will had his own phone activated now. 'Who the hell is he?'

'He knows what we did to Bruce Craven that night,' Charlotte said. 'How can he? He knows every detail. He has my necklace - it's here somewhere.'

'He's threatening us with the police, isn't he?'

Charlotte nodded.

'He's saying Bruce's body is buried in the paddling pool. He says it's been there for years. Nobody missed him; nobody was looking for him.'

'So how come he's supposed to have resigned? He walked out of here, I can't have killed him.'

The man was beginning to stir now. Charlotte grabbed the discarded roll of gaffer tape on the windowsill and taped his hands before he came around fully.

'Sit on his feet. Secure him. Don't let him get away. And don't call the police yet. I've a feeling I know who's with Lucia.'

Charlotte left Bruce, turned off her torch, and ran out onto the concrete balcony. Half by memory, half by touch, she made her way down the concrete staircase and silently began to head towards the pool. She could hear Lucia, still sobbing.

'It's okay Lucia, I'm here. It'll be over soon.'

As soon as she'd spoken, she moved, taking cover in the doorway of an arcade.

'Whatever you think you're doing, we've got you!' came a voice.

Jenna?

Charlotte followed the sound. She was over by the old gas cannister store.

'Why would you do this Jenna? Were you even there that night?'

As Jenna gave her answer, Charlotte began to move around the outskirts of the pool fence, towards the sound.

'I saw it all,' came the voice. She was nervous, unsure of what they were doing. 'I saw you hitting Bruce with a rock. I saw Will strangling him with his own hands. You're killers, Charlotte. And now it's time to pay.'

'We were friends, Jenna,' Charlotte continued. 'We are friends. We drank coffee together. Why would you do this? I don't understand ...'

'You were never really my friend Charlotte. You were always better than me. You did better in college, you always had the attention of the boys. And now, you're back to rub my nose in it. You and Will are still together after all these years. A lovely guest house, a lucrative business. And what do I get? More bad relationships with men like Bruce and living in a crappy bedsit at the age of fifty-four. We don't all have charmed lives you know. Life is tough for some of us ...'

Charlotte thought of Abi and her daughter. She'd made the best of a bad lot and was grateful for her life, in spite of its challenges.

She was making her way towards the gas canister store now, hoping that Jenna would carry on talking so that she could get in close without giving away her whereabouts. Suddenly, she became aware of a movement by her side and a fast panting.

Una?

She stroked the dog's head but maintained her silence.

'My life is changing Charlotte. I've kept your little secret for years, at a great cost to my own life. But now you're back, I figure it's time to start paying for all those years of freedom you had when you should have been in jail.'

A man's voice came out of the darkness. He was on the other side of the pool, also making his way slowly towards Jenna.

'Only Will and Charlotte didn't kill Bruce Craven, did they Jenna?'

George? What did he know about that night?

'I was on duty that night and saw most of it playing out. I saw Charlotte running back to her room and I went to find Will, who was looking for her. I watched as Bruce tried to strangle Will, and I was about to intervene when he overpowered him. I was watching it all, hidden in the gas cannister store. I saw Will return to his room and I saw what Will did. But there's another part of the story that you're not telling, isn't there Jenna?'

'Who are you?' Jenna shouted, rattled. 'Who the hell are you? I don't even remember you.'

'I watched you finish off Bruce Craven in that pool over there. I saw you squeeze his neck with your own hands. It was you who murdered Bruce Craven, Jenna, and it wasn't even in self-defence as it would have been for Will and Charlotte. And do you know why I never said anything Jenna? Do you know why I stayed quiet all these years?'

Charlotte was almost on Jenna now. George needed to keep talking.

'You're lying, that's not what happened...'

'We have three witnesses to what happened that night Jenna. I'd have kept quiet forever if you hadn't brought it out into the open again. And shall I tell you why I kept it quiet, Jenna? Because Bruce Craven deserved it. He's no innocent man. He was a nasty piece of work and we all know it. But you should have let it rest at that, Jenna. You shouldn't have re-opened old wounds.'

Charlotte was on her now, and George was close, approaching from the opposite direction.

'Don't come near me!' Jenna said. 'I've got a knife. He made me do it, Pat made me do it. The moment I told him what I'd seen when I read about you in the paper, he said we should do it. It wasn't me. He approached your daughter outside her school, I begged him not to.'

Charlotte was close enough now, moving fast to grasp at Jenna's hand. Jenna lashed out, slicing the side of Charlotte's arm. Una growled and leapt at her, throwing her to the ground, sending the knife hurtling across the floor to George's feet.

'It's over, Jenna. It's time we put this ghost to rest,' Charlotte said.

As George kicked away the knife, blue flashing lights could be seen at the far end of the holiday camp, just outside the old porter's lodge.

'Does that thug of a man of yours know what George knows?' Charlotte asked.

'No, he only knows about you and Will.'

'One moment,' Charlotte said. 'I need to speak to Will.'

EPILOGUE

Morecambe - Six Months After

'Congratulations George - I'm so pleased for you,' Charlotte said with a smile, giving him a hug and kissing him on the forehead. 'I can't think of a happier event to take place in the guest house. It's made my year!'

'It's so good to be able to put the past behind us at last,' Will said, shaking his hand. 'I'm just relieved that Isla has recovered so well. It was such a close call that night.'

Hearing her voice, Isla walked over to join them. It was hard to imagine her on that kitchen floor, out cold, surrounded by a pool of blood.

'Did I hear my name?' she asked.

'Here's the bride,' Will smiled. He gave Isla a hug and a kiss on the cheek.

'How are you?'

'I'm fine,' Isla said, shrugging it off. 'I complete my physio next week and then they'll give me the all-clear. I won't say it's been a walk in the park, but George here has made it all easy for me, running me to the hospital and back. We're lucky to have found each other.'

She reached out to squeeze George's hand.

Olli walked by with a plate filled with full champagne glasses.

'Anybody care for a top-up?' he asked.

'Here's the hero of the night,' George said. 'Isla wouldn't be here without you, young Olli, you did well that night, thank you.'

Olli's face reddened and a teenage girl, wearing the black skirt and white blouse of waiting staff, smiled at him.

'My hero!' she said, giving him a flirtatious grin.

Olli and the girl moved off together, mingling with the guests and offering drinks and nibbles.

'It was no thanks to me,' Charlotte said. 'I don't think I'll ever forgive myself for leaving you like that.'

'Enough!' Isla said, holding Charlotte's arm. 'You did everything you could, Charlotte. I'm here, aren't I? It was you who contacted Olli. I won't listen to you blaming yourself.'

'So, will you be retiring now you're a married woman?' Will asked, grinning cheekily at her. 'You know you're welcome here as long as you want a job. You choose the hours; we'll work around you. You too George, you've proved a big hit behind the bar. We'd love you both to stay on.'

'I think my security days are over now,' George laughed. 'But I thoroughly enjoy running the bar for you when you have the big parties in. How's that going now? You seem so busy nowadays.'

'It's going great,' Charlotte said. 'It's been the best thing that happened to us.'

She nodded towards Lucia, who was giggling with a friend in the corner, in between serving the guests.

'Since we've been employing serving staff for the big events, Lucia has found herself a friend now. She's got herself settled into Morecambe life, and she even admitted to me the other day that she loves it here. She prefers being by the sea to the city life of Bristol. It's worked well. And it's paying me a decent salary now. Things are good.'

'I'm just going out to check on Una,' Isla said. 'Poor thing is on her own out there.'

'Bring her in, she's fine!' Will said. 'So long as she's out of the kitchen, there's no problem with her being in the communal areas. You really don't have to leave her tied up out there, George.'

Isla left the group to attend to Una.

'Any news of Jenna's trial?' George asked. 'Silly girl, if she hadn't got mixed up in that mess, nobody would have ever known.'

'They took my offer and kept quiet about Bruce,' Charlotte said. 'As far as the police are concerned it's grievous bodily harm, abduction and extortion. Jenna will get stung with a murder investigation if they start talking about Bruce. Pat Harris thinks she made it all up - that's what I told him after we'd caught Jenna. A nasty piece of work he is, but he has previous form with the law, so he knows when to keep his mouth shut to reduce his prison sentence. And if they do talk, we stick to the story. As far as we were concerned, Bruce Craven walked away. It was Jenna who killed him, not Will or me. It's three against one. And the body is still there to prove it - if we have to go that far and reveal it.'

'Poor old Jenna,' said Will, 'She never managed to escape from men like Bruce Craven. They seem to have poisoned her life. Still, I guess we all make our choices. She didn't need to extort money from us. You just wanted to be her friend again. Her secret would have stayed buried with Bruce if she'd left it alone.'

George looked around, checking on where Isla was. Una had created a big distraction; a crowd had gathered to make a fuss of her.

'There's something I want to tell you both,' George said, indicating that they should lean in. 'I'm not a young man any more and I want you to know what really happened that night.'

'You mean there's more that we don't know?' Charlotte said.

'A little,' George replied. 'It's important to me that you know though, now it's all out in the open.'

'I still don't really understand how Bruce's body never got found,' Will said.

'That's just it,' George began to explain. 'There's one more part to the story that I need you to know. Jenna did kill Bruce Craven, but do you know what? I let her. I watched her squeezing his neck from the cover of the gas cannister area and I let her do it. I was going to stop her. But I'd seen what Bruce did to you two, how he tried to make your lives miserable. And I decided to let her get on with it.'

'My God George... shouldn't you have stopped her?'

'Let him speak, Charlotte,' Will urged.

'I watched Jenna sobbing as she walked off into the night. Jenna is not a killer by nature, she finished Bruce as an act of self-preservation. You and Will are not killers. Bruce Craven would have raped you that night, Charlotte. And he would quite happily have strangled Will, even though Will was trying to help him. And as for Jenna, she had landed herself in the same pickle as you did, Charlotte.

Bruce Craven chose to be that way. He has only himself to blame.'

George watched their expressions before continuing.

'After Jenna tried to cover up the body, I watched and waited a while. He was so heavy, she could barely move him. Once she'd left to return to her room, I went over to where the body was concealed. I made sure that Bruce was dead. And then I grabbed a builder's shovel and I dug a hole beneath the foundations so that when they poured that concrete in the following day, Bruce would never be found. And he's still there, nearly four decades on. Doesn't it say something that nobody ever came looking? That nobody missed him?'

'I still don't understand though,' said Will. 'Bruce handed in his resignation the next day. As far as the camp was concerned, he'd left without working his notice. That meant nobody was looking for him. It let me and Charlotte off the hook. And as for Jenna, she must have been wondering what happened for the past thirty-five years!'

'I wrote that note,' George said. 'You remember what that place was like: staff were arriving and going back home all the time. I wrote it out in the porter's lodge. I disguised my handwriting as best I could. But things were simpler back then, in 1984. There was no CCTV on the site, except for the arcades. It was easy back then.'

'So Bruce's body is still buried in the old paddling pool?' Charlotte said, watching as Lucia stroked Una. 'And it's about to get filled in with rubble and built over. Don't you think we should tell the police?'

'And screw up Jenna's life even more?' Will asked. 'She'll get her punishment. But it won't be anywhere near as severe as if she was found guilty of murder. Bruce is gone - he was a nasty piece of work. You and I now know we didn't kill him. We've lived with our guilt for years. It's time Bruce Craven stayed buried.'

'I still can't believe it. Bruce Craven was an evil man, but we're not the same, are we? Does it make us evil for keeping quiet?'

'You know, sometimes Charlotte, good people have to do bad things,' George said. 'I wish the world wasn't that way, but from time to time it's necessary. And truth be told, it makes the world a nicer place. Now let's get back to the wedding celebrations. I for one refuse to think about Bruce Craven for one more minute.'

CIRCLE OF LIES PREVIEW

1984 - Sandy Beaches Holiday Camp

The knock at the door came just after midnight. It was too late for a social call, even at a holiday camp which barely slept at night.

Jenna had been expecting it all day. She still couldn't believe what she'd done. It was more than twenty-four hours ago already, yet the nervous exhaustion she felt was every bit as intense as when she'd watched the life slipping away from him.

Had he really gone? It seemed unbelievable. One moment she was covering him in rubble, concealing the body, expecting him to leap up and grab her by her throat at any moment. If he did, he'd break it like a twig; his hands were so powerful. She'd felt those same hands caressing her body, touching her gently with affection and desire in the early stages of their relationship. But Bruce Craven was the kind of man a woman should avoid.

Jenna had spent the day like a stunned bull, waiting for

the final act of slaughter, knowing it would be coming soon, but not quite sure when. It was an adrenaline-fueled cocktail of fear, relief and exhilaration. She'd escaped him - at last - but at what cost to herself? Was the risk of being found out - of prison - any better than living with his dark, oppressive presence? She'd dug her own hole with Bruce and happily jumped into it. She'd even begun to pull the mud in on herself, right up to neck height. But when the opportunity presented itself, she decided to fight back and dig her way out; she believed she'd killed him. She'd tried to put an end to the violent bully who'd trapped her in an abusive relationship. And in doing so, the three of them had created a circle of lies and deceit - yet only she knew what had truly happened, only she had watched the entire tragedy playing out. Yet somehow – incredibly – Bruce had handed in his resignation and supposedly walked out of the holiday camp. How could that be?

She'd spent much of the day considering treachery. She could blame it on Will; she could pin it on Charlotte. If the police came, asking questions, she could deflect all the blame. Nobody saw what she saw. They all killed Bruce Craven; all three of them played their part. Charlotte struck him with a stone, Will strangled him with his bare hands, and she just finished off the job that they'd bungled. He was a formidable man; he took some killing. Surely he was dead?

There was another knock at the door, it was impatient now, more aggressive. Was this the police? Was her time up? Had they found Bruce's body in the foundations of the paddling pool, hauling it out of the newly poured concrete before it had time to set? Was he really alive, had he reported them all to the police? Maybe somebody saw what she did; perhaps they weren't the only ones wandering through Sandy Beaches Holiday Camp in the dead of night.

She had to think it through quickly now. Jenna had run through the scenarios several times. It was easiest to blame it on Will. He would not let Charlotte take the blame for her part in Bruce's assault. It was self-defence, after all. Bruce was trying to rape her on the beach at the time. Any woman would have done the same thing if the opportunity had presented itself.

As for Will, reluctantly, she had to admit that was also self-defence. He'd gone to see if Bruce needed help and, like the feral animal he was, he attacked the man who had come to his aid. She'd been terrified as she witnessed Bruce's pursuit of Will from her hiding place behind the gorse bush. The power and sheer velocity of the man was enough to paralyse anybody with fear. There was no doubt about it; it had been self-defence for Will. So, if she removed herself from the equation, her two friends would be charged with manslaughter at the very worst. They'd likely get off without a sentence, particularly if they told the court the truth about what had happened. And if Bruce was still alive? Who knew how he'd take his revenge.

As Jenna had searched her soul that day, she found that when push came to shove, she was lacking in the moral fibre that her parents had tried to instil in her from an early age. After all, in the eyes of the law, she was what Charlotte and Will were not. Jenna Phillips was a murderer. At least, she'd intended to murder Bruce. She hadn't finished off Bruce Craven in self-defence. She'd taken that last, agonised breath from him because she hated the man. She could no longer face the way he forced himself on her roughly in bed, the constant, eroding comments about her appearance and her behaviour, or the sense that she simply did not have the courage to walk away. Bruce Craven had to be stopped. At that time, in that place, caught as she was, Jenna could see no other way out.

Yet, she would happily throw her friends under the bus to avoid prison, if it came to that. The thought of the police coming to question her, taking her down to the station, getting fingerprints and those terrible prisoner photos that she'd seen on the TV and in the papers; the fear and shame of it all consumed her with terror. In the twenty-four hours or so since she thought Bruce Craven had drawn his last breath, Jenna had learned some harsh truths about herself. She was a coward, she was treacherous, and she would rather see her friends suffer than have to go through the process of seeking justice for Bruce Craven's attack. She was abdicating all responsibility. If this was the police at the door, she'd deny any culpability and point the finger at her friends.

There was a third knock. She heard the sound of some-body leaning against the door and giving it a push, trying to force it open. She'd have to answer it now; if she didn't, it sounded like they were coming in anyway. Would the police behave like that?

She looked at the LED alarm clock at the side of the bed. That was Bruce's. It was ten minutes past midnight. Bruce had supposedly left a letter with the admin depart-ment saying he was quitting his job at the holiday camp without notice. Jenna hadn't a clue how that had happened or who'd written that note. All she knew is that there was no way Bruce Craven was alive when she left him in the foun-dations of that pool and, even if he was, by some twist of fate, he had not come back to his room to collect his things.

Jenna walked up to the door, twisting the small handle on the Yale lock. Before she'd even completed the motion, the door was forced. Two men burst into the room, silently dangerous. One of them pushed his hand against her neck and propelled her over to the bed, lifting her up from the floor momentarily and throwing her down onto the mattress.

The other checked that they hadn't been seen, quietly closed the door, then locked it. He stood in front of the door, blocking it with his massive frame.

Jenna began to panic and drew breath to scream. The first man sat on the bed, his substantial weight compressing the mattress so that she rolled towards him. He put his finger to his mouth and indicated that she should be quiet.

From a sheath that was attached to his belt, he removed a large knife with serrations at the tip; the type a hunter might be seen with in an American movie. Slow and deliberate in his movements, he gently pressed the knifepoint into her groin, then ran it up to her stomach, pressing it in a little, moving to her neck, then levelling it up with her eyes.

'Such pretty eyes,' he said.

Jenna was motionless on the bed. They'd said three words between them, yet she already knew they were more dangerous than Bruce. He seemed like a lightweight in comparison. She just wanted to be rid of men like this; Jenna craved the end of this horrible violence.

'Where is Bruce Craven?' the man asked. His voice was steady and regulated; there wasn't a sign that he found this even mildly stressful. He was approaching the intimidation of Jenna much in the way that she'd place a cup of tea in front of one of her customers in the dining hall. It was an everyday occurrence to him, all in a day's work.

He placed his free hand on her thigh and moved it towards her groin, working underneath her nightshirt so that he was in direct contact with her flesh. His skin was smooth, but his hands were fat and threatening. She flinched.

'Where's Bruce Craven?' he asked again.

Jenna tried to speak. She couldn't find her voice. Her throat was dry and taut; the words would not come.

The man moved his hand a little further up. Jenna tensed again, fearful for what was coming.

'I don't know,' she managed to say.

'Where's Bruce Craven?' the man said again like this was the extent of his vocabulary.

She had her voice now. His hand was now gently massaging just below her groin, the knife perilously close to her right eye.

'No, please,' Jenna pleaded. 'I don't know. We argued last night. He never came back to the room. I've been waiting for him all day. Everybody says he left the holiday camp and went back home. Ask the people in the admin block. He left a letter. I promise he never came back.'

'Who saw what happened?' the second man asked. His voice was deep and gravelly; she'd never heard one like it before. It was as if he'd had some kind of throat problem in the past; it didn't sound right to her.

'Nobody, I swear. We argued in the pub last night. He stormed out. I thought I'd find him here. He wasn't in the room when I got back. I assumed he'd stayed in a friend's room, maybe even gone with another woman. I waited all night. When I went to work this morning, everybody was talking about it. Bruce Craven just quit. He went back home. It's a pretty shitty place to work; we just assumed he'd thrown the towel in. That's it, that's all I know.'

Jenna was sweating, in the few minutes that this exchange had taken, her nightshirt had become sodden with sweat.

The man with the abrasive voice moved closer to Jenna, who was still on the bed, not daring to move for fear of the knife.

'If you see Bruce Craven, tell him we're looking for him. He's not finished with us yet. And if I find out you're lying ... have you ever been with two men before? That look on your face tells me no. Well, we'll be back if we find you're lying to us. And next time we might even bring a friend. It'd be a shame not to make the most of a nice girl like you. Especially before we take your skin off and throw it in the waste paper basket.

Jenna closed her eyes tight shut as she used to when she was five years old, to repel the bogey man in the dark. She kept them closed for ten minutes after they'd left her room. She had never known fear like it in her life. But it was a fear that would find her once again, many years later.

Morecambe - Six Months After

The phone started to ring in the hall. Charlotte left the lounge to answer it.

'Hello, Lakes View Guest House, Charlotte Grayson speaking.'

'Hello, is that Charlotte Grayson as in Will and Charlotte Grayson?'

It was a woman's voice with a strong hint of a north-east accent.

'Yes, that's me. How can I help you?''

'I'm sorry it's short notice, but do you have a room available tonight and Saturday? I may extend beyond that, but I'll decide when I'm there is that's okay?'

Charlotte consulted the bookings. She could accommodate the booking and, with the exception of Barry McMillan's room, that gave them a full house for the weekend. She was relieved that they didn't have any events in the lounge that weekend, it was always all hands to the pumps whenever that happened.

'Yes, I can book you in on those dates. If you decide to stay, we've also got a couple of rooms free throughout the week. Whose name shall I book it in?'

'Mrs Bowker. Daisy Bowker.'

Charlotte took down her details, went through the credit card procedures and secured the booking in the online management system.

'Just one last question,' Charlotte said. 'What's your reason for visiting Morecambe, leisure or business?'

'A bit of both really,' Daisy replied. 'I'm researching my family history. I've got a relative whose last known whereabouts were Morecambe. I want to see if I can track him down.'

Charlotte's interest was piqued.

'Now that sounds interesting,' she said. 'We have a lovely local library and I can even recommend the local historian to you, he's really quite excellent. Jon Rogers is his name. He seems to know everything there is to know about Morecambe. I'm not sure if he works Saturdays, mind you.'

'Well actually, I wanted to book in at your guest house for a reason. I read about you and your husband online in a recent article about the guest house. I don't think you've had it very long, have you?'

Charlotte was tense now. This woman had sought them out rather than selecting them at random from a list of search results, as most guests did. She hesitated as she answered, nervous to find out more.

'Yes, we've been here for some time now. What was it that caught your eye? That story has been read by a lot of people, it's amazing how far the local newspaper travels.'

'Well, I saw that you and your husband met at the Sandy Beaches Holiday Camp in the eighties.'

Charlotte's stomach tightened, she felt sick.

'Yes ... that's right. It's been demolished now, they're building houses on it.'

'So, I've read,' Daisy continued. 'It looks like it's quite a project from what I've been able to find out about it. I'm trying to find somebody connected with the holiday camp, it's proving to be quite some task.'

Charlotte tried to silence the alarm bells that were sounding inside her head. Thousands of people passed through the Sandy Beaches Holiday Camp over the years. Some were staff but most were holiday-makers. She scolded herself for being too jumpy. This woman would come and go, there was nothing to worry about.

'Have you managed to track down the electoral roll or the phone books from the time? They can be quite useful,' Charlotte suggested.

'Oh yes, I've been through all the usual channels,' Daisy replied. 'I'm quite used to doing research like this, most people are much easier to find. But my half-brother is proving to be the proverbial needle in the haystack. He moved from Jesmond in 1984 and then I lose track of him completely. It's unusual for somebody to slip below the radar like that, particularly in these days of digital records. He even seemed to evade the Poll Tax and that took some doing.'

Charlotte knew the answer to her question already, but she had to ask it; she had to know. They hadn't even considered the possibility of a marriage breakdown, a broken family and a half-brother or half-sister. That prospect had passed them by completely.

'It sounds like you've got quite a task ahead of you,' Charlotte said, trying as best she could to keep a voice steady. 'Sandy Beaches was such a huge place, it's unlikely that I'd have met him. What was his name, just to be certain?'

'It was Bruce. My half-brother is called Bruce Craven.'

Carry on reading Circle of Lies today. Available now as an e-book or paperback.

AUTHOR NOTES

Left for Dead is probably my most personal thriller to date in that it very closely maps the summer of 1984 when my then-girlfriend - now wife - and I spent our first summer together as students at Pontins Middleton Tower site near Morecambe. As with Will and Charlotte, we were working off the overdrafts that we'd run up during term time and working at the camp gave us food, accommodation and income, sparing us from having to go our separate ways and spend the summer at our respective parental homes which were at opposite ends of the country.

The entire story is a complete figment of my imagination, I hasten to add, but the locations of the book have been born out of my own experiences working at the resort and visiting Morecambe over successive years.

The story is based upon my memories and experiences working on that holiday camp. The descriptions of the chalets, the moaning of the holiday-makers, the presence of the prune eaters and the brick and stone covered beach are for real. However, the camp on which the story is based is fictional, as are the characters in the story. I never met a Bruce Craven character while I was working there, neither was there a pool being built or a night watchman called George. The guest house is made up too - that should be enough assurances to keep the lawyers at bay!

Before I began writing the story, I dug out all of our old photographs from our time on the camp. There are pictures of us in the uniforms we had to wear when waiting on tables, as well as images from around the holiday camp. I've added these to a picture scrapbook at https://paulteague.net - just click on the **Psychological Thrillers** tab to check them out. You'll also find an excellent Flickr collection on that web page; it shows photos of the Pontins Middleton Tower site through the ages. It's hard to imagine now, in these days of cheap air travel and foreign holidays, but this is the type of home-grown holiday that the British used to enjoy.

I also returned to the holiday campsite before starting work on the book. It's now a retirement village - nothing is left of the previous site. You're still greeted by the Middleton Tower sign, and the tower itself is still there on the beachside, but the pub, the big ship structure and the arcades are all gone. Thousands of holiday-makers and hundreds of staff must have passed through there over the years. If that place could speak, it would have so many stories to tell.

It was strange writing about a time before computers; a lot of the time I had to really cast my mind back to recall how we did things back then. Even catching a bus to Morecambe was a logistics effort - you had to secure printed bus timetables first, and there was no cheating by doing an online Google search. There were no mobile phones either;

the first proper mobile phone I ever saw was in 1991, so it was all payphones and keeping some loose change in your pocket back then.

It's the same with the comings and goings of staff. It would have been very possible to just disappear in 1984, like Bruce does. There was no social media - we all communicated on the phone or via Royal Mail and I didn't even have access to a home phone in those days. I couldn't afford it. I used to write letters to my mum to keep her updated. Our payslips were generated electronically I believe, but we were paid in cash and we'd go and pick up our wages every week. When my wife and I left, we'd earned the money we needed and we did a deal with the holiday camp to let us go early. It was all managed verbally back then. If nobody was looking for you - as is the case with Bruce Craven - and nobody was found, you could disappear and never be seen again. It was the very early days of DNA back then, and by no means as routine as it is now.

Compare that with Charlotte's modern-day life and everything has changed. She can now get anonymous messages through Facebook, and she and her family message each other all the time. Her kids won't even use the phone, preferring instant messaging instead. Anonymous guest house bookings come in via online sites and the local newspaper can now be seen all over the world because the stories are placed online. It's all very different to the world of 1984 when Bruce Craven could bully and intimidate and there was no HR behavioural code to refer to.

If you've read any of my other thrillers, you'll know I have a soft spot for UK coastal resorts. As a former student at Lancaster, Morecambe was one of our summer destinations during our long student holidays. We used to go to

Frontierland - which was an excellent pleasure park in the resort - and frequent the arcades, most of which are still there. I still love a game of bingo too, by the way.

On a recent research visit to Morecambe, I was sad to see that Frontierland has now been completely levelled, ready for somebody to build the next supermarket, I suspect. Adventure Kingdom is my fictional version of Frontierland and will feature more heavily in Circle of Lies.

The pier has long gone - I am privileged to report that I once went to a party there in 1983, well before the fire which brought about its eventual demise.

I've managed to immortalise locations like the Old Roof Tree Inn at Middleton, Julian's Pantry and The Old Galleon restaurant which are - alas - all long gone, but enjoyed in the story as they were by myself and my wife all those years ago,

For the most observant readers, you'll have noticed that DCI Kate Summers makes an appearance in this book. She also features in my Don't Tell Meg trilogy. This is her home patch in my fictional world of psychological thrillers. Nigel Davies, the local newspaper reporter, will also make future appearances in my trilogy of books about Morecambe Bay. As a former BBC journalist, I'm familiar with the reporter's world, and it's one I'm happy to inhabit in my stories.

There are some observations made in this book which may seem a little far-fetched, but they are true about my time working on the holiday camp. For instance, my wife and I arrived as a couple, so we got one of the very few double beds that were available. They were in such short supply that I was actually offered money once to exchange it for two single beds. Also, the concept of chalet rash was revealed in that camp, which is what love bites were referred to back then. I'm pretty certain I'd never even seen a love bite until I went to Pontins - I was only 19 years old and we were much more naïve in those days - but they genuinely were worn like a badge of honour among the non-student staff. Working there was certainly an excellent education for life beyond our academic world.

The bars are for real too, and one of the things I liked best about the camp. The big ship structure was where the holiday-makers gathered in their hundreds at night. It was a great place to hang out, with the Bluecoats hosting entertainments (my Purple Coats are fictional!) and the resident house band Kaos entertaining the crowds every night.

I still have my 45 rpm vinyl single of the song that was played to encourage the children to bed at nine o'clock every night. It was called The Crocodile Song and was an inspired idea, aimed at getting the kids all lined up in a dancing march, then leading them out of the door where the parents were waiting to take them to bed. I've added that to my picture gallery, by the way. However far-fetched this stuff might seem, it was all for real.

I hope you enjoyed frequenting this seaside world as much as I did writing about it. It's been a wonderful trip down memory lane for me, and I've enjoyed creating the stories around Abi, Charlotte, Will and our favourite bad guy, Bruce Craven. There's more to come too, as the trilogy continues. We're not quite done with Bruce Craven yet as you'll find out in Circle of Lies and Truth Be Told.

The best way to stay in touch is to subscribe to receive my email updates at https://paulteague.net/thrillers, that way you'll never miss out on a new release or promotional offer.

In the meantime, thanks so much for reading Left for

Dead and if you're ever anywhere near Morecambe, call in if you can. Lots of money has been spent on regenerating the resort and it's looking great these days.

Paul Teague

ALSO BY PAUL J. TEAGUE

ABOUT THE AUTHOR

Hi, I'm Paul Teague, the author of the Morecambe Bay series and the Don't Tell Meg trilogy, as well as several other standalone psychological thrillers such as One Last Chance, Dead of Night and No More Secrets.

I'm a former broadcaster and journalist with the BBC, but I have also worked as a primary school teacher, a disc jockey, a shopkeeper, a waiter and a sales rep.

I've read thrillers all my life, starting with Enid Blyton's Famous Five series as a child, then graduating to James Hadley Chase, Harlan Coben, Linwood Barclay and Mark Edwards.

Let's get connected!
https://paulteague.net

This is a work of fiction. Names, characters, businesses, places, events and incidents are either the products of the author's imagination or used in a fictitious manner. Any resemblance to actual persons, living or dead, or actual events is purely coincidental.

All rights reserved. No part of this book may be reproduced or transmitted in any form or by any electronic or mechanical means, including photocopying, recording or by any information storage and retrieval system, without the written permission of the Author, except where permitted by law.

Copyright © 2019 Paul Teague writing as Paul J. Teague

All rights reserved

Lightning Source UK Ltd.
Milton Keynes UK
UKHW010643200322
400330UK00001B/68

9 781916 475106